Running Scared

Baycliff Valley Series: Book Four

H K Brown

First paperback edition October 2025

Book design by H K Brown

ISBN 979-8-9902545-6-5

Content Warning

Running Scared is a marriage-of-convenience, closed-door romance. It will push boundaries while fading to black when it threatens to get spicy. It's perfect for those who want the emotional rollercoaster while limiting the steam.

Please note that *Running Scared* contains content that may be sensitive to some readers. Some scenes include abuse, abandonment, suicidal thoughts, and past trauma.

Happy reading

Prologue

"I honestly don't know what you want from me," I state. "I'm not going to let the thought of my ex run me through the wringer again. Last time, it took me a week to feel some-what normal, only for you to do it again." I shift my weight on the couch, tucking a pillow behind my back for support.

I first started this journey with my therapist, Katie, a little over a year ago. When I found myself huddled on the shower floor, contemplating ending it all, I realized I needed help. No matter how tough life gets, suicide isn't the solution. I felt completely shattered, but there was still so much to live for.

At our first appointment, I could barely speak through my tears, as my life had just been turned upside down. But now, as she sits across from me, urging me to revisit the past that I'd rather forget, I feel the urge to shrink away . . . but I refuse to do so.

She leans back, bringing one leg up under the other, clearly ready to dive into our session. "I'm not trying to break you, Janelle. You've come such a long way. You should be proud of that. When you came to me nearly a year ago, you wouldn't even look me in my eyes, and yet here you are now, looking me head-on and saying no. That's a huge accomplishment."

"Then why do I feel so weak?" My shoulders sink as I absentmindedly tug at the frayed thread dangling from my pants. "Bryant took everything from me. I'm not the woman I once was. And yet . . . I still feel so broken sometimes."

People constantly tell me how strong I am. But inside, all I can think about is the life that was taken from us. I can say one thing for sure—Bryant provided a comfortable life for our family. My kids never wanted for anything. I didn't have to work a single day of our marriage. I got to be the stay-at-home wife and mother I dreamed of being while my kids were young. Just like my mom. Now, I have to constantly worry. Will I have enough money for gas this week? And what if Peter—our middle child—needs something for school again? I feel a knot form in my stomach just thinking about it. The memory of last year, when I could barely afford to put food on the table or pay for our basic necessities, still haunts me.

Now that I have SNAP benefits to help with food and a job as an EMT while I work to become a paramedic, I can afford these expenses a little easier. But just last year, I could barely afford to survive, let alone care for my three children on my own. I never could have imagined that I'd be the mom on the DHS—Oklahoma Department of Human Services—doorstep begging for help, but when you have kids counting on you for everything and an ex that won't help in any way, you do what you've got to do. So if that makes me strong, then so be it, but I still don't see it. I feel like I've failed my kids in so many ways.

"It takes time," Katie says. "The internal struggle that someone experiences after enduring a relationship like yours can last longer than many realize. Overcoming not only physical but also emotional abuse requires patience in the healing process. It won't happen overnight."

"I know. But it's been more than a year since he left. I should be further than I am by now. Shouldn't I?"

I was so in love with Bryant. Our arguments seemed like nothing compared to the intense passion we felt when we made up. We had been each other's first love, together since our sophomore year of high school when he bought me a bottle of Crush for Valentine's Day. There on the orange soda label was a note—*Will you be mine? Xoxox Bryant Fuller.* I thought it was the cutest thing ever and, of course, said yes.

When we were still going strong our senior year, I was convinced that we were meant to be together forever.

Now, looking back, I can see the red flags I missed. "There is no time frame. Everyone moves at their own pace. Considering all the challenges you've faced along the way, I think you're doing well."

"Challenges" is a kind way to put it. Since Bryant left, I've been through the wringer. He beat me within an inch of my life, landing me in the hospital for weeks. Once out, I had a long road of recovery ahead of me, all while figuring out how to take care of three kids on my own. Thank God for family—they've been my saving grace through all of this. But while my brothers have continued with their lives—Cam getting engaged and, shortly after, married; Pat healing and moving forward with his fiancée, Kim; and Tom being Tom—mine has been completely turned upside down. I'm thankful for their love and support throughout all of this, but it hasn't been easy. Trying to keep the peace doesn't allow me to completely open up to them. If I ever did, I would worry about them going after Bryant. They can be very protective, given that they are all cops. Well, Pat may never go back after what he went through, but we'll see. Without them, I wouldn't be where I am today. But I cannot say that it has been easy. I just wish the healing process would speed up, because I'm over it already.

At least, I hope I am.

"How about you tell me about the night that your ex took you out and things took a turn? Let's see how you get through it this time. Sometimes all it takes is for us to talk about it until we no longer break down."

I lean back against the couch and close my eyes, thinking back to our last date night.

I stand in front of the bedroom mirror, smoothing down my dress and feeling excited for a night out with Bryant. Since having Eric, I haven't left the house much, other than for short periods of time. But tonight, we're leaving Baycliff Valley behind for a trip into the city.

"You ready, babe?" he asks from the doorway. Bryant does a double take when he sees me standing here. With a smile on his face, he crosses the room and takes me in his arms. "You're wearing my favorite dress, you little minx."

I chuckle as his chin stubble drags over my bare skin and he leaves hot kisses across my shoulder. It's moments like these that I treasure the most. They've become all too rare lately. His touch feels different now, distant somehow, as if he might be repulsed by me. It's been like this since I shared the news of my pregnancy with our youngest. I knew Bryant didn't want more than two children, but I wasn't going to terminate our pregnancy. Eric may not have been planned, but I loved him the same. Bryant seemed to understand that, but he sure has changed since we've had him.

"It finally fits me again. Of course I'm wearing it. I know how much you like it."

Bryant stops trailing his lips along my shoulder and takes a step back to look, having me do a spin. "It looks nice. Another fifteen pounds or so and it'll fit a lot better."

"And how did that make you feel?" Katie asks.

I lift my head from the back of the couch and look over at her. "Like trash. I'd just had the man's baby months before he said that. A woman's body doesn't just bounce back after birth. When he initially said it, I remember swallowing down my feelings so that I didn't upset him. Now, it just makes me mad that I was such a coward. No man should ever talk to the woman they claim to love like that."

Katie's lips curl into a warm smile before she picks up her pen and jots down some notes on her paper. "What happened next? After you two made it to your destination."

"That's the thing—we never did."

"What do you mean?" she asks, as if she's never heard this story before.

All my muscles tense. "By the time we made it to OKC, he had gotten a call from Shelby—his secretary—asking that he meet her and a few others from the office for drinks. Since I was with him, he decided to take me with him, completely forgetting about our date night. When I made a fuss, he bought me a burger from the bar and let me sit at the table with them."

I unclench my fists and shake out my hands, noticing the crescent-shaped indentations my nails left on my palms. Just the thought of that night sets me on edge. Taking a deep breath, I lean back into the cushions of the couch, closing my eyes in an attempt to calm my thoughts.

I've been sitting here at the end of the booth filled with a bunch of Bryant's drunk and tipsy coworkers. To make things worse, Shelby won't keep her hands to herself, and no matter how many times I've tried to stop it, my husband has told me to keep my mouth shut. Drunk Bryant is not my favorite, and I think he is well past buzzed by now.

I lean into his side so that he can hear me. "Can we head home now? I'm sure Kim's ready to get back."

He raises a brow and then turns back to the table. "I better get the wife home. She'll just die if she lets herself have any fun."

"But, Bry," Shelby says. Her lips turn downward in a pout as she rests a hand on Bryant's arm, causing my blood to boil. "You can't leave me alone with the guys. It's no fun when you're not here."

I stand, taking Bryant's hand and tug. "Sorry to disappoint you, Shelby, but my husband and I will be leaving now." I can't just sit here and watch her hit on him while I do nothing.

Once he's up and on his feet, I march out to the car. When we're mere steps away, I turn, hand outstretched for the keys.

He slaps them down in my hand and hops into the passenger side as soon as it's unlocked. "You didn't have to be so rude in there, Janie. I don't know what came over you, but you were a real bi—"

"Don't you dare finish that sentence. You are the one who was letting Shelby hang off you like she's some kind of tree monkey or something, while your wife was sitting right next to you no less. I had every right to demand we leave."

"I can see this is having an effect on you," Katie interrupts. "How are you feeling at this moment?"

"I'm mad!" My chest rises on a huff. She nods, so I keep going. "I'm frustrated that I allowed him to treat me like that. No wonder Shelby thought that her behavior was okay. Not that it was in any way, but he should have stopped it. Heck, I was sitting right *there*. Then he had the gall to call me names afterward!" I throw my hands up in the air, stand from the couch, and start pacing. "If only I had stopped it there and called one of my brothers, maybe things wouldn't have gotten so out of hand." A tear rolls down my cheek as the memories of that night flood back in. I still don't understand how things went so sideways.

"You had no way of knowing what was coming."

"No, maybe I didn't, but he had never been that mean to me before either. I should have taken that as a sign."

Pulling into the driveway after the trip back home from the city, I'm ready to throw the car in park, go in and change, check on the kids, and take a blanket down to sleep on the couch. There is no way I will be sharing a bed with this man tonight. Not after the way he's spoken to me.

One look at Bryant, and Kim is out the door. I feel bad that I don't even get a chance to thank her properly, but that will have to wait until morning.

As Bryant heads up the stairs, I lock the doors and make sure all the lights are off except the one on the end table in the living room, since I plan on coming back down. Then I head up to check on the kids.

No sooner than my feet hit the landing to the second floor does Bryant grab me by the arm with his bruising grip and drag me into our bedroom.

Once the door is shut, I whirl around on him, hand on hip. "What the heck, Bryant? Don't you ever grab me like that again."

I yank free of his hold and walk toward the door, intending to check on the kids as planned. But Bryant grabs me violently by the hair and yanks me back, bringing me flush against his chest, causing my eyes to widen in surprise. My scalp burns as I try to break free.

His voice is a low growl in my ear when he finally speaks. "I'm about sick and tired of that mouth of yours. Maybe it's time to teach you a lesson."

"Please, Bryant. You've been drinking. Let's just sleep it off," I beg.

But my words fall on deaf ears as his hand snakes its way to my throat, squeezing with just enough force to make breathing difficult. I still my movements as tears prick at the corners of my eyes. I never imagined Bryant would ever harm me, even when he was drunk. But now, pressed against him, I know he can, and it terrifies me.

"Okay, let's stop here," Katie says, pulling me from my thoughts. "You did good today, Janelle. The once-broken woman who walked into my office has shown a lot of strength today."

I wipe at my tears with the tissue Katie hands me and smile as best I can. Despite my frustration with how this session turned out, I'm relieved to realize that I'm not so out of sorts that I can't drive myself home. I'm not where I'd like to be, but I am stronger than I was a year ago. I guess I'll take it.

"Same time next week?"

"Yeah, sounds good."

As I excuse myself from her office, I know there is still a lot of work to do before I can move on. But I have three littles counting on me. There's no way I'll ever give up.

Chapter One

Two Years Later

Watching the numbers on the gas pump climb higher and higher, I mentally calculate if I'll have to remove anything from my grocery list. This is my first month without SNAP benefits. Now that I'm a certified rescue paramedic and I'm supposed to be getting child support from Bryant, I make too much money to qualify for assistance anymore. It's frustrating because he hasn't paid a penny in months. And now with my benefits having been cut off, I know we're about to feel it. The kids having to sacrifice due to their parents' drama is not something I ever wanted. I wish DHS had given me a few months to catch up on bills before cutting off our help. Then I wouldn't have to worry so much. We used to fill up the trunk of our Suburban with groceries, but now, what we can get is so little that I'll be able to carry it all myself, excluding the heavy bag of dog food. My ninety-five-pound German shepherd, Thor, is a hungry boy. But he's worth every burger I have to give up.

When I saw the amount of my last paycheck, the first since my promotion, I was shocked to see that it had increased by around fifteen hundred dollars. I nearly choked. I knew the position came with a raise, but it was way more than I anticipated. My first thought was to pay off debt before anything else. That same day, the first thing I did was call and pay off one of my credit cards, then deactivated it. I still need to be frugal with our spending, but if each paycheck is similar, I should be in a good place financially in two or three months. I might not enjoy it, but it's part of the hole we've been in for so long.

The handle clicks, causing me to look up.

A hundred and ten dollars!

For *gas*?

This is ridiculous. If I didn't have three growing kids and a big ole dog, I might think about getting a smaller car. Especially with having to drive back and forth from Baycliff Valley to OKC so much.

"Hey, Mom?" Sage hollers from the car window. "Can we get a fountain drink?"

Instead of responding right away, I start calculating. If I don't buy seasoning packets and use what we have at home, I think I can do drinks. At least she's asking for something cheap, unlike Peter, who always wants a new game.

"Sure, angel. Each of you can get a small drink. Wanna find out what your brothers want and come in with me?"

Sage pulls her head back in, and a moment later, she's opening the door and hopping out. She's at my side by the time I have the nozzle back in the pump and am ready to go in and get my receipt. I pull her hood up over her head to keep the cold from hitting her ears. With it being the start of January, the weather is getting chilly. I'm just thankful there's no ice or snow yet.

I put an arm around her shoulder and move to the front of the car, looking both ways before we cross. "Did the boys tell you what they want?"

"Yup. Pete wants cherry soda, and Eric wants something lime or berry."

A gentleman opens the door for us. I look at him and nod in thanks, guiding Sage inside. We find the drink station, and I help her fill the cups.

"What are you getting?"

"Suicide!"

I roll my eyes. This kid. She came home from grabbing pizza with Tom and his best friend, Maddie, not long ago and, ever since, has been mixing every drink in the house together in one cup calling it 'suicide. Apparently, it was a fad when her uncle was in high school, and she intends to bring it back. I'm glad I missed that one. I've been on her about changing the name of it, though.

"Why not call it something else? That just sounds so . . . sad." I worry about the way someone might take it when she says that. I know she's saying it innocently, but still.

"I know, Mom, but I can't just rewrite history like that."

"Sure you can. Not many people your age would even know that it used to be called that. Maybe you can bring it back but with a better name."

"Excuse me." A woman squeezes between the two of us, grabbing a straw for her cup.

Sage and I gather the drinks and are heading to the front to pay when my phone rings.

"Hello?"

"Hey, J. You still in town?" Heather asks. She's one of my closest friends. I met her on day one of the job. We've worked together nearly every day since—well, until recently, due to my shift change with the new position.

"Yeah. We're about to head to the store. What's up?" I move up with the line.

"I was thinking that we could get the kids together for pizza tonight. I know it's your Friday, and my workweek starts tomorrow. I haven't seen you in a while and am having withdrawals."

I chuckle. "Sure. Can you come out to the house? I can be there by six."

"Sounds good. I'll buy tonight. See you then."

The line goes dead, and I move up to pay, then turn to let Sage know what the call was about.

"Awesome. Is she bringing Chris and Grace?"

"She is. That means that we need to go and get these groceries, then get home. Do you think you can help me keep Eric in line?"

"Sure."

When we make it to the car and hop in, Sage tells her brothers about the call. Peter removes an earbud from one of his ears so he can hear what she's saying. It wasn't long ago that I worried about her. There are times I still do, but I know that she's come a long way. Pete too. You cannot witness what they did at such a young age and not be scarred by it.

As the food sizzles on the stove, I turn and pour a mug of coffee for Bryant, making it just the way he likes it. I place it carefully on the counter, and I'm plating his breakfast when I hear his foot hit the bottom step. I brace myself, hoping not to set him off. Things with him have gotten intense ever since I walked in on him and Shelby at work. I swear they were kissing but I can't prove it. Once I have proof, though, things will change around here.

Straightening up and dusting myself off, I greet him softly with a smile. "Good morning." I lean in and kiss his cheek as he draws nearer.

He grumbles in response and takes a seat in front of his plate at the bar. Bryant sips his coffee before digging into his breakfast. As I walk towards the refrigerator, I hear the sound of his fork clattering against his plate, causing me to stop in my tracks. I quickly turn around to see a dark expression on his face as he stares at me, sending shivers down my spine. "You never listen, do you?" he says with disappointment in his tone.

I shake my head, trying to ignore his prodding, and hoping that he'll let it go. The kids will be up soon, and I don't want them to walk into another argument between us. But without warning, he's right behind me, my hair in his hand, and I'm being pulled back to the bar and shoved within an inch of his plate. My head throbs from his hold.

I struggle to try and free myself from his grasp, but he's too strong.

"What the hell is this?" he growls angrily.

"I don't know what you mean," I cry.

He pushes me away, releasing my hair and making me stumble into the wall behind me. "Are you going to answer me or stand there looking stupid?"

I flinch at the harshness of his voice. "I—I don't understand," I stutter. Tears stream down my face as I wrap my arms around my stomach, trying to process everything that's going on.

Sure, he's become more aggressive lately, but never where the kids could see. And he hasn't touched me like this since the last time he was drinking. Now, he's stone-cold sober. I wipe at my tears and hope that I can deescalate this before the kids wake up.

"How many times do I have to tell you to tie your hair back when you cook? Nobody wants it in their food. It's disgusting, Janelle!"

Before I can even process what's happening, Bryant sweeps his arm across the bar in front of him, sending hot food, plates, and coffee flying in my direction. I turn and cover my face as the hot liquid and food hits me.

Crying out in pain, I quickly bend and try to clean up the mess he's caused. I don't know what else to do other than try not to anger him any more than I already have.

Before I can even think of standing back up, Bryant hoists me from the floor and slams my back against the wall. I'm helpless, pinned here, only able to hope that our children remain asleep and unaware of what's happening.

Desperate for him to calm down, I apologize repeatedly in an attempt to reach him. A sharp pain shoots through my jaw as Bryant's hand strikes me, causing me to see stars.

"Don't look at me like that!"

My eyes meet his chest. Maybe if I do as he says, he'll calm down. In this moment, trapped against the wall with fear coursing through my body, all I can do is pray for strength.

Even though it's going on four years since that horrifying day, it still hurts knowing that my kids did, in fact, wake up and come down the stairs to find their mom in the fight of her life. Their cries stopped Bryant from harming me further, but when he left with them, all I could do was crawl across the field toward my brother's house, desperate to find help. Thank God Cam was on his way out for a run.

My kids should never have had to face that, especially at such a young age.

Bryant spent one year in jail and was then ordered to complete probation, as well as attend courses for domestic violence and parenting. In our last court hearing, he was granted supervised visitation with the kids. Every Monday after school, they get to see their father at the local DHS office for two hours. While not ideal, it's what the judge deemed appropriate.

Bryant still likes to give me a lot of grief, messing with me every chance he gets, but over the years, I've learned to go straight to my lawyer rather than dealing with it on my own.

We pull up in front of the local grocery store and I turn back to the kids. "Okay, we're going to keep our hands to ourselves and not ask for a thing. Got it? We're going to keep to the list and get in and out quickly."

"Got it," Eric says with a firm nod. Seeing as he's the youngest at almost five, he's the one I'm most worried about.

"Alright then. Let's go." After killing the car, I grab my bag and get out.

With Pete being ten and Sage twelve, this would be so much easier if I could send them around the store to help, but seeing as Bryant lives nearby, that's not happening. He's been known to show up while I'm here, and I'd rather avoid that if I can. I feel for the kids. I remember a childhood of freedom, being able to roam around the town and head into the woods surrounding our home, building tree houses and such. Don't get me wrong—the kids *do* have a tree house in the forest right behind the house, but I can see it from the kitchen window. If they're out of sight for too long, one of us adults goes out looking for them.

Sage has Eric out of his car seat by the time I open the back door. Rather than letting him join his siblings, I hoist him onto my hip as we head towards the line of shopping carts. I'm not ready to chase after him today.

"Momma, can we get the car?" he asks, eyes bright with excitement.

The store has those clunky green-and-yellow shopping carts shaped like cars. They never steer correctly, always veering awkwardly to one side. Right now, though, I'd rather deal with a stubborn cart than a cranky kid. "We'll get one, but if you get out even once or touch anything, I'll strap you into a regular cart, understood?"

He nods, extending his pinkie. "Promise."

I wrap my pinkie around his and press a kiss to his knuckles.

At the cart corral, I grab a cleaning wipe and sanitize the cart before securing him with the seat belt. After a bit of maneuvering to get the cart rolling straight, we navigate through the first half of the store.

When we reach the cereal aisle, I grab for an off-brand box, then catch sight of a small hand reaching for a box nearby with a superhero on the front as I'm putting mine in the cart. I glance at Sage, giving her a knowing look. "Angel, could you grab a big cart, please? It seems Eric's had enough of the car already."

Eric's hand snaps back, and he throws himself against the window opening in the car with enough force that the cart jolts into my stomach. "Sorry," he pouts.

"It's okay. But no extras today, alright?"

We continue with our shopping, picking up a jar of peanut butter, a loaf of bread, and a bunch of ripe bananas. I double back to snag a bag of flour and sugar before heading to the front of the store. Thankfully, the checkout lines are short, and we don't have to wait. With Sage taking the lead and me unloading from the side, we empty the cart in no time.

"Momma," Eric calls. "Can I have candy?"

He did so good through most of the store, only to be tempted at the checkout.

"No, sir. Not this time. We still have some of the cookies that Aunt Leah made at home."

"But, *Mom*," he cries.

"I said no," I say a little firmer.

Talk about mom guilt. Telling my child no to a three-dollar candy bar is crazy. Moments like this, even though they may be small to some, make me feel like I've failed them. It would have been different if I was telling him no because he'd had too many sweets already, but that's not the case. I already think I might have to put something back. If my calculations are right, the tax on the food might put me over by a few dollars. I can't keep adding to the costs.

Eric gets out of the cart and walks toward his siblings, standing with them while I check out.

By the time we get out and get loaded into the car, I'm ready to go home, change into my pj's, and crawl into bed, but I know that's still hours away for me.

Once we make it to the house and get the groceries unloaded, then Thor let out, I barely have time to pick up the house before Heather is knocking. Sage runs to the door to let her in. The kids make their way to the family room, where they already have a game set up on the TV.

One of my favorite things about this house is the open floor plan. It allows me to see the entire bottom floor, minus the closets and bathroom. Before, when Bryant lived here, there was a wall dividing the kitchen and dining area from the living space, but after my backside met the wall during the scuffle with Bryant, leaving a hole in the wall, I asked my brothers to take it down entirely, leaving two beautiful beams in its place. I couldn't be happier with that decision.

"Hey, girl," Heather says. She sets down a few boxes of pizza and then hangs her coat on the back of a chair.

"Hey. Thanks for bringing dinner. You really are a life-saver."

"No problem. I know how it is."

If anyone understands, it would be her. Well, not everything, but she is a twenty-six-year-old widow. Her husband passed away after a long battle with cancer, leaving her with two kids as she tries to figure it all out. She understands the part of being a single mom and trying to do it all on her own.

"Besides, it was my turn," she adds.

Grace runs in and pulls her mom's attention away for a moment before running back in the direction of the other kids.

I take out some paper plates and get the kids taken care of before I grab each of us a beer from the fridge. Thank God for brothers. They keep me stocked with beer so that they can have one when they come over and hang out.

"Thanks. How are things?" Heather asks.

I take a seat at the kitchen table with my pizza and beer, then fill her in on my week.

"Are you still going to take Val up on her offer of going on that double date with her?"

Val, Heather, and I used to work the same shift at the station and grew quite close during that time. Although Val and I aren't as close as Heather and I, we keep in touch, mainly through her cousin, Garrett—well, Courtney Garrett, but we go by last names at work—who is now my work partner since I'm on a different shift. This date has been in the works for nearly a year. Val's been trying to get Heather and me to rejoin the dating scene. She's the type who seems to go out every other weekend or more, not in any rush to settle down. Meanwhile, both Heather and I had thought we were settled down for good.

It takes time.

I wipe my mouth and swallow the bite I was chewing. "Yeah, Katie thinks I'm ready, that it might be good for me to step out of my comfort zone. I'm not so sure about putting myself out there again, but it has been several years. It's not like I'm getting any younger."

Up until my last session, I had been dead set against dating again. Of course, I want the companionship, the cuddling, the fun parts of dating, but I don't know if I can ever open up enough to fully invest. But Katie says I'll never know unless I try. I'm still hesitant and not at all ready to jump into anything serious, but I am looking forward to getting out of the house and feeling like a woman again. It's been so long since I felt like more than just a mom.

Chapter Two

I lean forward on the couch in Katie's office, my elbows pressing into my knees, fingers interlaced. Across from me, she tilts her head, pen poised over her notepad. I was braced for our usual: reciting the trauma that Bryant left behind. But instead, she's thrown me for a loop.

Katie leans back in her black leather chair and fixes me with a soft, expectant stare, as she waits for me to answer her.

I shake my head, dislodging the disbelief. "Sorry . . . what did you just ask?"

She taps her pen against the notebook in her lap. "Now that you're ready to date again, it's just as important to remember the green flags. Tell me, you met in high school, married right after graduation—what kept you together? What moments made you think, 'This is who I want to spend my life with'?" She crosses one ankle over the other, eyes filled with encouragement.

My chest tightens, and I lean back against the couch cushions, nails pressing into my palms. My stomach flips at the thought of those happy memories. They're still hard to reconcile with who I know as Bryant now. But as Katie's gaze holds mine, I nod and close my eyes, letting the past unfold.

I stand near the foot of my bed, adjusting the gown over my simple white sundress underneath. Today is graduation day. After the ceremony, I'll officially be on my own—well, almost. Like my older brothers, I chose my piece of land where Dad will park the travel trailer tomorrow. It's a Cameron family rite of passage. My heart races at the thought of moving out of my parents' house and finding my footing in the world. This is everything I've been working toward. It's a bit scary, but at least they'll still be close by.

There's a knock at the door. I turn around just in time to see Bryant slip into view. His dark hair curls at the nape of his neck, a telling sign that he's in need of another haircut. When his brown eyes meet mine, it brings a smile to my face. He pushes the door wide and walks in, taking me in from head to toe.

"Spin for me," he says. I chuckle as I twirl, and Bryant whistles appreciatively. "My God, Janie, you are downright gorgeous." He steps closer, his eyes soft, and offers me his hand. I place mine in his, and he draws me in for a kiss.

I swear, I love this man.

"Y'all best leave this door open and keep the kisses PG—Dad won't hesitate to grab his shotgun!" Tom, my youngest brother, says from the doorway. When I pick up a shoe off the ground and hurl it his way, he takes off down the hallway, his laughter echoing off the walls.

Bryant chuckles, brushing a stray piece of hair from my cheek. "No shotgun needed," he promises. He leans close, so only I can hear. "I'll be a gentleman . . . at least until you're wearing my ring."

His words tingle along my skin, and my smile grows so big it almost hurts.

A single tear slides down my cheek as I remember the next night in my cramped travel trailer parked on my piece of land. Bryant came over to help me unpack and have our first ever dinner in my new home. After dinner, he kneeled beside me and pulled a cheap silver band from his pocket, asking me to be his forever. That night, I gave him everything.

"What is it about that memory that makes it so hard to share?" Katie asks.

I reach for the tissue she offers. "Even though I'm glad I'm no longer with him, I can't help but hurt when I think of those times. We were so happy. I built my world around him. It stings, knowing those happy moments are now tainted by the trauma he inflicted. So many years of my life were wasted on a man who doesn't even love me. I don't regret our time together, though—he did give me three amazing kids."

Katie nods. "Did those times fade quickly, or did they last through your marriage?"

I pause, thinking back over our marriage. "We had what felt like a lifetime of happy times before things changed."

With Sage napping in her playpen in the living room, I make my way into the kitchen and take out the makings for cheeseburger mac. I begin chopping an onion, which of course burns my eyes, then brown the ground beef, finally stirring in the elbow macaroni.

Tonight, I'm telling Bryant that I'm pregnant again. My throat goes dry at the thought. Another baby before I'm even twenty. Who'd have guessed? Not me, that's for sure. But that's why I decided to stay home after high school—to start our family. Sage came as a surprise. We found out about her just months after I moved out of my parents' house. They were so mad at me at first, but seeing as Bryant married me before she came, all is right again.

Now, with nearly three years of marriage behind us, two babies, and Bryant's new job, life is looking up. Soon, we'll be able to pay off the loan that Mom and Dad cosigned for the house build and then everything should be smooth sailing afterward.

I'll be able to go to work in a couple of years, when the kids are in school, and then it's just building our nest egg.

When the front door opens, I wipe my hands on the tea towel draped over my shoulder and step into the living area. The moment Bryant spots me, he smiles brightly and steps out of his shoes, then heads my way, pulling me in for a hug and kiss. "How are my girls today?"

I lean in, inhaling the comforting scent that is Bryant. He presses a quick kiss to my temple before stepping further into the living room to peek at Sage.

"We're good," I call back. "Dinner's almost ready. Care to join me?"

"Let me run upstairs and get changed, then I'm all yours."

While he's taking care of that, I go into the kitchen and turn the flame to a simmer, then put a lid on the pot.

"Janelle?" Bryant hollers down the stairs. "Is there something you should tell me?"

My smile grows so wide it makes my cheeks ache. He's spotted the pregnancy test resting on the counter. "I do," I say, turning to face the stairs. "Come on down so I can tell you."

Footsteps thunder overhead until he's at the bottom step. When he reaches for me, Bryant pulls me in and spins me, causing me to gasp as my feet leave the floor. When he settles *me back down, I look at his smiling face and lean in for a quick kiss.*

"You're going to be a daddy again."

Laughter bursts from him. He releases me, sinks to his knees, and presses kisses along my still-flat stomach. "Janie," he murmurs, looking up at me, "you've made me the happiest man alive. I love you so much." He leans in and kisses my stomach again. "And I already love you, too, little one. I promise I'll be the best daddy I can be. You already have the world's best mommy."

Those were some of the happiest years of my life.

"Did he react similarly with all of the pregnancies?" Katie asks.

"No," I reply, shaking my head as memories flood back. "After having Peter, Bryant sat me down and let me know that he was done having kids. Two was enough for him. I may not have liked it, but I understood. We were so young, and two felt manageable. The fight didn't come until he asked me to get my tubes tied."

"You didn't want that?" Katie inquires.

"No. The thought of never having kids again was too much for me. I wanted to keep that door open. I mean, we were still so young. So I chose the pill, and Bryant took precautions of his own."

"Yet you still got pregnant. What happened there?"

I shift on the couch, tucking a cushion behind my back to get comfortable. "Surprises happen. I was taking my pill religiously, but after an office party, Bryant was careless."

He didn't take the news of the pregnancy well at all.

"Was Bryant okay with Eric after he was born?" Katie asks.

"He was. I mean, he wasn't hateful, at least. But things weren't the same as they were before. Bryant's interactions with Eric were sparse, almost like he was a stranger in his own home. The late-night feedings, diaper changes, they were on my shoulders alone. I sat by and watched as Bryant began to pull away, but there was nothing I could do to stop it. Every attempt I made to bridge the gap only seemed to make him pull away further."

"That makes sense with the timing of you coming to see me then. I assume things spiraled from there?"

In the early months of Eric's life, Bryant was like a ghost in our home. My mom would come over, allowing me to catch up on housework or get a few hours of sleep here and there. She knew we were hurting, but held on to the hope that things would eventually get better.

The first time Bryant hit me, he had been drinking. I wanted to believe it was a one-time thing, especially since he was so remorseful the next day. But his drinking became a thing for him, and his absences around the house became longer and longer. By the time Eric was six or seven months old, our arguments had become as regular as clockwork. I walked through our home as if on eggshells all the time. I was afraid of setting him off. So yeah, that's when things truly began to spiral.

"Yeah," I reply simply.

"I'm sorry that you had to face that," Katie says, her voice gentle, "but you truly have come such a long way since you started seeing me." She leans forward slightly, her eyes searching mine. "Do you think you could pick up on some of those signs Bryant showed if they were to happen again?"

I nod confidently. "Oh yeah. Not only did I live it, but I see it at work too. I don't think I'd have a problem with it now. At least I hope not."

Katie smiles as she jots something down in her notebook. She looks up again, meeting my gaze. "So now that you're getting back into the dating scene, do you think you're ready?"

I shift in my seat. Just thinking about getting back out there makes me nervous. "I'm not sure that I'm fully ready, but then again, I want to do it. It's weird, really. I think once I'm out there, I'll be fine, but taking that first step is scary. I haven't dated anyone since high school."

Looking down at her notepad, she taps the paper with her pen, then meets my eyes again. "You mentioned once, a while back, that there was a guy you met at your brother's place that you liked, but you felt guilty for finding him attractive, and when he asked you on a date, you shot him down right away. Do you think you'd still feel guilty if that were to happen today?"

I hope not. The man Katie is talking about is none other than Elijah Boyd. A friend of the Whitfield family, Maddie basically grew up with him.

After a long, exhausting day at work followed by hours in class, Tom called to invite me to a barbecue. I was hesitant at first, so I called Mom and asked if she'd mind keeping the kids for another hour or two. She reassured me that all was fine. "Go, have fun," she told me. "If you're still there by eight, I'll have Dad bring the kids to you." Relief washes over me as I park at Tom's, savoring a rare moment free from the demands of motherhood, work, or school. The aroma of grilling meat drifts through the air, brought on by Maddie's siblings' impromptu visit.

Walking up the path to my brother's yard, I pass Maddie's youngest brothers, the twins, and flash them a grin, then go in search of Tom. But my steps falter at the sight of a man standing beside Cam. He glances my way and smiles, stirring feelings I thought had been buried with Bryant.

A pang of guilt twists within me. I vowed my life to my ex, and though he left me, moving on seems impossible.

Cam's voice pulls me from my thoughts. "There she is. Come on over, Janie. Have you met Eli yet? He came down with Maddie's brothers."

My eyes return to the man, Eli, whose gaze is locked on mine. He's handsome, his blue eyes almost violet in the fading sunlight. Though not as tall as Cam, he's close. Where my brothers are bulky, Eli is lean, his sleeves stretched taut over his arms.

A flutter I haven't felt in years takes root, and I'm ready to run.

"I might not be ready for anything serious, but the thought of dating again is both intimidating and thrilling," I answer honestly.

Maybe it's time to get out there and meet new people—just not anyone who makes me feel like Eli does. I'm not ready for the level of commitment that comes with those kinds of feelings just yet.

Chapter Three

I swing the rear doors of the ambulance shut and toss the trash into the bin, then head up the stairs toward the gym. Thank God the rig is finally clean and stocked. My shoulders ache from today's calls—a diabetic collapse, a pediatric asthma attack, and a live birth in a woman's closet. They kept us busy today, and it's not even midweek. At least I'll get in a quick workout and a hot shower before the drive home.

My hand closes on the gym door handle when Lieutenant Hugh's voice comes from down the hall. "Cameron, you've got a call from the school—line one."

I pull away from the door and sprint down the hallway to an empty office. I drop into the squeaky swivel chair, lift the receiver, and put it to my ear. "This is Janelle." The school rarely ever calls me at work.

"Hello, Janelle, this is Mrs. Christy, the principal at Baycliff Valley School. Your children are fine, but your ex-husband is here in the office, causing a bit of a scene. He's demanding that we release the kids to him and his girlfriend, but the last documents that we have from two years ago state that he has limited visitation and that it's monitored. Mr. Fuller claims that's changed. Can you confirm?"

I've been wondering when he'd pull his next stunt. He always seems to behave at the beginning of a new relationship.

"No, ma'am. There's been no change. That order still stands." I glance up at the clock on the wall. 2:47 p.m. "I'm finishing up here. I'll be there soon."

"Thank you."

"You're welcome. See you soon." I hang up and go in search of Lieutenant Hugh. Moments later, I find him down in the open bay, wiping his greasy hands on a rag.

He glances up from the polished fire engine. "Everything good?"

I shake my head. "No. Bryant's at the school trying to get the kids. I need to go. My rig is already clean and fully stocked."

"Go. Val just walked in; I'll have her clock in early. Holler if you need anything."

I nod, relief running through me. "Thanks."

I head for the locker room, skipping the showers this time. I grab my duffel and my phone and keys from the top shelf of my cubby, then jog toward my car, adrenaline propelling me out the front doors.

I pull into the small parking lot just outside of the school. The town is so small that all the grades are clustered in the same area, just in separate buildings. At the office entrance,

I press the button and wait for the click that signals I can enter.

Once inside, I'm greeted by Officer Andrews. His face is as familiar as the hallways to me; he's the same officer on duty as when I was a student here years ago. From what I've heard, this might be his last year.

"Afternoon, Ms. Cameron," he says with a nod.

"Afternoon, Officer Andrews," I reply.

"Right this way." He motions me toward the office door, which is normally propped open but now sits closed, a testament to how loud Bryant must have made himself.

"Mrs. Christy is waiting in her office," he announces as he opens the door for me. He guides me past the reception desk to another closed door at the back of the room. Andrews pauses, then pushes it open. I cringe as, even from the other end of the hallway, Bryant's voice ricochets off the walls.

At the far end of the hallway, Andrews knocks, then cracks the door open. "Ms. Cameron is here."

A woman's muffled reply drifts out. "Let her in."

Andrews swings the door wide, then leaves to grab a chair for me. While he's gone, I offer Mrs. Christy a polite smile. She's sitting behind a large desk, shoulders squared. She looks as if she's had more than enough of Bryant already.

Opposite her, Bryant sits with his new girlfriend, I presume, a blonde woman in a pale-blue dress whose shoulders slump slightly as she offers me a tentative smile.

I step toward her and extend my hand. "Hello. I'm Janelle Cameron. Who might you be?"

She slips hers in mine. "I'm Milly, Bryant's girlfriend."

Before I can say more, Bryant snarls, "Get your paws off her."

I pull back, my palms raised in surrender.

Milly's cheeks flush, and she tucks a stray curl behind her ear. She places a hand on his arm, murmuring something I barely catch—"Calm." She lifts her face and offers me a soft, apologetic smile. "I'm sorry. It's been a long day. He didn't mean to snap."

Oh, he meant it, I think, but I don't voice it out loud. I just hope she knows what she's getting herself into. She seems sweet. I'll have to try and keep an eye out for her. I'd hate for Bryant to hurt another innocent woman.

Officer Andrews returns with another chair and positions it on the side of Mrs. Christy's desk, away from Bryant. I take my seat so this, whatever this is, can get started.

Mrs. Christy clears her throat and looks from me to Bryant. "Now that we're all here," she says, "we can work at getting on the same page. Ms. Cameron, you state that the existing visitation agreement stands. Mr. Fuller, unless you present a new court order, I won't be able to release the children from school to you. Do you have such a document?"

I watch Bryant's jaw work as though he's grinding his teeth. I'm sure Mrs. Christy's told him this already. Why he thinks it'll be different now that I'm here is lost on me.

Finally, Bryant runs a hand through his hair and exhales hard. "No. My lawyer didn't give it to me." He glances at Milly, who soothes him with reassuring strokes along his arm.

Of course he doesn't have it, because there isn't one!

"Then we cannot release the children to you," Mrs. Christy says firmly. She shifts her gaze back to me. "Ms. Cameron, this agreement is two years old. Can you provide updated documentation? I must follow the paperwork before me unless shown otherwise."

"That is from our last court hearing, but I'll call my lawyer tomorrow and see if he can get me something stating that nothing has changed."

Bryant's voice cracks with frustration. "I just wanted to take the kids out for a meal so they could meet Milly. Why can't I do that?"

Mrs. Christy's expression remains impassive. "Rules are rules, Mr. Fuller." She looks back at Andrews. "Officer Andrews, would you walk Mr. Fuller and his guest out to their car? I need to speak with Ms. Cameron."

My stomach twists into knots. The weight of her words makes me feel like I'm being summoned to the principal's office all over again. In a way, I guess I have been.

Officer Andrews gives a brief nod, his expression unreadable, as he strides toward the door, gesturing for them to follow him.

Bryant takes a step closer, towering over me. His voice drops to a whisper as he leans in. "This isn't over, Janelle. Far from it."

I clasp my hands tightly in my lap, my fingers trembling slightly, but I sit upright, determined not to show any sign of fear. He'll never hold power over me again.

The door clicks shut, snapping me back to the present.

Mrs. Christy clears her throat softly to regain my attention. "Ms. Cameron," she begins, her voice tinged with a hint of sympathy.

"Janelle, please," I interject, offering a small smile. "Now that he's gone, there's no need for formalities."

She returns my smile with a nod. "Thank you, Janelle. I hate to add more to your plate, but after the commotion your ex stirred up today, I'm afraid I'll have to do just that."

I sigh, resigning myself to what she's about to say.

"Your kids are so well behaved, and I hate to do this, but Mr. Fuller disrupted things to the point that I had to ask my secretary to put the classrooms on lockdown. That is not something we want for any of our students."

"Of course. But what can we do?" I ask.

"As of tomorrow, I'd like your children to start distance learning," she states, her voice firm yet regretful.

"For how long?" I ask, panic bubbling up inside me. How am I supposed to juggle my job *and* help my kids with online school? Maybe Mom can help, but she already does so much for us.

"I've scheduled a meeting for you to come in and talk with me the week before spring break. If anything changes before then, you can always call me, and we'll arrange to meet sooner. Otherwise, we'll discuss everything then."

My phone rings, causing me to jump. I pull it out of my pocket, and when I see Maddie's name flash across the screen, I silence it.

"You can go ahead and take it. We're finished here, unless you have anything to add. I've already sent someone to help the kids pack up what they'll need to take home. If you'd like, I can ask Officer Andrews to walk them out to your car himself when they're ready."

"That would be nice, thank you." I stand from the chair and extend my hand to shake hers. Despite being frustrated, there's no sense in arguing with her. I don't blame her for making this decision. Even if I hate it.

As I make my way out of the office, I pull out my phone and dial Maddie.

"Hello?"

"Hey, Mads. What's up?" I ask, weaving through the now-busy hallway.

"I was calling to see what you were doing tonight. Your brother's working, and I'm bored," she replies.

As I near the exit, a small group of kids rush past, laughter trailing behind them. One of them holds the door open, and I nod in thanks, then step out and head towards my SUV. "I've got to call my boss, but other than that, not much. Do you want to come over?"

"Everything okay?" Maddie asks.

Settling into the driver's seat, I insert the key, and the engine rumbles to life. I begin recounting the events that just happened. "I guess we're okay. But now I have to figure out what to do with the kids for a few months. It's different when I'm expecting a break, but this is so unexpected, I don't have anything planned."

"What a jerk. I'm sorry you're still having to deal with him. You deserve so much better. Why don't you take your vacation and come to Charleston with me?"

The idea of a getaway tempts me, but the reality is it's not possible right now. "That sounds like a dream come true, but I can't afford that yet."

"My treat. You'd be doing me a favor, really," she insists. I know she has more money than all of the Camerons com- bined, but I still don't like taking charity, and that's what this feels like.

A knock on the rear hatch startles me. I glance in the mirror and see Officer Andrews standing there with the kids, a patient smile on his face. I press the button to open the hatch. "I've got to get. The kids just came out. I'll see you in a few."

"Call your boss and see if you can take your vacation, and leave the rest up to me. Oh, and don't cook anything. You need a night off. Dinner's on me tonight."

Before I can protest, the call ends with a decisive click, leaving me smiling at the thought of a much-needed break. I won't argue with her buying dinner, but I'll draw the line at paying for a vacation.

Chapter Four

Garrett, my partner at work, races us through the city streets to the scene of a building collapse. As we pull around the corner, my heart pounds faster at the sight ahead of me. I peer out the window—the right side of a three-story building has caved in. I can't even begin to imagine the sheer force it must have taken to destroy a building like this.

I jump out of the rig and quickly make my way to the back, where Lieutenant Hugh waits with urgent information. "What are we working with?" I ask, my voice laced with adrenaline.

"We have three people trapped in the stairwell," he replies. "One may need stabilization on scene. My team is still working on clearing the path. I'll follow up as soon as they have it ready. Can you handle things out here until then?"

I nod confidently, but inside, I'm trembling with fear and uncertainty. This is my first big scene since the promotion, and it's my turn to take the lead. I inhale deeply, trying to steady myself. There's no time for self-doubt.

Garrett opens the hatch so I can grab my gear and mentally prepare myself for what lies ahead. "This is Garrett on 14 Rescue," she calls in, her voice strained with tension. "We need another rig on scene ASAP."

As we wait for the all clear so I can get in there, Luka, one of the fire and rescue members, walks out of the building with a woman in his arms. I holler back at Garrett, letting her know I'm on it, and head that way. This is going to be a long day; I just hope we don't lose anybody.

Thank God it's my Friday. I'm ready to go home and hug my babies.

I open the back door to my Suburban and throw my bag in before shutting it. I'm finally off work, on vacation, and ready to head home. It has been one heck of a tiring shift today. I typically work four twelve-hour shifts a week, but this week, I picked up an extra day, and it was brutal. After the building collapse—thankfully, there was only one serious injury, the others minor—we responded to a five-car pileup.

I'm bone tired.

I've never been good with confined spaces, and that only got worse after Bryant. I can say, after today, with one hundred percent surety, that I still don't like them. When Garrett and I made it back to the station and the next crew showed up, I cleaned up, hit the gym to blow off some steam, and am just now leaving. Normally, after my shift is over, I spend a good hour working out before heading home. I need that time to clear my head.

When I get home, my kids deserve all of me.

"Hey, Cameron?" Hugh hollers.

I turn with my hand still on my door handle, ready to get in.

"Good job today."

"You too." I open the door and turn back. "Are you and Sherry coming out for Eric's party still?"

"We wouldn't miss it. See you tomorrow."

I hop in and turn on the heat. I would normally go home and cook dinner, but tonight, I'll make an exception. Cooking is out of the question. I open my glove box and dig for the twenty I've stashed for a night like this. After I check in with Mom, I'm going to go get a bag of two-dollar burgers and fries. I feel bad that she's been with the kids so much this week, but since they will be schooling virtually for a while, I don't have much of a choice right now.

Me: *Sorry I'm late. Long day. I'll stop and grab dinner, and be there soon.*

Mom: *No rush, Janie. We're just fine. See you when you get here. Love you.*

Me: *Love you, too, Mom.*

I secure my phone in the hands-free holder and leave the parking lot, on the hunt for an affordable—if that's even possible these days—fast-food joint. Once I get there, I park and place my order. I know that cooking would be the wise thing to do, but I've adjusted my budget so that it's not as tight anymore. Paying off two credit cards has made a big difference. The money I would usually use to make those payments is now reserved for leisure or, in this instance, a cheap burger. Since it usually takes a few minutes for the food to come out, I decide to recline my seat and close my eyes, savoring the moment before they bring out dinner. I'm definitely ready to call it a night.

I could fall asleep right here and now.

There's a rap on the window, startling me. I turn and see a young woman holding up my takeout bag.

I sit up and unroll the window with a smile. "Sorry. I thought I could rest my eyes while I was waiting. You guys aren't normally this fast." I fish out the twenty from my cupholder and hand it over.

She hands me the bag with a bright smile. "No problem, ma'am. Have a nice evening."

"You too."

I reach over to the passenger seat and buckle the bag in before backing up and heading across the way to the interstate. I learned the hard way to buckle in my bags a long time ago. There is no better lesson than trying to get sweet-and-sour sauce out of tan carpets.

After merging onto the interstate, I crank the radio up and try to amp myself up. Knowing my kids, when I get home, they'll be little balls of energy, ready to eat and play. I'm glad that I have most weekends off with them.

As I drive into the final stretch of the Cameron Farm, I can finally relax, knowing I'm home and ready for the weekend. The Cameron Farm (or Farms, depending on who you ask) covers almost 150 acres. We all live just a short golf cart or gator ride from one another. This arrangement is ideal for my kids and has been a tremendous support since my divorce.

After parking, I hop out and go to grab my bag from the back, then move to the front to grab the food. Hearing the door, I look up as Eric runs out.

"Momma!" He looks back over his shoulder and yells, "Mom's home!"

I set my bag on the ground as he hops down the stairs and runs my way, just in time for me to catch him. He's not as small as he once was, so he nearly knocks me over when he's running full force. And I'm not a small woman by any means. Though for an almost thirty-year-old mom of three who works out a lot, I don't think wearing a size sixteen is too bad. At least that's what Heather likes to tell me. I've put on a lot of muscle mass since my marriage. It's part of the job, I guess. Lifting people all the time will do that to you.

"Hey, buddy." I pull back from his embrace. "Were you good for Grandma?"

I am so thankful that my family is willing to pitch in and help with the kids. There is no way that I could afford childcare for them if not. Not like the older two would want to go anyway.

Eric nods. "Yup."

I look up to see my mom walking down the stairs behind Peter and Sage. Thor runs off to take care of his business, not bothered by my homecoming. Mom smiles and wraps her sweater tighter around her.

"Go give Grandma hugs."

The kids run over and wrap her in their arms. I'm not far behind.

"Thanks, Mom."

"No problem. I love spending time with the kids. You know that. I better get a move on, though. Dad said he's about to put the rolls in the oven if I'm not home soon, and you know how bad the hockey pucks he makes are."

I chuckle. Dad can grill with the best of them, but he is not a cook when it comes to the kitchen. Cam and Pat took after him there. I thought Tom did, too, at first, but he seems to be getting a little better nowadays.

Peter grabs my bag from the ground and tosses it over his shoulder before sticking his nose back in his game.

"Thanks, Pete." I turn back to look at Mom. "I'll take that as my cue to get the kids inside and fed. Thanks again for watching them. Love you."

"Love you, too, Janie."

Mom walks out through the gate and closes it behind her. I turn and catch up with my kids, who are walking ahead of me. At the door, I glance back and whistle for Thor to join us inside, then head straight for the sink to wash up. I plate up our food while Sage feeds Thor. After the plates are set around the table, I call the kids over. I really enjoy these meals with them—no phones or other devices allowed. Despite our busy schedules, it's one thing that will never change in our family. Even with my parents and brothers—you can often find us gathered around a table, enjoying a meal or playing games.

With Eric's birthday celebration tomorrow, followed by the double date I agreed to the day after, and our upcoming trip to Charleston with Tom's now girlfriend, Maddie—yeah, she talked me into it—I want to savor every moment I have left. The kids are growing up way too fast, and now that I'm working, time seems to be passing even more quickly.

"How about a game after dinner and cleanup?"

"Can we invite Uncle Pat?" Eric asks.

"I guess if you want to." I was kind of hoping for some time with the kids myself, but who am I to say no? I did work all day when it was my one guaranteed day with them. "Did you guys have fun with Grandma?"

"Yeah, we got to go see Aunt Leah and the babies," Sage says. "She told me that I can come to the girls' lunch next time, if it's okay with you."

"She did, did she? That was nice of her to offer."

For going on two years now, since right before Leah had the babies, all of us ladies—my sisters-in-law, Mom, and some close family friends—have been getting together for lunch monthly out here on the farm. Most of the time, there are no kids, but we have been known to bring them from time to time.

"As long as your behavior is good and you get all of your schoolwork done, I don't see an issue with that."

Sage shoots her fist up in the air triumphantly.

"What about you boys? Are you going to hang out with the guys?"

While the ladies get together, the guys try to get together too. They've been known to take that time and fix the fence along the property, go fishing, or get together for beer and games. We never really know what they'll get up to until they do it.

"I figured I'd just hang in my room and play video games," Peter answers.

"Yeah," Eric replies. "We'll be in his room, playing games."

Peter raises a brow as he looks at me, then at his brother, but surprises me by letting it go.

"I'll see if Uncle Cam can pick y'all up," I state.

"I don't think they're getting together this month," Sage says. "Aunt Leah said something about Uncle Cam and Mark having to work."

I swallow the bite in my mouth before responding. "I'll find out. A lot of times, they still get together even if a few of them have to work." Not always, but I know that they try.

The rest of dinner flies by with conversation about a new game that Pete found and would like to try out and the party tomorrow. Before long, we're cleaning up, then finding our way to the family room. Pete pulls up a racing game on the TV and Eric grabs my phone to call Pat.

While I'm worn out, I cannot imagine closing out my night any other way.

I lean down and kiss Eric on the forehead. "Good night, bud. I love you."

"Love you, too, Momma." He turns over and cuddles Thor. After giving Thor his nightly pets, I head toward the door, which I leave cracked open as I turn off the light.

I make a quick stop off at the doorway of the others' rooms. After nearly dying due to Bryant's actions, I've made it a habit to tell my loved ones how much they mean to me daily. Especially the kids. I don't want one day to go by where they have to question the way I feel.

When my feet hit the bottom step, I come to a stop. I thought Pat would've left by now, but instead, I find him standing at the kitchen sink washing the dishes.

I walk over to his side and shoulder-bump him. "Thank you."

"You're welcome." He rinses the last plate and hands it to me so I can towel dry it. "Sage told me that you have a date this weekend. Do you think you're ready for that?"

"I'm not sure. My therapist does, though. I miss the companionship, but I'm not sure that I'm ready to open up to let anyone in fully. At least not yet."

He takes two beers from the fridge, handing me one before walking around the island and taking a seat. "Is it a good idea to date someone if you're not willing to open up to them? Janie, you have a lot to give to someone, but it goes both ways. You can't expect to start a relationship and expect the guy to open up while you hold back. That's just asking for things to end badly."

My walls are there for a reason.

I walk around and take a seat next to Pat. "I'm not looking for anything serious right now. I only want to dip my toes into the dating pool, not dive in."

"I hope you know what you're doing." He takes a long pull from his drink before setting it back down. "You could meet the man of your dreams and still be holding on to those walls so tight that you miss out. I don't want that for you, but even worse would be the kids. Janie, they've already lost their father. They don't need to lose another." He smiles softly. "Just promise me that you won't bring anyone around the kids unless you're certain that it could lead to something long-term. They've been through enough already."

I love my kids with all my heart. The thought of them being hurt again guts me.

"I know you'd never do anything to hurt the kids intentionally. But trauma changes people." He pauses. Pat hasn't been the same since the incident that left him scarred inside and out. Aside from Katie, he's been the most supportive. Sometimes, he just sits quietly beside me, saying nothing, yet his presence offers me all the comfort I need. "I worry about you falling for someone who knows how to say just what you want to hear."

I want to argue, but his words strike a nerve, and I'm suddenly filled with doubt. Can I truly trust my own judgment after everything I've been through?

Chapter Five

The next morning, I put my headphones on and open the patient portal, waiting on Katie to join our session. I'm not big on meeting virtually, but considering that Eric's party is this afternoon, this is the best we could do.

A chime sounds in my ear, alerting me to her video call.

"Hello?"

"How are you today?"

"I'm good, and you?" I always seem to have a hard time starting out. No matter how many sessions we have, I think I will always want to ask how she is too. That's just how I am.

"I'm good. How was your week?"

"It was a busy one." I tell her about the calls I went out on this week and all the things that are coming up this weekend. As I continue, my mind keeps circling back to the incident with Bryant at the school. "I don't know if I told you or not, but Bryant went to the kids' school last week and tried to get them to release the kids to him."

"You didn't. Is everyone okay?"

"Yeah, we're good." I fill her in on everything that happened.

"And how do you feel about it now?"

"I'm still mad that my kids can't go to class and be with their friends because their father can't be a mature adult. But I'm handling it. I called my lawyer to get the paper Mrs. Christy asked for, and in return, my lawyer asked that they write a letter about the incident for him to keep in my file."

"I'm glad that you got it handled. The last thing you need right now is more of his drama."

"I know, right?"

"Well, I think you're handling things really well, considering." There's a brief pause while she looks at her notebook. "Didn't you tell me that you had a date this weekend? How did that go?"

I nod my head and begin fidgeting. "I do. It's scheduled for tomorrow evening. If I'm honest, I'm not really looking forward to it. I'm more excited about our trip to Charleston than I am the date."

"Why is that?" Katie asks.

I fiddle with the cord of my headphones as my knee bounces. "Well, the guy that I'm supposed to go on a date with sort of reminds me of Bryant—Val showed me a picture once and, I swear, they could be brothers." I chew on my bottom lip. "And um . . . uh, as much as I hate to admit it, I can't stop thinking about Elijah. After talking about him at our last session and then to Maddie about staying in her family's home, where he lives, it's brought him to the forefront of my thoughts."

"I can see why." The corner of her mouth lifts in a slow smile. "Care to elaborate on Elijah? From my understanding, you two met at a barbeque. What happened?"

I tuck a stray strand of hair behind my ear and glance toward the window. "We did. I mean, I had heard about him a few times from Maddie, seeing as his mom is their house manager, so they were as close as siblings."

Those flutters that I felt the moment my eyes landed on Elijah don't go away—not completely anyway. After Cam walks away to help Tom on the grill, Eli joins me where I've taken up stock on the grass nearby. Now, we've been talking for God only knows how long. Conversation with him is easy. So far, I've learned that he's a momma's boy, big time. I don't think it's in a creepy way, but in a sweet way where he takes care of her.

"You're really an EMT?" Eli asks.

"Yeah, I am. Soon, I hope to be a rescue paramedic. Better pay, more stability for my kids, and a better schedule. The work is hard, but I grew up in a family of cops. It was kind of expected that I'd be some sort of emergency personnel."

Eli places his hand on my arm, and instead of flinching, I feel a spark. It's terrifying. The man standing before me stirs emotions I haven't experienced in so long, and I don't know how to deal with it.

He must see the conflict written on my face and pulls his hand back before offering a small smile. "That's impressive."

"Thanks. What is it that you do for work?"

"I'm a security consultant. Basically, I travel a lot and look at companies' security systems, then tell them how they can improve them. I'm working my way up to becoming a security engineer. I really don't want to travel so much anymore."

Our conversation gets cut short when Dad stops by with the kids. I hadn't realized it was already so late. The kids run off toward their uncles as dad walks my way.

"Dad, this is Eli. Eli, this is my father, Butch," I say.

"We met earlier today," Dad says. "Elijah came over with Tom and helped Peter and me load hay into the barn." Dad flashes me a smile. "Eli and Pete seemed to bond over some game he was playing."

Eli's cheeks turn pink. "I noticed Peter was playing an older version of the game and asked if he'd tried the latest one. A client of mine developed it and gave me a few copies. I thought that I could send him one if he didn't already have it."

"You really don't have to," I insist.

"It's no trouble. They're just collecting dust at home."

"Well, I guess that would be fine, if you don't mind. I'm sure Peter would appreciate it."

He hands me his phone to put my number in so we can chat more about the game later.

"I should head home now," Dad interjects. He calls the kids over for a hug, and I smile at Eli. "Be good for Mom. We'll see you tomorrow."

As Dad talks to the kids, Eli leans in to speak privately with me. "I had fun tonight."

"Same here," I reply.

"How about we continue this over coffee tomorrow morning?"

Who knew such a simple question could trigger every alarm in my body?

"No!" I nearly shout. "Sorry, I can't. I'm . . . uh . . . busy." The look of worry on his face makes me want to explain, but the panic I'm feeling won't let me stop.

Before I can say another word, I gather the kids and quickly head to my SUV, not worried about what anyone thinks of me making a show.

Once inside, I rest my head on the steering wheel and let out a sigh. I made a fool of myself in front of the first man *who has stirred feelings in me since my divorce.* Way to go, Janelle. *If he texts me after this, I'll need to apologize, or at least explain my panic.*

"So saying no to Elijah was just a knee-jerk reaction. How would you feel if he asked you out again now?"

I chuckle. "I think I scared him off. We've texted a bit since then, just casual chats, but he hasn't made any attempt to ask me out again."

She writes something down on her notepad, then looks back at the screen. "How do you feel about that?"

"I'm a bit disappointed, but also happy. I know that if I were to date Eli, things would most likely get serious. He's close with my family, and I can't see him dating me to just date me. I don't think I'm ready for anything serious just yet."

The timer chimes in the background, letting me know that my hour is up.

"That's our time for today. What do you think about starting up every-other-week sessions? I think that maybe soon, we can even go to once a month. But let's get you through the start of your dates first."

"Oh, wow. Okay. If you think I'm ready for that, then I guess we can give it a shot."

"You can always text me or call the office and set something up in between if you need me. But I think you're ready. You've come so far since we started talking."

The thought of not having her to vent to on a weekly basis is terrifying, but I guess if I'm ever really going to move on, this is a step in the right direction. I just hope that I'm ready for it.

I pause to straighten out my T-shirt and jeans in front of the mirror. Even though I'm keeping it casual today, I still want to look presentable. It can be hard to look at myself without hearing Bryant's words echoing in my mind. I still see all the imperfections—the stretch marks and extra pounds he always pointed out—but I'm working on it. For everything that I see that I don't like, I try to find something that I do, like my eyes, a brown so deep a lot of people say they're black, and my smile that Mom and Dad paid a pretty penny to get straight with braces. The physical scars Bryant left may have healed, but the emotional ones I'm still working on. Katie believes I'm ready to move on, yet moments like this make me question if I ever will be. I shake my head and remind myself not to let Bryant have the power to drag me back into the depression I've fought so hard to overcome.

I try and reach deep within for my Grammy's words. "Janie, dear, you are a beauty. Any man worth a dang will stop in his tracks and move heaven and earth to be with you." She would often tell me this when I stayed the weekend with her. We would sit at her organ and play her favorite song, one that she dubbed mine—"Beautiful Brown Eyes" by The Brothers Four. I have the sheet music up in my attic somewhere. I really should get that out now that I have her organ in my home. It's been ages since I've played. Those moments spent at that organ with her are some of my fondest memories. I sure do miss her. None of us could have imagined her passing right after Cam's twins were born. Grammy was such a strong-willed woman, we all thought she'd be around forever.

I wipe away tears as I think about her and glance at the clock on my bedside table in surprise—it's already ten in the morning! "Shoot, I'll never finish everything at this rate."

I quickly slip on my tennis shoes and head downstairs to start preparing for the day. With coffee brewing in the background, I move through the house like a madwoman, making sure everything is perfect for the celebration. Today is Eric's fifth birthday, and the first *large* party we've had for him since the divorce. Though my anxiety is through the roof at the thought of everyone being here, I know it's time to try.

We deserve to celebrate after everything we've been through.

With the kids out of school today and them getting to stay up late last night, they're all still asleep, or at least still in their rooms. For now.

I walk into the kitchen and pour myself a cup of coffee, sipping on it as I make a mental note of all the things left to do.

The sound of footsteps above me causes me to smile. The kids are up, and the quiet of the house is about to change. While I enjoy it being quiet, I love hearing the laughter of my kids more.

"Hey, Mom." Sage walks into the kitchen and smiles at me. She's still in her sleep shorts, tank top, and pink animal-paw slippers. In this moment, she looks like my little baby girl, all rumpled, with her long strawberry-blonde hair sticking out every which way. If only she were batting her baby blues up at me like she used to. Though she's nearly the same five-foot-three as me already. I may be looking up at her one day if she doesn't slow down.

"Good morning, angel. Sleep well?"

"Once Eric quit yelling about it being his birthday, I did." She opens the fridge and grabs the milk, then pulls down a box of cereal from the top of the fridge. "Do you think I can have a cup of coffee this morning? I'm still tired. I don't want to fall asleep at the party."

Seeing as how Sage is now a preteen—I still can't seem to wrap my head around that one sometimes—and I was drinking coffee with Mom at the age of ten, I guess one cup won't hurt.

"Sure, but let's limit it to one cup, okay?"

"Thanks, Mom." Sage puts her bowl down on the island, leans over, and kisses my cheek.

I smile. I'm so glad that my baby girl is back. There for a while, I thought for sure the depression would take her under. We all still have our hard days, with Peter having more than the rest of us, but for the most part, life is better than it has been in years.

"Want another cup?" she asks.

"I'd love one, thanks. My cup is over by the pot already."

I put my back against the center island as I hear the clicking of dog paws heading our way and brace for impact as Thor runs down the stairs. No matter how much training he's been through, I cannot get this boy to stop jumping on me when it's time to go out or be fed. My big ole fur baby scares the heck out of most people—that is, until they get to know him. He'd rather lick you than bite—though I'm also not saying that he won't bite. The way he growls at Bryant makes me wonder if he would if given the chance.

"After you eat, I need you to let Thor out back."

Sage wrinkles her nose but doesn't argue. After handing me my cup of coffee, she gives Thor his breakfast and then gets back to hers.

A knock at the front door interrupts my time with my daughter. I turn in time to see Cam walking in.

"Hey, Janie." Cam greets me with a smile as he reaches for my cup of coffee and takes a sip. The only ones who still call me that are my close family members. To everyone else, I go by J. And honestly, I prefer it that way. "Thanks. How did you know I needed this?"

I playfully punch his shoulder before heading to the coffee pot to pour another cup.

He leans down to give Sage a kiss on her forehead, then pets Thor, who makes his presence known. "Leah sent me to see if you need help setting up."

I take a sip of my steaming-hot coffee. "I need all the help I can get. Kim said she'd swing by and pick up Eric and Peter to take them into town for haircuts while I set up for the party. Are you sure you want to help?" I ask. "It's a lot of work, and you look like you need a bed more than anything else."

Cam walks over to the table in the corner and plops down in a chair, nearly dousing himself in the hot coffee. He sets it down and rubs the bridge of his nose before looking my way. "I'm here, so put me to work. Just make sure to keep the coffee strong and endless."

Sage, now done with her cereal, lets Thor out and then heads back upstairs.

I move to sit with my brother. "Did the babies not let you sleep last night?"

"I got maybe two hours. Kelly was up most of the night screaming."

I reach out and touch his shoulder. "Is she okay?"

Cam nods and downs nearly his whole cup. I scoot mine across the table to him. At this point, he needs it more than I do. "She is. The doc said she's just teething. Apparently, this is normal."

"Yeah, it can be pretty miserable for both the kids and the parents."

Cam finishes off my coffee, then nods. "So what can I do?"

"How about you head up to the guest room and take a nap? There's plenty that I can do that I don't need help with. I'll send one of the kids up to get you by noon if you're not down yet. Then you can help me move stuff around."

"Are you sure?"

"I am."

"I might not say it often enough, but you're the best sister ever." Cam stands and rubs the top of my head. "Thanks, sis."

I chuckle. "No problem."

Cam turns and head up the stairs just as my phone begins to chime.

Bryant: *Tell Eric that I said happy birthday and that I'll see him when he gets back since I can't be at his party.*

Me: *I'll let him know.*

Bryant: *This would be a lot easier if I could just see my kids, Janelle.*

Me: *I'm not doing this with you, Bryant.*

I'm sure he only wants to bait me. If it weren't for the fact that we have kids together, he would have been blocked by now. I know I could limit his access to me and make him contact my lawyer, but for some reason, I haven't.

If only we could co-parent without all this drama.

Chapter Six

The next afternoon, Sage and I rush around, getting ready for the ladies' lunch. I planned on making pasta salad but that took a turn when I got sidetracked and overcooked it. There's no way that I'm taking that to lunch. At the last minute, we managed to throw together a pot of macaroni and cheese instead. Since we'll be out of town, we needed to use the milk and cheese anyway. It worked out in the end. Even though it's my turn to host, the ladies took pity on me, and Kim opened her home instead. Since we had Eric's party here yesterday and we're leaving for Charleston in the morning, there was no way I could do it.

"Are you about ready, angel?"

"Ready."

I grab the potholders and the pot as we head toward the door.

Earlier today, Dad and Pat came by to get the boys for a guys' day out. Tom will be spending the day with Maddie before we leave tomorrow, and Cam had to work, so their gathering did get canceled after all.

Once outside, Sage turns and locks the door while I head toward the golf cart. In no time, we're at Kim's and heading inside.

"Knock, knock," I say, sticking my head in the door.

"Come on in," Kim says.

Sage shuts the door behind us as we make our way through the living area toward the dining room in the back. Their house is a bit on the smaller side compared to the rest of our houses. Pat never has been one to need much room.

"Hey, girl," Leah says as we walk in.

"Hey."

"Aunt Leah," Sage says. She walks in past me and goes straight to her aunt, taking Kelly right away, before making her way back to the couch.

I set the pot down on the counter, waving to the others as I move closer to Leah.

"Are you guys ready for tomorrow or do you have a lot left to do?" she asks.

"I think we're pretty much ready to go for the most part. Dad's taking the kids to visit Bryant this evening while I'm on my date. Those are the last things on my to-do list. Of course I'll double-check later, but I think we're ready." If all goes well, we'll be on our way to Charleston in no time.

"That's good, I hope all goes well. Are you ready to see Eli?"

My stomach does a little flip at the thought. "I figured that he'd be out for work. Do you really think he'll be there?" I bite the inside of my lip.

"I don't know for sure, but I can't imagine him missing out on the gala."

Mom walks over, kissing me on the cheek with a "Hey, Janie" before handing Noah over and walking back to the kitchen.

I'd really like to see him again, but the thought of him actually being there makes me nervous. Dwelling on it too much would probably have me repacking my whole suitcase. So, I opt for a more relaxed approach and try to ignore it.

"Everything's going to be okay. I doubt that I'll even run into him. He travels a lot, so I'm sure he'll get there on the day of the gala and then head out again right after." I lean in to kiss Noah and catch whiff of a smell that should not exist in a kitchen full of good food, causing my nose to wrinkle.

Leah grabs her son from my arms, lifting his bum to her nose before echoing my earlier expression. "I'm going to get these two changed before lunch. Just do me a favor, will you?"

I nod. "Sure."

"When you see Eli, and I'm sure you will, don't push him away out of habit. If you're really rejoining the dating pool, maybe he deserves a chance too."

The thought of him taking me out on a date causes my heart to race. Knowing him, Eli is a man who would not want a single date. He'd want a lot more than one. The thought scares the heck out of me.

Later that evening, I walk out of my closet and find Sage and Heather lying on my bed. I do a full spin, and when they shake their head no, I turn and walk right back in.

"What do you even wear for a first date? I haven't been on one in thirteen years." Geez, that makes me feel old! Twenty-nine isn't technically over the hill, right?

"Wear your red wrap dress," Heather suggests.

"No, the black pencil skirt and green button-up," Sage argues.

"How about neither? We're going for casual here. How about jeans and a dress shirt?"

Sage comes running into the closet and pulls out a pair of dark skinny jeans, the green silk button-up that she spoke of, and my nice pair of black wedges. "Try this."

"Honey, I doubt they'll even fit me anymore." I'm not fat, but I have hit the gym a lot since buying them. I'm short and curvy, and no matter how much I work out, that won't go away. I'll never be slim again.

After slipping on Sage's choice—which fits like a glove—I step out to stand in front of the mirror.

"Wow. Nice choice, Sage." Heather gives her a high five and smiles at me in the mirror. "I don't think you have to worry about it not fitting you. They look better on you now than when you bought them."

I must admit, I look dang good. The emerald-green top makes my brown eyes pop. My chestnut-brown hair, down in waves to my midback, and makeup are flawless thanks to Heather, and now my outfit is perfect too.

"I almost regret wasting this on a date that I'm pretty sure will go nowhere."

"Why do you say that?" Heather asks.

I hear the door open and close downstairs, and Thor starts yipping, letting me know it's someone he knows and approves of.

"Will you go down and see if that's your brothers?" I ask Sage.

"Sure." She hops off the bed and exits my room as I turn to face Heather.

"I know that I said I'm ready to date, but what if I'm not? Can I really put myself out there again? I mean, come on. Look how long Bryant and I were together before he turned into the man that left me in the way he did."

Heather scoots off the bed and is at my side in the blink of an eye. "What your jerk of an ex did has nothing to do with this. From all I've heard about him, I think I agree with your therapist. Bryant is a narcissist, and he had you under his thumb for far too long. It was bound to explode at some point. That does *not* mean that you will fall for that again. You'll do things a lot differently this time. Plus, you have me this time around."

I move to sit at the end of my bed so I can put on my shoes. "What does having you in my life this time have anything to do with me dating?"

"Do you honestly think I'll sit back and not say anything if I think the guy doesn't deserve you? That's not happening, J. I'm not going to be rude or all up in your business, but if I see red flags, I'm going to make it known."

The door opens and Sage walks back in with a big smile on her face. "The boys are home. Grandpa dropped them off. He also brought us dinner and said that he'll be back in time for our visit with Dad."

I stand and make my way toward the door. "Thanks, angel." I turn back to look at Heather. "Are you sure that you're okay to stay?"

"I'm here, aren't I?" She smiles and nudges me so that I exit my room. "I'll be calling you at seven. If the date is going well, tell me where you keep the fever patches, but if not, use that as an excuse to leave."

Before I take my first step down the stairs, I look over my shoulder and smile. "Have I told you that I love you?"

Heather laughs as I start down the stairs. "Nope, but it goes both ways. I'd expect the same from you."

"You got it."

As soon as my feet touch the bottom step, I glance across the living room and see my boys standing there with big grins, each clutching a colorful bouquet of flowers in their hands.

My goodness, they're growing up way too fast.

Peter is the spitting image of his father at his age, with brown hair, brown eyes, and a slender build, but at ten, he's already an inch taller than me. He gets his height from my brothers.

And then there's my baby. Five going on fifty. Eric takes more after my side of the family than anything. When he was two, his pictures looked exactly like Tom's at that age. His dirty-blond hair curls at the back when he needs a trim, and his ocean-blue eyes are so sweet. Eric still hasn't lost all his baby weight in his cheeks yet. I know it's only a matter of time, but I'll soak in this stage as long as he'll let me.

But now that they're standing before me in their church suits, hair combed back, my eyes burn with unshed tears.

"Aw, boys. What's this all about?" My heart swells at the kind gesture.

"We wanted to make sure that you got flowers," Eric explains. "You look very pretty, Momma," he adds, his cheeks dimpling with a shy smile.

"You do," Peter adds.

As I approach them, the sweet smell of the flowers fills the air. I accept the bouquets, trying to hold back happy tears as I bend down to wrap the boys in a hug, pressing a grateful kiss atop each of their heads. "This is sweet of you. Thank you, boys. I love them."

"These two are going to make some girls fall hard and fast if this is how they treat their mom."

I turn to look at Heather, a smile spreading across my face at her prediction. It makes my heart happy to know that my boys have good, strong men like my dad and brothers in their lives to show them how their partner should be treated rather than taking what their father did and holding on to that as what a relationship should be like.

"I agree. The boys are going to make fine husbands one day, if that's what they want to be. I'm proud of you boys." I walk to the kitchen, Sage hot on my tail, and pull down two vases from the top cabinet. "Care to help me? It's not too often that we have flowers in the house."

Sage takes one of the vases and begins to put water in it, along with the packet from the bouquet. I show her how to trim the bottom off each of the stems, and we start putting together two beautiful arrangements. The fragrance of freshly cut flowers is something that reminds me of a happier time. When Bryant and I first started dating, he bought me a small arrangement of carnations. *No.* I shake the thought away. I've worked too hard to get rid of my thoughts of him to go back there now.

"How's this?" Sage asks.

"That's beautiful, angel." She did a good job, better than I could have ever done at her age. "How about you take it into the family room and put it on one side of the mantel, then come back for this one?"

Thor sticks his nose up on the counter, trying to see if there are any scraps for him.

"Pete, let Thor out please. And, bud, I want you to go ahead and get him fed before dinner."

My phone chimes, letting me know that it's time for me to head out so that I can make it to my date on time. My heart picks up a beat and nerves begin to kick in. I haven't dated anyone in so long. What if I make a complete fool of myself?

Putting aside my worries, I gather the scraps from the flowers and throw them away before walking to the living room where Heather sits, phone in hand.

"It's time," I say when she looks up.

She tosses her phone aside and stands. She walks around the couch and stands in front of me. After her last-minute primping, she hands me my coat and purse. Turning me to the door, she gives me a little nudge. "You've got this. You are beautiful, you are smart, you are the prize. If you need an out before I call, go to the bathroom and text me. I'll get you out in a hot second."

I turn back around once I reach the door. "I don't know if I can do this."

"Sure you can. It's just nerves. Besides, just think of this as practice. You said yourself that you don't see this date going anywhere. Take the pressure off yourself and just go out and enjoy a free dinner." She turns her head and hollers out, "Kids, come say bye to Mom. It's time for her to head out."

Eric and Sage join us by the door. I give them each a quick hug before stepping out onto the porch as Peter is walking up the stairs.

"Heading out?" he asks.

"Yeah," I say. "Help Heather out, will you?"

He nods. "M'kay."

"I'll be back as soon as I can. Love you guys." I lean in and kiss his head on my way out.

Even though this date is not one that I am looking forward to, in a way, I am happy to finally be moving forward.
I've let Bryant put my life on hold for way too long.

Chapter Seven

Pulling up outside of Angelo's, a fine-dining Italian restaurant, I step out of my car and hand the valet my keys. I look to the right when I hear Val holler my name, then smile and walk her way. She's standing there with two men, one I've seen her with before. I guess he must be her date for the evening.

She pulls me in for a quick hug and kisses me on my cheek. "Your date, Scott, seems nice. Ethan swears that he's a good guy. They went to school together, but haven't hung out in a few years." She pulls back, and I nod.

Scott steps forward and extends his hand out to shake mine. He seems nice. He has a decent smile—nothing that makes my stomach flutter, and I swear he reminds me of Bryant. They could be brothers—both with brown hair, brown eyes, a stocky build, and similar features. Yeah, there's no chance of romance here, that's for sure.

"It's nice to meet you. Janelle, right?"

"Yeah, nice to meet you too." He seems as thrilled as I am to be here. At least he's being polite.

"Shall we?" Ethan asks. He extends his arm out to Val, which she takes and heads toward the door of the restaurant.

Scott follows his lead, and I accept. We make our way inside and weave through the bustling restaurant, following the host to our table. The soft hum of conversation and clinking of silverware surrounds us. Scott steps ahead, pulling out a chair, inviting me to sit. I lower myself into the seat, appreciating the small courtesy. He then takes his place across from me, beside Ethan, who is already scanning the menu. Maybe Heather had a point. This isn't so terrible.

"Can I get you all something to drink?" the hostess asks. When Val orders a chardonnay, I echo her order before grabbing my menu.

"Oh, ritzy taste. Nice to know," Scott says.

I raise my brow, but the night is still young, so I file it away for later. For all I know, he meant it in a decent way rather than as an underhanded slight, the way I'm used to.

Val shakes her head in disapproval but doesn't voice her opinion either. "What are you going to have?" she asks me.

It all looks so good. "I'm between the chicken parmesan and the farro mafaldine with black truffle butter and mushrooms." Val scrunches her nose a little, causing me to chuckle. "It's not often that I get to eat something that isn't kid approved."

"You have kids?" Scott asks. He looks from me to Ethan and back.

"I do. I have three."

His eyes widen just enough that I notice. As he shifts in his seat, I catch him glance toward the exit briefly as if he's ready to run. Watching his reaction, I feel a twinge of relief that I approached this date with low expectations. But it does make me wonder how many more will react the same way.

"Is that a problem?" Val asks. She looks over at Ethan and raises a brow.

"I thought with you being in your thirties, it wouldn't have been an issue. A lot of women our age have kids by now," Ethan says to Scott.

"It's not that it's a huge turnoff, but three . . . Do they at least live with their dad?"

Every muscle in my body tenses as I fight to maintain my composure.

If my kids are going to be an issue when I attempt to date, then I guess I can write dating off altogether. My kids are here to stay. I won't let his question cause me to snap, though, no matter how much I want to.

I close my eyes and inhale deeply, allowing air to fill my lungs and calm my racing heart, then open them and look across at him. "No, they do not," I say firmly, "and they never will, as long as I'm around to prevent it." I close the menu and place it neatly on the tabletop. Rising from my seat, I look around the table, my gaze softening slightly on Val. "I'm sorry, but this isn't going to work. Val, Ethan, I hope you both have a pleasant evening, but it's time for me to go." I turn and make my way toward the exit, my steps firm and purposeful. By the time I reach the valet and she gets my car back to me, I have my phone out and am already dialing Heather.

"That bad, huh?"

"Ugh." I tip the valet and hop into my car. "Worse." I go over the happenings of the night as I pull out of the parking lot, heading east on Reno.

"Do you think he meant it the way you took it? What if he really was just curious if the kids lived with you or their dad? I mean, if he wasn't told about the kids, then I'm sure he wasn't told about Bryant either."

"Maybe not." Downtown is buzzing with activity tonight; the cars are creeping along in what seems like an endless line. We come to a standstill, just far enough from the traffic light that I know it'll turn red again at least one more time before I make it through the intersection. "Either way, from the moment we met, I sensed that he wasn't interested."

"Are you sure it was him and not you?"

"Maybe it was a combination of both of us. But I did show up and was going to give it a go, until he was so rude." The light turns green, allowing us to creep up a few more car lengths. "I'm on my way home now. How are the kids?"

"They're fine. Take your time getting back home," she assures me. "It's not often that you have the chance to get out like this. Go walk through the gardens or catch a show. Treat yourself to dinner since you walked out on yours. I'll be here for another hour or two. Use this time and just let loose."

"I don't have that kind of money; I'm supposed to be paying bills off. Besides, there's so much to do at home," I protest. I grip the wheel, even as I glance at the fast-food sign in the distance. "I'll just grab a two-dollar burger on the way home. I'll be fine. Besides, I know you have a lot to do too. A mom's job is never done."

As the light turns green again, we inch through the intersection.

"You're right, it's not, but everything will be here when you return, just as mine will be when I get back." Her voice softens a fraction before she continues. "J, you need some time for yourself too. There's more to Janelle than just being a mom and paying bills. This is the perfect opportunity. I'm not telling you to spend hundreds of dollars, but forty or fifty will give you a night that we both know you desperately need."

"I know you're right," I admit reluctantly. "But this life is all I've known for a while now. I feel guilty even thinking about it." The thought of leaving my kids in her care while I indulge in something purely for myself weighs heavily on my conscience. It was hard enough to accept help while I went on a date, but this . . . this is different. It makes me feel selfish.

"That's why you need this so badly," she insists. "Go and have some fun. The kids are fine. We'll be here when you get home."

Relenting, I pull into an event parking lot just past the stadium that has a spot near the back. "I'll take you up on it this time because I know I really do need a break, but when I come back from Charleston, I expect to return the favor."

"Done. I'm not even about to argue. Being a single mom sucks sometimes."

I don't know how she does it. After losing Bryant, it took me years to even think about dating again. Her husband, Jacob, had been gone for two years when she finally decided to get out there again. Luckily, she and Jacob had time to talk about it before he passed, and he made her promise to try to find love again.

"Thor!" Heather yells. "Get *off* me. Peter, come and get this furry beast off me, please."

Good thing I'm parked, because the thought of my big ole German shepherd launching himself onto her while she's laid out the couch has me chuckling so hard that I nearly snort. Thor seems to have a sixth sense for detecting when someone is in relaxation mode, and once he does, he's on a mission to smash it—literally.

"Gee, thanks. Your fur baby just about flattened me and all you can do is laugh?"

"Pretty much," I quip. "Isn't there some saying about best friends? Like, 'I'll help you up after I finish laughing,' or something? Besides, weren't you the one howling when Thor sent me flying into that mud puddle last spring?"

"I couldn't help it," she retorts. "It's not like you were hurt or anything. You were just covered in mud. You reminded me of that swamp creature from that movie we watched together. It was hilarious."

"See, that's exactly my point. I know you're not hurt. Besides, it's funny." I know Heather would be in stitches if Thor had chosen me as his victim; she'd probably even document the whole thing with photos before lending a hand. "And I'm not even in town, so I can't help you. My hands are tied."

I hear some rustling on her end, followed by her thanking Peter. "Alright, go out and have some fun. No rush. I'll be here until your dad picks up the kids."

"I guess I'll see you when I see you then. Thanks, Heather, for everything."

"It's what we do. Now, go have some fun."

Before I get the chance to reply, the line goes dead.

I haven't done anything for me in a long time. Thinking of myself as a mom, daughter, sister, and coworker doesn't leave much room for anything else. I don't even know what *I* like anymore. I guess it's high time that I figure that out.

I push through the door of Downtown Sweets, and warm air filled with the hint of cinnamon and sugar wraps around me. "Be with you in a minute," a voice from behind the glass case calls out.

"No rush."

I walk to the counter and take a peek at the display case. Golden croissants—filled with chocolate, banana, blueberry, and even peach—catch my attention.

"Sorry about the wait. How can I help you?"

I point. "One of each croissant, plus a half-dozen oatmeal cookies to go, please." Before I can stop myself, I add, "I'd also like a black coffee and a slice of seven-layer for here."

She makes quick work of my order and hands me my mug. I claim a seat by the front window, the one facing the street so I can people watch. It's a bit on the cold side, so this is a much-needed warming station.

Gazing out the window, I notice Bryant leaning against the wall outside a store just down and across from here, looking in my direction. I quickly slouch in my seat, hoping he hasn't spotted me. When Milly exits the store a moment later, he pulls her into his arms. As he moves in to kiss her, I attempt to avert my gaze, but freeze when he waves at me midkiss.

How can someone you once loved be such a creep? It makes me hesitant to get serious with anyone again. My choice in men isn't exactly stellar. Who's to say the next guy I choose will be any better?

An hour later, I hop back into the car and crank up the heater. Exploring downtown OKC was way more enjoyable than I remembered, but it's freezing out there. Thank God I wore pants, or I'd have frozen. I had a great time—aside from spotting Bryant—even in the cold. Things have really changed around here over the past few years. There's so much to explore, and I've only scratched the surface. Turns out, this was exactly what I needed.

I pull out my phone as I'm waiting on the windshield to defrost. It's been pinging with texts for a while now. If the messages were about the kids, I would've gotten a call, so I've left my phone alone until now, wanting to enjoy my time out. I pull up the ladies' group chat first.

Maddie: *I don't know why I wait until the last minute to pack! Ugh.*

Kim: *I can come over and help in a bit. Pat mentioned getting out of the house anyway. Maybe he can come and keep Tom company.*

Maddie: *Sounds good to me.*

Leah: *Sorry, ladies, I'm out.*

Kayla: *Same here. I'm not feeling too well tonight.*

I guess I can afford to stop by for a few and help. I mean, Dad's got my kids anyway. There really is no need to rush home. *Look at me making strides already.*

Me: *I'm leaving the city now. I can be that way in a few.*
Maddie: *OMG I love y'all. Thank you, ladies. See you soon.*
Me: *See you.*

I back out of our group chat and see a text from Bryant. Not wanting to ruin my good mood, I ignore it. There's nothing he could've said that would change my mind about leaving tomorrow. I already got the go-ahead from my lawyer and that's all that matters.

When I spot a text from Eli, though, I'm taken aback. I haven't heard from him in a little over a month now. Why would he be messaging me all of a sudden? It's not like we talk all that often.

Eli: *Hey, Peach. How are you and the kids doing? Mom told me that y'all will be coming with Maddie to stay awhile. I hope I get to see you while you're here. Does Pete still like racing games?*

Peach. He's the only one who has a nickname for me other than J or Janie. Even though I know I shouldn't, I kind of love it.

Me: *Hello, Eli. We're good. You? We leave in the morning. Will you be there? Maddie wasn't sure. Pete has nearly every racing game, except the newest one that came out last week.*

Eli: *I'm good. I'm currently finishing a job in Georgia. I was supposed to leave yesterday, but it got delayed. I'm scheduled to go home tonight. Don't count on me just in case it gets pushed back again.*

I begin to respond, but then I notice the three dots appear and vanish. I pause, waiting on what he'll say next.

Eli: *Sorry to cut this short but I've just been called back. Gotta go. I hope I get to see you and the kids soon.*
Me: *Stay safe. Talk to you soon.*

I want to see him again, but given the emotions he had me feeling the last time I saw him, I'm not sure if that's a good idea. It's not that there's anything wrong with him; actually, it's quite the opposite—he's practically perfect, or as perfect as anyone with flaws can be. Eli could have his pick of women, yet he still shows interest in me. I don't understand why. I'd hate to let my walls down with him and just set myself up for heartbreak. I've experienced enough of that for a lifetime.

Chapter Eight

We've been at Maddie's family's home—or, should I say, *mansion*—in Charleston for three days now, and I must admit, I adore it here. Inside the estate, the ceilings are high and the floors are marble. Many areas in the home have a well-lived-in feeling, but the front of the home is so grand that I was scared to let my kids out of my sight at first. Maddie assured me that we would be fine; her nieces and nephews run around here all the time. The tension between Maddie and her mom is so palpable, it made me uncomfortable at first, but as long as we keep our distance as much as possible, everything seems to be fine.

Eli was here when we arrived and hasn't left since. He said he's taking some much-needed time off work. I thought it was a bit too convenient, but it's been quite nice having him around. He, his mom, and his grandma live in their own apartment off the side of the mansion. His mom, who took over as the house manager when his grandma retired, stays nearby in case she's needed.

As soon as Pete saw Eli, he practically glued himself to him and hasn't left his side since, unless I insist. Eli assured me that Peter's not bothering him, so I haven't protested too much. It's nice that Peter has a good man to look up to. I just hope that it doesn't upset him too much when we head back home and Eli doesn't come with us.

To be completely honest, there's a small part of me that might miss him, too, just a little. Since we met a few years ago, I've tried to keep some distance between us. But now, staying under the same roof as him, it's nearly impossible. When I called Heather to tell her he's here, she practically pleaded with me to relax a bit. But that's what I'm trying to avoid. There's something familiar about Eli, and becoming relaxed would be too easy to do. I can't shake the feeling that allowing him in would make it incredibly difficult to leave. If I let my guard down, I could very well be in trouble.

There's a part of me that's drawn to that connection, even as I resist it. He lives in Charleston! Even if I were ready to let him in now that I've begun dating, it would only result in heartbreak. I can't leave Oklahoma, and with his mom and grandmother in Charleston, I'm certain he wouldn't want to leave either.

It just wouldn't work.

Not that he's asked me out again anyway.

"Mom!" Sage hollers from the kitchen.

"Coming." I stand from the couch and look over at Eric and Cheyanne—Maddie's niece, who's similar in age to Eric—and point my finger at my son. "You be good while I'm out of the room. No more hiding where we can't find you, and please . . . quit running in front of people."

"Got it." He smiles. "Wanna build a fort, Chey?"

They move over to the large couch and start taking the cushions off as I head into the kitchen. Lord help us all, those two are a handful for sure.

Sage, Anna, and Ms. Emmy are all standing at the island. Anna hands potholders to Sage and moves to open the oven door as Maddie walks in behind me.

"I'm just in time," Maddie states.

She and I head over to the island and each pull up a barstool. Being in this home has been good for me and the kids. Sage has officially become the baker's assistant, a title given by Ms. Emmy herself. Anna took me grocery shopping, claiming she wanted to avoid buying anything we might dislike. And as for Eric, if he and Cheyanne aren't best friends already, I'm not sure what they are.

It's been a while since I've seen my kids this happy. They're close with my family back in Oklahoma, but this is a new level of attention for them—something they never had with Bryant's family. Since his mom and dad moved to Florida the year after Peter was born, we've seen them twice.

Eli walks into the room while looking over his shoulder toward the kids in the living room. My heart sinks into my stomach. I haven't checked on Eric in a few minutes and he's gone quiet.

This isn't good.

"Are you sure that's okay for those two to be doing?" Eli asks.

I look at Maddie, then to Eli, and take off in that direction.

"Eric!" I shout as I reach the doorway, stopping in my tracks.

Cheyanne is on the floor, hidden beneath a heap of couch pillows, laughing. Eric stands on the couch arm, grinning with his arms spread wide as if he's an airplane. He leaps into the air, ready to land on the pillows—and Cheyanne. Just as his feet lift off the couch, Eli races across the room with incredible speed, his arms extended. He leans over the back and grabs Eric midair, halting his fall.

My heart feels like it's about to explode. What on earth could have possessed Eric to do something like this? He knows better.

I walk over to the couch where Eli has Eric sitting on the back. I lean down so that we're now face-to-face. "I don't know what you were thinking, son. You know better than to do something like that." I close my eyes and take a steady breath. I cannot let my worry come across as yelling.

"But, Mom," he tries. "I was just playing."

"Don't you 'but Mom' me," I start. "You could have hurt her. That's not how a young man should treat a woman."

I glance over at Eli, standing silently, and feel a wave of gratitude for him being here to catch Eric. Yet, embarrassment washes over me at the same time, just thinking of him witnessing this chaos. Why would someone like him be interested in someone like me, whose life is such a mess? *He's not interested, at least not anymore,* I tell myself. If he was, he would have spoken up, but he hasn't. Not since he first asked me out and I turned him down. What does it matter if he still likes me or not? I'm not ready to date a man like him anyway.

"I wasn't trying to hurt her, I promise," Eric replies.

"I know, bud, but you can't do that. Okay? Accidents happen all the time, and wouldn't you feel bad if she got hurt?" I want to wrap him in my arms and cuddle my baby, but I know I can't. I have to teach him right from wrong.

"Like when Daddy hurt you?" Eric asks.

I glance over at Maddie, who is sitting on the floor with Cheyanne in her lap now. When she shifts her gaze to Eli,

I notice him looking so tense that he might crack a tooth if he's not careful.

Mentally noting his expression for future reference, I turn my attention back to Eric. Now is not the time to bring up Bryant. "I know you don't want to hurt her, so can you please be more careful?"

"Yeah. Sorry, Momma." He wraps me in his arms for a moment, then hops down and runs to the kitchen.

As soon as Eric turns the corner and is out of sight, I feel the tension leaving my body. What breaks my heart is knowing that the time for the kids to start questioning Bryant's abuse is finally here. Sure, they've mentioned it, but they've never really asked me why. How do I explain to them that their father, someone they should admire, holds such deep resentment toward me?

Tears threaten to spill over as I feel a prickling sensation around my eyes and nose. As if he knows the battle brewing within me, Eli steps forward with open arms and wraps me in a comforting hug. My head tucked below his chin, I'm pressed against his firm chest, and the metal of what appears to be a necklace of some sort. This hug is the kind of embrace that feels like a weighted blanket, second only to the ones my children give me.

"How about we go watch a movie in my living area?" he suggests. "I'll ask Mom to keep an eye on the kids so you can have time to decompress."

I pull back and look up at him. Even though Eli is short compared to my brothers, he's still tall enough that I have to look up at him. "I can't do that, Eli. She already has a whole mansion to run."

"Sage is helping Grandma make dinner. Pete's in my room playing games, and I'm sure that won't change any-

time soon. The only one she'd have to really watch is Eric.
I can even ask Maddie and Ari to keep an eye on him. I'm
sure it won't be any trouble."

A tear escapes. Maybe I do need to take a moment. Eric
mentioning his father's abuse touched a nerve I'm not prepared to face just yet.

Eli carefully brushes his thumb over my cheek, wiping
the tear away with a touch that sends warmth through me.
"Let's get you settled and then I'll come take care of the
rest." He pulls back, his touch tender, as he entwines his
fingers with mine. With a soft smile, he guides me through
the hall, leading us toward the living area he shares with his
mom and grandma.

My heart hurts, knowing how good things could be between Eli and me if only I'd have taken the chance when I
had it.

I open my eyes and spot a smiling Eli at the other end of the
couch. I must have fallen asleep after he brought me back
here. Heck, I don't even remember him starting a movie.

"Have a good nap?"

I nod. "How long have I been out?"

He glances at his watch, then lifts his gaze back to meet
mine. "A little over an hour."

I shift and swing my legs over the edge of the couch,
feeling the plush carpet beneath my bare feet. As I sit up

straight, the blanket that Eli must have put over me during my nap slips off and pools onto the floor at my feet. "I don't know what came over me. I never nap like that. I better go check on the kids."

Eli extends his hand and places it on my arm, the warmth of his touch anchoring me to the spot. "I checked on them not even ten minutes ago. All is good. You might as well enjoy your free time while you have it." Why do people keep telling me to take time for myself? Eli must be able to read my frustration, because he continues. "I'm not trying to tell you what to do. If you want to go and check on them for yourself, I'm not going to stop you. It would be nice to hang out for a bit, though. We haven't had much time together since you got here."

I stand and start folding the blanket as I think about what he said. "Are you sure this isn't just a way to get me to go on a date with you?" What the heck am I even saying? I was just wondering what it would've been like if I had taken that chance.

Eli chuckles lightly. "All I asked was for you to hang out with me." A smile tugs at the edges of his mouth, but then his expression turns sober. "Why are you so against us dating?"

"You live here, and I'm in Oklahoma. I don't see that changing." I smile sadly. "Do you think that maybe we can just be friends?"

Eli nods. "I'd have never asked you out in the first place if I wasn't willing to move if and when things got serious. I know you have kids, and I would never dream of uprooting them for my own convenience. But if friendship is all that you're comfortable with, then friends it is." His gaze softens, sincerity etched in his features. "I'd much rather have you in my life than not."

As his words sink in, a flutter of nerves dance in my stomach. I never even thought of him being willing to move for me. That is not something Bryant would have done. Would I be willing to consider Eli giving all of this up for me? Why do I keep jumping ten steps ahead when it comes to this man?

"Just let me peek in on the kids and then I'll be back."

He leans forward with a smile, grabbing the popcorn that I didn't even notice was there. "I'll be here waiting."

I slide my feet into my house shoes and head toward the main part of the house. I wish I could get out of my head when it comes to Eli. Just the thought of him has me feeling out of sorts. My heart tells me to take a leap of faith and see if he still wants that date, but the cautious side of me reminds myself that I can't afford to lose myself in a man again.

But what if he's worth it?

What if I don't lose myself but instead gain a true partner?

I shake my head, trying to rid myself of the thought. *Friends.* He said we can be *friends.* Let's just focus on that.

Chapter Nine

I double over, clutching my side as I laugh uncontrollably. "No way!" I exclaim.

Eli just finished telling me about his beach trip with the Whitfields a couple of years ago, where while attempting to swim, he lost his swimming trunks to the ocean. Not only did the others not have a spare pair, but they made him marinate in his embarrassment, pointing and laughing like he was a comedy special.

"They helped you eventually, I assume."

"Yeah. Rick waded in with a towel, forming a makeshift wall while I covered up."

"Did you ever find your shorts?" I ask, still giggling.

"They were gone with the wind—or the waves, rather. Now, whether I'm in the pool or the sea, I make sure my shorts are on good and tight before getting in."

I can't stop chuckling as a thought comes to mind. "Why not wear a Speedo? Those aren't falling off because of a wave, that's for sure."

He points at me while grinning. "This girl right here," he announces to an imaginary audience, "is a comedian, folks!"

"You know it." I stand, wrapping an arm around my waist as I take a bow.

Eli laughs right along with me as I take my seat again. I've had a lot more fun hanging out with him than I could have ever imagined. I almost hate to think that I'll be leaving in a matter of days.

I'm glad that I came back to hang out like he suggested. Sometimes, it's hard to push past the guilt of leaving my kids in other people's care so that I can do something for myself. I really need to work on that. But mom guilt is not easy to push through.

"Would you mind if I ask you something?" Eli inquires.

"Ask away." I curl my legs beneath me, shifting until I'm facing him. Absently, I reach for a couch pillow, pulling it close to rest on my lap.

"What was Eric talking about earlier, when he said that his dad hurt you? I've heard that your ex was no good, but I never thought that . . . Well, when Maddie said that he hurt you and all, I just thought that it was the normal pain in ending a relationship."

I knew this conversation would happen eventually, yet I still had hoped that Eli might have forgotten. I should've known better. Now, as the moment looms over me, I'm torn. Am I prepared to tell him about the abuse that Bryant put me through? Clutching the couch pillow tighter, I find myself wavering. Can I really trust Eli enough to lower my defenses and be vulnerable with him?

Eli shifts on the couch, inching closer until our knees are touching, causing butterflies to take flight in my stomach. He takes my hand in his, fingers intertwining with mine, warm and reassuring, as his other hand gently lifts my chin with a soft tap so that my eyes meet his. "You don't have to tell me anything that makes you uncomfortable," he says. His voice is soothing. "I want to know what happened, but not if it means causing you pain." His finger leaves my chin, and a gentle smile spreads across his face. "What do you say to some ice cream? I'm pretty sure we still have some of that chocolate-chip strawberry you couldn't get enough of." He gives my hand a light squeeze before rising from the couch. As he turns away, I reach out, my fingers brushing against his arm to halt his movement.

He gazes down at me with a gentle smile.

"It's not that I don't want to share with you, Elijah. It's just that . . . I fear you'll see me as someone who is broken. You've never treated me that way before, and I'm afraid that if I open up about something so . . . personal, you might."

He lowers himself onto the edge of the couch, angling slightly as he places his hand over mine. "I would never see you as broken. I can sense you've been through something intense, but you're here. You've overcome it." With a soft touch, he lifts his hand to cradle my cheek, wiping away a stray tear I didn't even realize had fallen. "I'm going to get that ice cream now. When I return, if you want to talk about it, we can. If not, that's okay too."

Eli stands and heads toward the kitchen, and this time, I let him go.

The thought of telling anyone else about Bryant is scary. I've worked through so much in therapy, but the pain my marriage caused me and my children is still there.

After what Eric said, though, I feel like I owe Eli something. Maybe I'll just say a little bit.

When Eli returns with our bowls of ice cream a few minutes later, we sit on the couch, quiet, the only sound that of our spoons clinking against the bowls as we eat. The weight of our previous conversation sits heavy on my shoulders. Aside from confiding in a select few that had to know—the judge, police, my family, and Katie—I haven't told anyone about what happened with Bryant. Not even Heather knows. I've told her fragments of the story, but I've never felt the need to tell her everything that happened.

After I eat the last bite of my ice cream and place the empty bowl on the coffee table, I decide to share with Eli. Maybe it's due to him not pushing, giving me the option to tell or not. But I feel ready to share. With him at least.

"I'd like to tell you what happened . . ."

As I begin to speak, Eli's face grows serious, his eyes locking onto mine, ice cream forgotten. His body is tense, but he remains silent, giving me the space to continue. I can see the battle of emotions brewing behind his eyes as I start, but he remains quiet. His support encourages me to carry on and let him hear it all.

"In the start of our relationship, everything was amazing. You know that exhilarating feeling when everything feels perfect? You hold on to it as long as you can." I tell Eli about how Bryant and I first met in high school and then got pregnant right after graduating. "When Peter was born, we were on cloud nine. We thought we had it all—Bryant had landed his dream job, and we had our home and our family. It was everything we had ever dreamed of." I brush away a tear that escapes down my cheek. "Once Pete turned four, we started talking about me attending trade school. With both kids set to be in school the next fall, it felt like the right time. I lived my dream of staying home with my kids when they were little, and now that they were about to go to school, it was time for me to go after my dream career."

"Is that when you became an EMT?" Eli asks.

"No, that's when I found out I was pregnant with Eric." I smile gently through my tears as the memories of sharing the news with Bryant flood back. The way he showed me his temper by putting a hole in the wall and getting in my face, telling me it was all my fault that I had ruined his life. Those memories are a bit harder to share, so I'd rather keep them buried if I can. "That led to our first major blowup. It got so intense that I took the kids and spent the weekend at my parents' house." I fill Eli in about everything from the cheating to the hurtful words spoken to the abuse. I end up sharing much more than I originally intended, but once it's all out in the open, I feel like a weight has been lifted.

I wait for Eli to say something. Only, he's still quiet and looking at me, not moving a muscle. Finally, when I'm about to ask if he's okay, he responds.

"Wow, that's . . . that's a lot to process." He places his bowl on the coffee table and scoots closer. "I already thought you were strong, but now I'm in complete awe of just how true that is. Not many people can endure what you have and still manage to laugh and be open like you are. I'm incredibly proud of you. Being able to call you my friend is just . . . wow." He gently takes my hand and gives it a squeeze. "Thank you for trusting me with that part of your life. It couldn't have been easy to share. I won't take it for granted." He flashes an embarrassed grin and adds, "This may seem a bit silly, but my mom and grandma are really into hugging. Would it be alright if I gave you one?"

I grin and agree. "I think I'd like that."

As soon as Eli wraps me in his arms, it's as if the world fades away. How is it possible for a hug to feel so inti-mate? This embrace somehow seems to heal a tiny part of my heart. I close my eyes, my head tucking in below his chin, cherishing the warmth and safety of this connection, neither of us willing to break the spell and let go.

The cool metal of his necklace brushes against my cheek, and I reach up, tracing it with my fingers. Dangling from the gold chain is a ring that catches my eye—a vintage engagement band, maybe.

"It was my grandma's wedding ring," Eli explains, his voice a soft rumble above me. "She and Grandpa were married for fifty-two years before he passed."

"It's beautiful," I reply, admiring the simple elegance of the thin gold band. There are five small diamonds flush with the band, the center stone slightly larger than the others. It's designed for practicality, to be worn in daily life. The fact that he wears this close to his heart speaks volumes to the man Eli is. I close my eyes and inhale, ready to lose myself in the moment.

That is, until our moment is interrupted when someone clears their throat behind us.

Eli pulls away abruptly, taking his warmth and sense of safety with him.

Feeling let down, I glance back to identify the intruder and find Anna beaming back at us.

"Sorry to interrupt, Eli, but Eleanor is looking for you."

I turn back in time to see him stand and say, "Can you tell her that I'll be there in a minute?"

Anna nods and turns to leave.

Eli offers me his hand, which I accept. "I better get out there. Thank you for spending this time with me. I'd love to do it again. Maybe I can even take you and the kids out to the beach or aquarium or something before you leave."

I nod in agreement. "That would be nice. Thank you."

Eli guides us back to the main area of the house, where I join his mom, his grandma, and Sage in the kitchen, while he heads off to find Maddie's mother. Anna informs me that Peter and Eric are off playing flag football with some of Maddie's siblings. I walk to the sink and begin washing my hands as Anna slides up next to me and bumps my hip with hers.

"I can see why my son's been hung up on you now. I hope you two figure it out. The four of you would be a nice addition to the family."

I used to find it amusing when Tom would choke on his own saliva. I couldn't fathom how that could happen, but now, I definitely get it.

Anna chuckles as she pats me on the back. "There's no pressure here. I just wanted to let you know that I approve. Even if that means my son moves away from home." She passes me a hand towel, giving my hand a gentle squeeze, before turning back to the others.

I inhale deeply to calm my nerves. The idea of being with Eli is exciting yet frightening. What if we were to begin a relationship and it became serious enough for him to move in, only for something to go wrong? Would he end up resenting me and leave, abandoning me and my children? We've already experienced so much loss; I don't know how we would cope if *he* walked away.

Will I ever truly be ready to let a good man into my life?

Allowing one into my world also means letting him into my children's. Sure, Eli is already involved in their lives, but being a friend is a whole different story than being a partner.

Sage walks over to me as I turn back to face the others. I smile at her and pull her in for a side hug. "Have you been having fun with Anna and Ms. Emmy?"

"Yup. They said that they're going to teach me how to make okra soup tonight. I also get to make the cornbread all by myself."

"That's great, angel. I'm sure everything will be amazing. You really are good in the kitchen. Maybe one day you'll be running the restaurant with your Aunt Leah."

"Maybe."

Ms. Emmy walks our way, a smile plastered across her face. "Are you ready to start dinner now, sweetheart?"

I lean in and kiss Sage's cheek. "You go ahead. I'll pull up a stool and watch you. I might even take some pictures to send back home."

As I settle onto a barstool, Eli strolls through the kitchen, stopping to kiss both his mom and grandma on the cheek.

"Why don't you grab a stool, son? We could use another taste-tester," Anna says.

"I'd be happy to help."

I snap a picture of Sage as she works closely with Ms. Emmy on prepping the okra.

Eli takes a seat next to me and leans in. "I think my mom is trying to play matchmaker with us."

"I think so too."

"Do you mind if I join you?"

"Not at all."

I grin at the phone while snapping another picture, capturing all three of them—Ms. Emmy, Sage, and Anna. Sage looks so happy here with them. I'll need to print several copies of this one. I'm certain Sage will want one for herself.

Eli leans in closer, his eyes focused on the photo. "Would you mind sending me that one? I don't have many where Mom is smiling like that."

"No problem," I reply. I tap on my phone screen to attach the image, then send it his way.

"We're going to have to take more pictures before y'all leave," Eli suggests. "I don't know when we'll see each other next."

The thought makes the back of my eyes sting with unshed tears. How is it that I can't bring myself to date him, yet the idea of not seeing him every day fills me with a sense of loss?

"Yeah, sure," I agree, trying to keep my voice steady. "Maybe we can video chat when you're not at work. I know the kids will want to say hi if they can."

"Just the kids?" he asks, a teasing note in his voice.

"No, not just the kids," I respond. My cheeks warm as I look away, feeling a shy smile tug at my lips.

He places a hand on my knee and gives a playful squeeze, then drops his voice to a soft whisper meant only for me. "Just friends, right? No pressure. But if you ever change your mind, just say the word. My answer will always be yes."

I look into his eyes, the closeness of his face just an inch away, causing my heart to race with an intense urge to close the gap and seal his lips with mine. But when Eric hollers my name, I retreat, feeling my cheeks flush as I draw back into myself.

What am I doing? I almost just kissed Eli.

But would that have really been a mistake?

Chapter Ten

Eli pulls open the glass door of the restaurant, stepping aside to let the kids and me walk in first. It's been a busy, fun-filled day out. Earlier today, Eli kept his word and took us to the beach. It's been a cool fifty-nine degrees outside most of the day, but we kept warm with our hoodies as we played volleyball and then flew a kite. After shaking sand from our clothes and changing into something clean, Eli drove us to Crawlies, a family-friendly eatery, for dinner. Until now, our day out hasn't cost a dime, thanks to Maddie lending us everything we needed for the beach. Now, I'm a little nervous about how much this dinner's going to cost me, hoping that the overtime I worked last week will cover it.

As we near the hostess counter, Eric attempts to dart past. I hurry to catch him, snatching his arm before he gets too far.

The hostess, a young woman with a friendly smile, glances at Eli. "Welcome to Crawlies. How many are in your party?"

"Five," Eli replies.

Eric starts squirming so I hoist him onto my hip. "You can't run in around here, bud," I whisper firmly.

"But I wanna see the fish!" he insists, his eyes wide.

Fish? I hadn't noticed any when we entered, though I was preoccupied with keeping Eric from darting into the dining area. Now, I take a moment to scan the restaurant for these fish.

"Over there!" Eric exclaims, taking my head in his hands and turning it with such speed that I wince. "See them now?"

Sure enough, at the far back of the restaurant, a massive tank with brightly colored fish stretches nearly the entire length of the wall. I'm not sure how Eric managed to spot it so quickly after stepping through the doors.

"If it's okay with your mom, and you promise to stay in your seat to eat your meal, I'll ask if we can sit near the tank," Eli says.

I glance at him, eyebrows slightly raised. It's not that I mind sitting there, but I wish he had consulted me first. If Eli doesn't follow through on this promise, Eric's heart will break. I know it's not that big of a deal to some, but to a kid who's been let down so much in his short life, this gesture is huge.

"I didn't mean to overstep," Eli says, his voice laced with sincerity. "I was only trying to help."

"It's fine," I reply, offering a reassuring smile. As Eli steps over to the hostess stand to update her about our seating, I get Eric's attention. "You have to promise me that you'll be good," I say softly. "Eli did something nice for us today. Now show him just how good I know you can be."

Eric extends his pinkie finger, hooking it with mine in a promise. I press a kiss to his thumb and smile as he whispers, "Pinkie promise."

Eli returns, giving Pete a playful pat on the head, causing him to look up from his game. "We're on the list for a seat near the tank," Eli announces with a grin.

Eric stretches out his arms, wanting to be passed to Eli. Without hesitation, he scoops him up, settling Eric on his hip as if he's always done this. I turn back to the other two. Peter is lost to his game, while Sage is focused on my phone as she texts her friend.

I extend my hand with a knowing look. "Devices, please."

"But—" Peter begins to protest, his voice rising slightly.

"Don't you 'but' me," I state. "You know the rules about games at the table."

"We're not at the table yet," he mumbles under his breath.

Sage hands over the phone with a sigh, then snatches the game console from Peter, passing it to me. "You better quit arguing or she'll keep them," Sage says.

I nod in thanks and tuck the devices away in the small bag slung over my shoulder and glance back towards Eric and Eli, while Peter grumbles to Sage about his game not being saved.

"I think it's impressive how you limit their screen time and don't allow it during meals. Not many parents do that anymore," Eli says, his voice full of admiration.

"Thank you. It's a challenge, but I want to know what's going on in their lives. I know someone who doesn't limit her kids and I've seen her struggle in getting her kids to open up. They'll barely set down their devices and look at her, much less talk to her. I can't imagine living that way. So if I have to set rules about device usage, then that's what I'll do."

"Eli, party of five," the hostess says.

I turn around and motion for the kids to come with us as we head to the table.

Today has truly been incredible. Eli has seamlessly incorporated himself into our family and has even taken some of the parenting stress off my shoulders with ease. I don't know how he's done it so effortlessly, but it has me wondering whether giving him a chance would be such a bad thing after all.

Now that the kids are finally in bed, I quietly make my way toward the kitchen. The events of the day play through my mind on a loop, making it impossible for me to sit still. As I approach the kitchen doorway, I freeze in place, caught off guard by the scene playing out before me. In the dimly lit kitchen, Anna and Eli are midspin, dancing slowly to a melody Anna is singing. A song that I don't recognize.

There's something heartwarming about watching a grown man enjoying his mother's company this way. Yet, I can't help but feel like I'm intruding on a private moment. Nixing my plans for a late-night snack, I begin to back away when Anna's voice stops me. "Janelle, don't leave because of us. Why don't you come join us?"

I turn back and find Eli's eyes with mine, a warm smile on his face. "Come on. Mom just put some milk on to boil."

I hesitantly walk toward them, not wanting to intrude. As I approach, Anna gracefully steps aside, and Eli extends his hand to me. "Care to dance?"

"I've already interrupted enough. I don't want to disrupt your special moment," I reply, feeling a bit awkward.

"It'd be my honor if you'd take over," Anna insists. "I need to check on the milk."

With a nod, I step forward to take Anna's place, slipping my right hand into Eli's and the other on his shoulder. Eli flashes me a smile before he expertly twirls me around the kitchen, our feet gliding smoothly over the tiled floor.

His movements are confident, as if he's been doing this his whole life. As he spins me around the room, it feels like we've been whisked away to a ballroom, just the two of us. Everything and everyone else disappearing.

"Wow, you're a great dancer. When did you learn to do this?"

Eli's gaze softens, and his voice takes on a bit of emotion. "One night, I think I was around ten, when I found Mom in tears. Dad had left us maybe a year before that. Thanks to Mr. Whitfield taking me under his wing, I wasn't that angry kid whose dad left anymore. I was the man of our house and wanted to help cheer Mom up. But I didn't know how to." He looks down at me and smiles. "Then I remembered her love for dancing. So I turned on some music and asked her to join me. Over time, it kind of became our thing." His cheeks flush as he glances at Anna, who's now pouring the hot milk into cups. "When I was about sixteen, my father popped back into our lives for about a month, and I asked one of my teachers to teach me some more steps. I knew it was only a matter of time before he left again." A chuckle escapes him. "I'd do just about anything to make her happy . . . even if it meant making a fool of myself."

"Oh, Eli," I whisper, my voice quivering as my eyes gloss over. That's got to be the sweetest thing I've heard. "I'm sorry you felt the weight of being the man of the house, having to take care of your mom. That wasn't your responsibility as a child." I never considered that Peter might feel the need to take care of me when I struggle, like Eli did with Anna. I know Pete's tried to help wherever he can. "I'm happy you two have such a wonderful bond. I hope for the same kind of connection with my own kids when they're older."

Eli's eyes soften, a gentle smile spreading across his face. "You will, I'm sure of it. You're a wonderful mom. Your strength and the love you have for your children amaze me."

The sincerity in his voice tugs at my heartstrings, making it hard to resist the feelings stirring within me. I lean close, resting my head against Eli's firm chest, feeling the steady rhythm of his heartbeat. He guides me around the kitchen, his arms wrapped securely around me. Even without any music playing, Eli and I sway together, lost in the moment. Any thoughts of Anna, or anyone else being present in the room, have slipped from our minds.

"Can I ask you something?" Eli's voice is soft, almost hesitant.

I nod, looking up into his eyes. "Anything."

His gaze holds mine, a flicker of vulnerability crossing his face. "Will you be my plus-one to the gala?" Then he quickly adds, "As my friend, of course."

Why do I feel so disappointed, even if friends is what I want?

I pull back slightly to see his eyes better, a smile playing on my lips. "I'd love to be your plus-one, Eli."

Why am I holding back? It's Eli, after all. Maddie has known him forever; surely, if he was a bad guy, she'd know by now.

We stop moving, still wrapped in each other's arms in the middle of the kitchen. My heart races wildly in my chest, yet I have no urge to pull away. Standing here in Eli's arms, I find peace, warmth, safety, and a sense of belonging that I haven't known for so long. To step away would hurt more than I'm willing to admit.

Our eyes meet, and the world around us fades away.

Slowly, as if drawn together by an invisible force, our lips meet in a feather-light yet electric kiss that takes my breath away. In this moment, a vision of a happy future flashes before me—one with so much happiness, laughter, and countless kisses like this one.

A door squeaks nearby, and I flinch, pulling back abruptly. My hand flies to my mouth in shock. Oh my God, what have I done? I haven't kissed anyone since Bryant. And I chose Eli, a man who lives on the other side of the country?

Eli reaches a hand toward me, but I shake my head, not wanting him to touch me.

There are so many reasons not to be with Eli, and yet all I want is him. What if I let him in and I ruin it? What if he moves to Oklahoma, misses his family, and decides to leave?

I can't do this.

Through the haze of unshed tears, I look up at him. "I'm . . . I'm sorry." I spin around, tears falling down my cheeks, and run down the hallway toward my room, praying desperately that Eli doesn't end up hating me after this.

Chapter Eleven

We've been back from Charleston for almost a week now. The morning after Elijah and I shared that glorious kiss that I can't quit thinking about, he took me aside to reassure me that there were no hard feelings and he still wanted me to be his plus-one. I struggled with the embarrassment over me running away at first, but we spent so much time together in the following days that by the time the gala arrived, it had faded. Dancing with Eli, twirling around the ballroom in our elegant formal wear, made me want to turn back time and kiss him again.

That was, until our dreamy moment turned into a nightmare when Maddie's ex, Ashton, abducted her from the ballroom, bringing everything to a halt. While Tom and Maddie's father joined the police in searching for her, Eli and I stayed behind to help manage things around there. Thankfully, it didn't take them more than a few hours to find her. Now, she's safe and back on the farm with Tom. I can't imagine what he would've done if anything had happened to the love of his life.

Since returning home, there's been this emptiness in me. I knew forming a friendship with Eli, and then kissing him, would make it hard to leave, but this is nuts. The kids have even been a bit mopey, as if I'm not the only one feeling it. Even though I've slipped back into the rhythm of work and our daily routine, something feels off, like we're missing something—or maybe . . . someone.

I move through the kitchen, plating up dinner. The delicious aroma wafts through the house, causing my stomach to growl. I haven't made chicken-fried chicken in a very long time.

The sounds of the kids arguing over the remote filters in from the family room. I put a stop to it by dealing out a few tasks. "Peter, take Thor out, please. Eric, make sure he gets his dinner. Sage, come help me set the table."

With their tasks assigned, I quickly grab my laptop.

During my now almost-nightly call with Eli last night, I mentioned how much the kids missed him. I was shocked when he suggested we do a video call with them tonight at dinner. I haven't told them about the call yet, just in case something comes up. I don't want them to be disappointed.

I make it back to the table and place my laptop in the empty spot, opening the app to set up for the call. Just the thought of seeing him again has my hand shaking as I finish up.

I hurry to the restroom, splashing water on my face and smoothing down my hair, double-checking to ensure there's no gravy splatter on my shirt. I really wish I had time to change, but it's too late for that now.

Just as I finish, Peter's voice echoes in from the other room. "Mom, Eli's calling."

"Answer it. I'll be right there," I reply.

I take a deep breath and glance at my reflection in the mirror. My heart flutters with a mix of excitement and nerves. "Calm down, Janelle. He's just a friend."

I hurry back to the dining room, eager to see Eli's familiar face on the screen.

As I approach the table, I spot my children leaning over it, surrounding my laptop. On the screen, Eli, with his tousled hair and kind grin, immediately locks eyes with me.

"Okay, kids, take your seats, please," I say. "You'll each get your turn to speak with Eli. There's no rush to blurt everything out at once."

Eli gives me a wink, and I feel warmth creeping up my neck. I'm sure I'm blushing from this simple yet disarming gesture.

"Hey, Peach. You look nice."

I glance at my outfit and feel like chuckling. I have no clue what he sees in me. I'm still wearing the leggings and T-shirt I threw on for my gym session after work. I did manage to clean my face a little and fix my hair into a high ponytail instead of leaving it in a messy bun, but I didn't put much effort into my appearance. Just moments ago, I was doubting my choices. Even though Eli says I look nice, I have a feeling he's only saying that to be nice.

"Thank you," I say as I sit down.

I wonder what he sees when he looks at me. The reality of my hectic life means I have no time to pamper myself like I used to. Beneath this shirt lies a network of stretch marks all over my skin, and no matter how many hours I spend at the gym, the "mom flab," as Bryant called it, from having three kids, is not going away.

Eli may think I look nice, but he doesn't see what I do.

"Did Mom tell you that I finished that level we were working on before we left?" Peter asks.

When we left Charleston, Eli was adamant that Peter take the game they had been trying to beat during our visit. I started to decline, but couldn't do it. The game was important to the both of them, and Peter had grown so attached to Eli that I couldn't bring myself to take that away from him as well.

"She did. I'm proud of you, Pete. I don't think I could have managed it myself. We'll have to play online soon. Maybe this weekend."

"Yeah, man, that'd be cool." Peter glances at me and genuinely smiles, the corners of his eyes crinkling. I've missed that smile so much. My heart warms, knowing that, just maybe, Pete isn't lost to his depression. In the blink of an eye, he picks up his fork and digs in.

I look over to find that Eli and Eric are carrying on a conversation as they both eat their dinners.

"Dude. No way," Eli says. "You're going to have to show me. I don't think I've ever seen a robot dog that looks like Thor."

Eric looks over at me with questioning eyes. "Can I go get my dog? *Please.*" He drags out the *please* for a moment, making me want to smile at his attempt.

"After you finish your dinner."

"Fine." His shoulders slump, but he turns back to his plate and digs in anyway.

Eli catches my eye for a moment, and I smile back at him. "What about you, Sage? What have you been up to since you left?" he asks.

Sage plasters on a big smile before she starts. "I got Mom to take me to the store and we got all the stuff so I could make okra soup and cornbread all on my own. I even made cookies earlier. Wanna see?"

"I would love that, but maybe you can save it until after we finish dinner. I can grab Mom and Grandma so they can see too."

"Really? That would be so cool."

"Of course. They've missed having you around. I'm sure they'd be happy to know that you took what they taught you back to Oklahoma."

This guy, I swear. He's almost too perfect to be real.

I've been doing a lot of thinking since we spent all that time together back in Charleston—honestly, not just about Eli. I've realized that I'm simply not ready for another serious relationship right now. I don't mind going on dates, but I'm not ready to commit to anything long-term just yet.

Not even with Eli.

In some ways, it hurts, because I'm aware that if I allow him in, things would no doubt become serious. My children adore him, and it's easy to understand why. The more time I spend with him, whether online or face-to-face, the more difficult it becomes to resist falling for him. However, until I'm ready to embrace the idea of sharing my heart, home, and children with someone else, I'm not ready to date with the goal of forming a serious relationship.

And I know Eli would not date me for any other reason than to get serious.

"Mom," Peter says, gaining my attention. "Eli was talking to you."

"Oh. Sorry, I spaced out there for a minute. What's up?"

"I was just asking if you guys would like to get together when I come to town. I have a meeting with Damon next month. I should be there for the weekend. Maybe we can get out and do something. What do you say?"

Damon is married to Leah's sister's best friend. He runs a tech security company. Maybe this will be that promotion that Eli has been searching for.

I look around the table at my kids, who look back at me with hopeful eyes. I nod. "Sure, that sounds like fun. Maybe we can take them to the Jump Zone. They love that place."

"Sounds good to me. I'll message you the details of when I'll be there as soon as we get it ironed out."

After finishing his dinner, Eric carries his plate to the sink before he heads to his bedroom to get the robotic German shepherd that Maddie and Tom gave him for Christmas. The call continues for another thirty minutes, allowing each of the kids to spend time with Eli and have a brief chat with his mom and grandma before we all say goodbye.

Eli and I don't get to talk much before he has to go, but he says that he'll call me back later tonight. Is it strange to feel disappointed in myself for keeping someone who fits into my family so well at arm's length?

As I feel a sting in the back of my eyes, I get up and collect my dishes, preparing for our nightly routine. I can't let myself dwell on this when there's still so much to do.

I step out of the steamy bathroom, my hair still dripping down my back and my body wrapped in a towel. The sound of my phone ringing has me rushing across the room, nearly slipping on the floor. I hit answer just in time.

"Hello?" I say, slightly breathless.

"Hey, Peach. Sorry I'm calling so late. I didn't wake you, did I?" Eli's voice crackles through the speaker, warm and apologetic.

"No. I just got out of the shower. Give me a minute, will you? I've got to get dressed real quick."

Eli erupts into a coughing fit, causing me to pause. It's then that I realize what I said, and my cheeks blaze with heat. I hadn't meant to tease him—it's just that with Eli, I'm so comfortable that I didn't even think twice.

I hurry to my dresser, flinging open the bottom drawer, where I keep my nightclothes, and pull out a pair of sleep shorts and a matching tank. I quickly dry off, then change and pick up my towel, rubbing it through my hair as I make my way back across the room.

"Sorry about that," I say as I press the speaker button on the phone and toss it onto my bed. I fling my damp towel into the hamper before plopping down near my phone. "You caught me as I was finishing up my shower."

"You could've called me back. Do you want me to let you go so you can finish up?"

"Nope. I'm good. What's up?" I reach over toward the nightstand and grab a bottle of lotion. I squeeze a dollop in my hands and cup them together to warm it up before applying it to my legs.

"Not much. I just wanted to talk. We didn't get to do much of that earlier. How are you?"

"I'm tired, but good. How about you?"

"I'm fine. What's got you so tired?"

I begin telling him about the busy week I've had at work. It seems like now that Old Man Winter has hit the state, it's been one call after the next. Between house fires, falls on the ice, and our normal calls, there wasn't a lull in our workweek. Then to top it all off, I came back home and had to play catchup around here, with the ever-growing pile of laundry, grocery shopping, stack of bills, and normal daily tasks. "It's just been a lot. Sometimes I feel like I'll never be able to come up for air."

"I can see that. Is that why you had such a hard time relaxing while you were here?"

"Pretty much. A single mom's job is never done. If I sit still for too long, I start to feel guilty, as if I should be doing something. Essentially, I'm Mom *and* Dad, the nurturer *and* the punisher. *Everything* falls on my shoulders."

"After my dad left, I watched Mom struggle to do it all on her own. Granted, we lived with the Whitfields and Grandma, so she had a lot of help. But she still had to fill the shoes of an absent father. I'm sorry you're going through that. I'll never understand how a man can walk away from his children like that." He clears his throat. "I wish there was something I could do to help. You have a lot on your plate and deserve to have a moment to yourself every so often."

It's nice to hear that he understands where I'm coming from. I lie back against the headboard, rearranging the pillows for a more comfortable position. This is one of the few items I managed to replace after Bryant left. I absolutely refused to keep sleeping in the bed I had once shared with my abuser. Although financial constraints prevented me from making more changes around the house, replacing the bed was something I was determined to do. I pull my blanket up, snugly tucking it around me, and exhale a sigh as I settle in. This is the one place I come to let the stress of the day melt away.

"There's really nothing you can do, but your offer means a lot to me. I do have some support. My family helps with the kids when I'm at work, and my dad takes them to their visitations with my ex, which keeps me from seeing Bryant too often." After this last one where Milly showed up with him, I'm not sure if I should be going too. God only knows what Bryant is saying to the kids behind my back. "Heather is also a big help. But . . ." I stop myself, not wanting to expose myself too much.

"But what?" Eli prompts.

"It's nothing," I reply.

"I know you better than that. You don't mention things without reason," Eli insists.

"Fine," I sigh. "It's just not the same as having a partner. I know that I'm not ready for a serious relationship yet, but I miss having a life partner. It's tough navigating life alone without that one person to lean on, someone who is always there to support me, who I can relax with at the end of the day, knowing they have my back no matter what."

I don't tell him this part, but more than anything else, I

miss being held, kissed, and honestly, I miss feeling like a woman.

Chapter Twelve

I step onto the treadmill, adjusting the settings for a five-mile run, eager to leave the workweek behind. I'd rather leave the stress of the job at work than bring it home with me. Winter always brings a surge of calls that has us rushing between scenes.

I set the pace to a steady jog and pop in my earbuds, losing myself in a playlist that drowns out the world. This hour is my sanctuary, a time to clear my mind before heading back to the chaos of home life. I make it a point to hit the gym daily on workdays, but on Fridays, I push myself further, squeezing in an extra five miles because I know my weekends are too packed for workouts.

Tonight, Heather is coming over for a movie night with the kids. I can already picture the family room being transformed into our little theater, popcorn bowls in hand, and the kids laughing and teasing each other. If it's anything like last time, I'll be finding popcorn for the next week. It'll be worth it though.

Tomorrow's to-do list is long, with a trip to town so that I can run to the grocery store and finish up my errands if the roads are passable.

Garrett hops onto the treadmill beside me, her ponytail bouncing with each movement. I glance over and give her a warm smile, pulling out my earbud to hear her better over the hum of the machines.

"I heard Val set you up on another date," she says, raising an eyebrow. "You know, you don't have to keep agreeing to them, right?" She lets out a small laugh, her feet pounding steadily against the treadmill.

"Yeah, I know." I may have been reluctant to go, but I still agreed.

Val, her cousin, is the only one on the team who goes by her first name, probably because she shares the same last name as my partner. At least for now. Garrett is engaged and has every intention of taking her fiancé's last name once they're married.

Jordan, another coworker, pushes the door open and enters the room. The weights clatter as he adjusts them, then he pulls out his phone to play his music and settles down to work out. Some people in the gym don't care who else is around; they'll play their music without worrying about disturbing others. Jordan is one of them.

Garrett is now quiet. I'm relieved because I'm not in the mood to discuss my love life—or lack thereof—once again. However, I do feel sympathy for her. She and Jordan used to be close friends, but things became tense between them after she introduced him to her fiancé. I'm not sure why. I've known them since they first met, and I never noticed any signs that Jordan was interested in Garrett. However, his behavior since meeting Jasper suggests otherwise.

As I reach the five-mile mark on the treadmill, I press the button to slow it down to a gentle walk. My phone buzzes insistently in the cupholder, and the screen lights up with a call. I glance at it but decide not to answer. Although my shift is over, I'm still at the gym inside the building. I try to keep my personal affairs separate from my professional life. Well, maybe not entirely, but when "Eli" flashes on the screen? That's a conversation I'd rather not have within these walls. I can already picture the teasing smirks and jabs I'd get from my coworkers if they overheard us chatting.

Finally bringing the treadmill to a halt, I wipe the sweat from my brow and leap off, reaching for my water bottle. Tilting it back, I gulp down the rest, feeling the cool liquid sliding down my throat. As I grab my phone from the cupholder, I glance over at Garrett, who is still pounding away on the adjacent treadmill. "See you in a few days."

She gives me a thumbs-up as she keeps her pace.

On my way towards the door, I toss my empty bottle in the trash and give Jordan a casual two-finger wave as I pass by. My skin feels sticky, and I'm pretty sure I stink. All I can think about is a nice, long shower and getting out of here. Let the weekend begin.

I slide into the driver's seat of my Suburban and put the key in the ignition. As the engine rumbles to life, I reach out and shut my door. While the car idles, I fish my phone out of my pocket and quickly type out a message to Mom.

Me: *Heading home, just waiting for the car to warm up. Need anything?*

In no time at all, she replies.

Mom: *We're good. Drive carefully. Dad said it's starting to get icy out by the interstate.*
Me: *Thanks, will do. See you guys soon.*

I place my phone in the cradle of the hands-free device, remembering that Eli called a few minutes ago. I pull up his number and dial, then crank the heater, feeling the first gust of warm air begin to circulate as I wait for him to pick up.

"Hello?" Eli answers.

"Hey. Sorry I missed you. I was with my coworkers. What's up?"

"No problem. I was just calling to see what you were up to. I'm bored. There hasn't been much work lately."

I shift the car into reverse and cautiously back out of the parking spot, the tires crunching over the packed snow and ice below. Living so far away means the commute is much longer, especially in conditions like these. With the roads slick from the first winter storm of the season, I choose to drive home at a slow and steady pace. I'm thankful for my reliable vehicle; without it, keeping this job would be out of the question.

"Sorry," I say. "I had to back out of the parking lot, and with it being icy, I needed to concentrate."

"Should I let you go? You can always call me back later."

"No. I'm fine. Honestly, I feel better knowing that some-one's on the phone with me while I drive home."

I merge onto the interstate and align my car with the tracks left by other drivers throughout the day. I'm relieved to see only two other vehicles in sight. Not having gotten winter tires yet, I'm a little worried. I'd much prefer to keep my distance if possible.

"Are the roads really that bad?"

"Yeah. The first storm that came through seems to have been worse than what they called for. It's all ice right now and I didn't have the time to get my car maintenanced before it hit."

Just as the words leave my mouth, the car jolts forward as it hits a patch of black ice. My heart leaps into my throat as the tires lose their grip and I start to skid. I let loose a screech before my instincts kick in—I've lived in Oklahoma all my life, and this isn't my first rodeo. I lift my foot from the gas pedal, my hands gripping the steering wheel with white-knuckled intensity.

"Janelle, are you okay?" Eli asks, sounding worried.

I can't be distracted by him right now, so I ignore him in my efforts to gain back control of my car. My mind races with the mantra Dad drilled into us when he taught us to drive on the ice: Don't touch the brakes. The world seems to blur around me until, finally, the tires regain purchase on the snow beneath. The tension in my shoulders eases as I gently press the gas pedal, my breath escaping in a long, shaky sigh of relief.

"I'm okay," I murmur, my voice barely a whisper. "I'm okay." I repeat the words, louder this time so Eli can hear me.

"Thank God. You scared the heck out of me. What happened?" After I explain, he lets out a deep breath. "Can't you just call off when the weather gets this bad?"

"Eli, I'm a paramedic. They rely on me to show up as scheduled. If I don't, it could mean life or death for someone."

He lets out another sigh. "I understand. I'm just concerned about you driving on icy roads. Could you stay in the city until the weather improves?"

"No, I can't do that. My kids need me at home. Remember, I'm a single mom."

"I know. I guess I just thought with your whole family out on the farm that maybe someone could help you out with the kids while you stayed where it's safest."

I know he means well, but I can't help but get a little frustrated. "I'm sure my family would lend a hand without hesitation, but why involve them when the kids are my responsibility? I can just go home and do it myself. They have their own lives to live. Besides, they do enough already."

"I wish you had more help is all."

"I know you do. It is what it is, though." I turn on my blinker and get into the right lane as my exit comes into view. "I love my kids, and I couldn't imagine not having them with me all the time. If it means that I work myself to the bone to give them a good life, so be it. I'm happy to do it." As I steer onto the off-ramp, the wheels crunch over the icy surface. "Hold on. I'm getting off the interstate now. Dad says it's an icy mess out here." I turn on my blinker and head toward Baycliff Valley.

Dad was right; the road is as slick as an ice-skating rink. As my car begins to slide down the hill, I grip the steering wheel tightly, trying to angle it just right for the turn at the bottom. My heart races. I take a deep breath, easing my grip, and gently press the accelerator, inching forward with caution as I gain traction once more.

I'll be happy once winter is over.

"It's really difficult for you to accept help, isn't it?"

I steer my car along the gravel driveway leading to Cameron Farms, the only home I've ever known. The crunch of rocks beneath the tires brings back memories, some comforting, others haunting. I love this place, yet every time the sight of my house comes into view, Bryant's shadow looms over me. What he did to us is etched into my mind, a constant replay of the day he drove away with our children, their faces pressed against the car windows, fading into the distance. I don't know how to make it stop. Katie says that day triggered PTSD that may never go away, but taking back my life and home will help. In my mind, I know my kids are okay; they're with my family. But after what we went through, I have to see them for myself. Even if that means driving from the city on an interstate covered in a sheet of ice.

"In a way, yes. But there's more to it. After what we went through, I think needing that closeness is normal."

Eli is quiet a moment. "I can see that. I'm sorry for mentioning it. I just don't like that you drove all that way by yourself on the ice. Someone should have been with you."

"I wasn't really alone, Eli. I had you with me."

"It's not the same, Peach. If something had gone wrong, I would've only been on the phone to hear it. I wouldn't have been able to reach you. Do you know what that would've done to me?"

I pull my car into my driveway and shift it into park. "I hadn't considered it that way. But I'm not sure what else to do. I need to work, and there's no one available to drive me or pick me up. I can't just stop working. We need the money." I lean over to grab my bag from between the seats.

"Hey, I'm home now. Can I call you back later? I want to make sure my mom gets home before it gets any colder."

"Of course," he says. "I hope I didn't upset you. I'm honestly just worried about your safety."

"You didn't. I wish things were different too. I just don't know what to do to change it."

"There's not much you can do," he huffs. "I'll let you go. Tell the kids I say hey. If you have time, maybe we can video chat tomorrow."

"Tomorrow night, maybe. It's my turn to host the ladies' lunch."

"Sounds good. How about you message me when you're starting dinner, and I can eat with y'all again?"

"Okay. Talk to you later."

After disconnecting the call, I lean my head back against the car seat, exhaling slowly as I try to calm the anxiety running through me. It's not just the adrenaline from the drive home that has my nerves on edge tonight. Usually, the only people who worry about me are my family and Heather. But Eli is different. He seems determined to peel away my defenses like layers of an onion, inching closer, no matter how much I try to resist.

Chapter Thirteen

The next morning, I push open the door of Heavenly Brew, a coffee shop and bakery in downtown OKC, and I'm immediately wrapped in warmth. The air smells of coffee and freshly baked pastries. I walk past a table of day-old bread and pastries and stop at the counter, where an elderly woman wearing an embroidered apron and dark-rimmed glasses smiles at me. This place reminds me of a grandma's kitchen, with all the lace doilies and mismatched colors. Val was right—this place is cute.

"Welcome to Heavenly Brew. I'll be with you in a moment."

I nod in acknowledgment and then look up at the chalkboard menu along the back wall as the woman works on another customer's order. In ten-ish minutes, I'll be meeting Darren, the second guy Val has set me up with. All I know is that he works at the local hospital and has a six-year-old daughter he adores. But since I woke up this morning, guilt has had my stomach in knots. Eli and I may not be an item, but the idea of him hearing about this date makes me want to call it off. I nearly did, but decided against it, then immediately hopped in the car, getting here early so I didn't talk myself out of it.

"Sorry about the wait. What can I get for you?" the woman behind the counter asks.

I clear my throat. "A large white-chocolate macadamia latte, please. And a spinach, egg white, and Swiss croissant."

She jots it down, then peeks over her glasses. "Name?"

Before I can answer, the bell above the door tinkles. I turn and spot him, the guy from the picture Val showed me—easily over six feet, shoulders broad beneath a charcoal blazer, salt-and-pepper hair combed back. His chocolate-brown eyes sweep the room until they find me, and he grins.

"Janelle?" His voice is low and confident.

"That's me."

The barista clears her throat. "Anything else?"

Darren steps closer, stopping just in front of me. "I'll take the biggest black coffee you have and a chocolate croissant, please." He reaches around me to drop money on the counter, telling her to keep the change. Then he turns back to me and offers a firm handshake. His palm is warm, slightly calloused. "Nice to meet you, Janelle."

I swallow. Val may have outdone herself this time.

"Nice to meet you," I echo, then nod toward the window. "Shall we get a table?"

He follows me to a round bistro table near the window and slides my chair out for me. Once I sit, he walks around and settles in directly across from me.

So far, so good.

He's kind, easy on the eyes, and there's a friendly vibe between us. This is just the low-key connection I told myself I wanted. So why do I feel disappointed?

Darren leans forward, forearms resting on the table, his voice soft. "So Val said you're a rescue paramedic. Do you like it?"

I push a stray hair behind my ear and nod. "I do. It's hard work, but I love making a difference."

The server sets our plates down. I offer a quick smile in return, then settle back in my chair.

"I heard you work at the hospital. What is it that you do?" I wrap my fingers around the warm cup in front of me and take a cautious sip.

"I'm an ER nurse. There's still some stigma out there about guys in nursing, but I wouldn't trade it."

I've never understood why there are stigmas around certain jobs. You should be free to do what you love doing. "Must be tough, juggling that kind of schedule with a kid at home." I take another sip of my heavenly latte. "I have three kids myself. Leaving them so much is hard. I'm always second-guessing my choices."

He finishes chewing, then wipes his mouth. "I get it. My mom and sister trade off watching Emma when I'm on shift. If Em hated it, I'd have to rethink these hours. But being able to provide so well for her and still do what I love? It's worth it."

Easy conversation, mostly about our jobs and kids, carries on long enough that we both finish our meals. There are no sparks, but the easy back-and-forth feels . . . nice.

Darren's phone buzzes against the table. He glances at it, then at me. "Sorry, I've got to take this. It's the hospital." I nod, and while he answers, I get up to grab another latte, making it back to my seat just as he's hanging up. "The ER needs me. Big pileup on I-40."

My heart lurches. "Don't worry about me. Go. I understand."

He stands, grabs his coat, and smiles. "Mind if I call you later? I'd love a part two."

Before I can overthink it, I smile. "I'd like that."

He brushes a quick kiss to my cheek and hurries off.

I sit back against the chair, my fingers wrapped around my latte, thinking about Darren's goodbye kiss. It felt more like a sibling goodbye than one of a date. Not that I wanted a kiss, but still. I shift in my seat, certain that no amount of small talk or shared laughter will change what I feel—nothing. There was no spark. When he calls, I'll have to let him down gently. I don't want to upset him in any way. He's a sweet guy, after all. I like him—as a friend, nothing more. Now I understand what Pat meant by not leading anyone on. I need to be on the same ground as my date.

I glance toward the door as its bell chimes. Milly slips in, her blonde hair falling over one shoulder. If she'd waited five more minutes, she would've missed me.

Milly orders her cappuccino, then spots me while waiting and heads to my table. "Hey, Janelle. Mind if I sit?" she asks, sliding into the chair opposite me.

"Of course not," I reply. Bryant brought Milly with him to his visitation with the kids before we left for Charleston. Dad confirmed what I was feeling when I met her at the school—she's too good for Bryant.

"How are the kids? And your trip to Charleston—was it as good as you hoped?" she asks, leaning forward with genuine curiosity.

"They're great. We had a blast." The memory of Charleston makes me smile. Eli's family was so inviting—the Whitfields, too, but they're more business than anything. Eli's family, however, was the best part. Before my guilt sets in over not telling Eli about my date with Darren, I fish out my phone and pull up the pictures I took. My favorite is the one of him and the kids sitting on the floor around a board game. When they saw me get out my phone, he pulled the kids into him, causing them to laugh.

Milly's eyes light up as she looks up at me. "Oh my goodness—Eric's face! Was he really playing football with them?" She chuckles.

I laugh, remembering Eric scrambling up to the top of the dogpile while Maddie's family, Eli, and Tom were playing flag football. "Yep. I think he thought he was Hulk Hogan or something."

Milly's gaze shifts past me toward the window. I follow her line of sight and my stomach twists. There's Bryant, standing across the street, hands shoved deep in his jacket pockets, eyes trained on our table. When I catch his stare, he straightens and quickly heads our way.

I lower my voice so that only she can hear me and place my hand on hers. "I hope you know what you're doing with him, Milly. I'd hate to hear that he hurt you."

Milly's hand squeezes mine. "I know you guys didn't end well, but he's good to me."

I swallow a lump of worry. "He can be danger—" My voice falters as Bryant closes the gap between us, stepping up to our table.

"Mills, we've got to go." He nods at the counter, where a barista just called out an order. "Grab that. I'll meet you by the door.

Milly stands, tucks a strand of hair behind her ear, and flashes me a quick, apologetic grin. "Nice seeing you again."

I force a small smile. "You too. Take care."

The moment she's gone, Bryant leans forward, his voice dropping to a dangerous whisper. The scent of mint and something much harder hits my nose, telling me that he's been drinking again. "Back off, Janelle. Talk about me again and you'll regret it." He straightens, his threat hanging in the air.

"Bryant?" Milly's soft voice comes from behind him, sounding curious.

He quickly stands to full height, a practiced smile spreading across his face as he turns to face her. "Ready?" he asks, his tone suddenly light and cheerful.

Her eyes flicker to mine for a brief second, a question in them, before she returns his smile and nods. "Yeah. Is everything okay here?"

"Yup. I was just looking at the photos of Eric playing football. He's growing up so fast, it's hard to believe. I miss my boy so much." He wraps an arm around Milly's waist, guiding her toward the exit.

She looks over his shoulder, her eyes catching mine, and waves. "See you later."

I smile and wave back before glancing down at my phone. The photo I'd been showing Milly just moments ago is still on the screen.

My hands tremble slightly as I stand from my seat, throw away my empty cup, and walk to my car parked just outside. Even after all these years, Bryant can still get to me. I hate the power he still holds over my emotions. I need to make a note to give my number to Milly in case she ever needs anything.

As I'm reaching for the door handle of my car, my phone begins to ring in my pocket. I pull it out and answer without looking.

"Hello?"

"Hey, Peach. You're not busy, are you?" Eli asks.

A smile spreads across my face, and my nerves begin to settle. He always seems to know when I need to talk, even miles away. I open the door to my SUV and slip inside. "No, I'm just about to head home. What's up?"

"I'm sitting at the airport right now and thought I'd check in," he replies, the faint hum of airport announcements echoing in the background. "Did you get your shopping done?"

When we spoke last night, I told him that I had to get groceries today. Which I do. I'll be heading there next. "No, not yet. I had a date." I try to hurry past that little bit and add, "Where are you going this time?"

I turn the key in the ignition, and my phone automatically connects to the car's Bluetooth system, allowing Eli's voice to fill the cab. "I'm taking a quick trip to New York," he says. "I should be back in a day or two. But that's nothing. What I really want to know about is this date. I thought you weren't ready for that. What made you change your mind?" His tone is light and teasing, yet I can sense the curiosity behind his words since I've been pretty firm about not wanting to date him.

"Val set it up a while ago. I almost canceled at the last minute, but then decided to go through with it."

"How'd it go?"

"It went well enough, I suppose. Darren is a nice guy."

Eli clears his throat before continuing. "That's good. I'm happy for you. Do you think he'll be the lucky *one*?"

I lean my head against my headrest. "There wasn't a spark. So when he calls, I plan on letting him know that there won't be another."

"Well, that's good news," Eli says.

I chuckle. "And why is that?"

"As long as you're not in a committed relationship, there's still hope for me," Eli says. A brief silence stretches between us. "Hey, Peach, I gotta go. They just announced boarding for my flight. I'll try and call you later. Tell the kids hi for me."

"Will do. Travel safely and let me know when you get there," I reply.

"Will do," he answers.

How is it that a single conversation with Eli, even with that tinge of jealousy in his voice, can ease my tension so fast?

I shift the car into drive and head toward the grocery store. There's no sense in driving myself crazy by overanalyzing my feelings.

Chapter Fourteen

I rush down the stairs, my feet thudding against each step, and head straight for the door. The ice from the other night is nothing compared to the looming storm that's headed our way now. Despite the potentially harsh conditions, those of us living on the farm plan to get together in a few hours. What was supposed to be a ladies' lunch has now turned into games with the whole family. It's rare for all of us to be off work at the same time anymore, but it's finally happened, so this impromptu game night is something I'm looking forward to.

Finally, I reach the front door, feeling the cold metal handle beneath my hand, and swing it open to welcome Heather and the kids inside. As soon as Gracie walks in, she shrugs off her coat, letting it fall into a heap on the floor. I bend down to pick it up before hanging it on the hook beside the door.

Heather had bundled herself and the kids up in their coats and gloves to make the trek from her home a few miles down the road to stay the weekend with me and the kids. Every year, when the ice hits like this, her home loses power. Luckily, my family room has a wood-burning fireplace. I've also got a hefty generator ready to keep the kitchen and a few space heaters going. My family room is just big enough that we're able to pull out all the sleeping bags, push the couch against the wall, and have a sleepover with the kids.

"Pete!" I holler. "Grab your coat and shoes, and help Heather and Chris bring their stuff in, please."

Heather puts her duffel bag into my arms, followed by Grace's smaller one, before she and Chris head back out to their car. Heather always packs up most of her fridge and freezer—there's no point in losing a whole stock of food to the power outage. Not when I've got ample room to store it all.

"Come on, Gracie, baby. Let's go find Sage." I place my hand on her shoulder and steer her toward the back of the house. After getting her settled in with Sage and Eric, I make my way toward the garage, where I keep my drink fridge. This is where we'll store Heather's items so they don't get all mixed up with mine. As they carry in the bags, I start organizing the groceries to ensure everything fits. To make space for Heather's groceries, I remove the case of beer that Cam left the other day. After finishing, I discard the bags and make my way inside.

As I step into the kitchen, the scene before me makes me chuckle. Thor is sitting at Heather's feet, his tail sweeping back and forth rapidly across the floor as he waits for her command.

Heather, dressed in her favorite yellow sweater, leans down slightly, meeting Thor's hopeful gaze with a smile. "You're going to be nice to me this time, right, buddy?"

He hops along the floor in front of her, hoping to get the treat she holds in her hand.

"No more jumping on me when I'm lying down. Agreed?" She holds out her hand for him to shake. When he does, she tosses the bone to him and smiles as he runs off with it. "You better hold up your end of the deal or there'll be no more of those when I visit."

She spins around, her eyes locking onto mine, and I can't hold my laughter back anymore. "Have we sunk so low that we're threatening our pets now?"

"Nope. Just yours. Mine's an innocent little girl," she replies.

I glance past her shoulder and see her dog, Lucky, losing her bladder in my dining room. "Yeah, she's a gem. Is that why she's over there making a puddle on my floor?"

Heather whirls around so quickly that she has to steady herself by gripping my countertop. "Lucky! No! You know better." She hurries over, bending down to grab Lucky by the collar. "You should've told me you needed to go outside," she scolds gently.

"Thor. Outside!" I call out.

He comes running in from the family room, his ears perked up, and follows Heather to the door.

As she takes them outside, I head upstairs to grab a sweater. Despite the heat being on, the house is chilly. I pick my phone up from the nightstand and notice a missed call from Eli. Rather than returning the call, I decide to send a text.

Me: *Sorry I missed your call. I was helping Heather get settled. She's staying with me for a few days until the worst of this next storm is over. What's up?*

Without waiting for a reply, I slip my phone into my back pocket and head downstairs. I make my way to the kitchen and begin gathering ingredients for lunch. After we finish eating, Heather and I will set out some snacks and get everything ready for game night. She and the kids have come to enough game nights now that Mom has started calling her an honorary Cameron.

With the weather moving in, I'm almost certain nobody will stay for long this evening. They'll all want to get home and bunker down.

Heather strolls into the kitchen and sidles up to the counter beside me. She grabs the loaf of bread and begins setting out enough for each of us to have a sandwich. While she makes them, I set out the plates and begin adding apple slices and string cheese to each. In a matter of minutes, lunch is served. Not that hungry, I set a few apple slices and a cheese aside to snack on while Heather and I start getting the snack table ready for game night. As I stretch on my tiptoes to grab one of the larger ceramic bowls on the top shelf, my phone begins to ring.

"Can you get that?" I call over my shoulder, trying not to lose my balance.

Heather steps closer and reaches into my back pocket, grabbing my phone. She answers, "Hello?" There's a brief pause. "Yeah. Hold on a minute."

Finally, I manage to grab the bowl. With a sigh of relief, I pivot, placing it down on the kitchen island. "Who is it?" I ask.

Her eyebrows arch playfully, and an amused smile spreads across her lips. "It's your *lover boy*, Eli."

I swat at her, causing her to giggle and scoot away to the other side of the island, but not before I grab my phone from her hand. I take a deep breath and place it to my ear. "Hey. What's up?"

"Nothing much. I just called to see what you were up to."

I tap the speaker button on my phone and put it on the bar. "Heather and I are getting the snacks ready for game night tonight. She can hear you by the way; you're on speaker." I grab the mixing bowl and start pouring in the pretzels, cheese balls, nuts, and candy pieces.

"Hey, Heather," Eli responds.

"Hello, Eli."

"Is it a family game night?" Eli asks.

"Yeah. Everyone should be showing up within an hour." Once all the ingredients are in the bowl, I stick my hands in and begin mixing. "What are your plans for tonight?"

"I'm going to cook dinner for my mom and grandma since it's their day off. I don't want them worrying about looking after me. I think we might watch a movie afterward. There's this one that Mom has been wanting to watch for a while now. I might check if we can stream it."

I glance over at Heather, noticing the way she places her hand over her heart and blinks dramatically, as if she's been swept away by a romantic scene. A chuckle bubbles up inside me, but I hold it back and opt to toss a pretzel across the island at her instead.

"That's awfully sweet of you," I say, raising an eyebrow with a playful smirk at Heather. I really do love how good Eli is to his mom and grandma. "Do you know what the movie is called?"

"I don't but I'm sure it won't be hard to find. She said it came out a few years back. It's about a woman who protects her family against a home invasion."

I glance over at my phone in surprise. "I never would've taken your sweet momma as a woman who likes action movies. I thought of her as a romantic."

Eli chuckles. "Well, if it weren't for me and my father, you might be right. After he left us, she had to step into the father role and developed a bit of an edge—" Suddenly, Eli's attention shifts away from our call. "It's Janelle," he explains to someone else. "Yeah, you want to say hi?"

Heather, standing across from me, raises an eyebrow, silently questioning the interruption.

"Hey, Peach?"

The use of his nickname for me has Heather smiling softly.

"Yeah. I'm here," I reply.

"Mom and Grandma just walked in. They'd like to say hi."

I reach for the hand towel beside me, a nervous flutter rising in my stomach at the thought of talking to his mom and grandma again. I take a deep breath, trying to calm the anxiety. "Okay," I say, with a shaky smile. "Put them on."

"You're on speaker," Eli says.

"Hi Anna. Hi Ms. Emmy. How are y'all?"

"We're good. Just missing you all. How are you? And the kids?" Anna asks.

I smile. These ladies are beyond sweet and welcoming. "We're good. Sage has been cooking up a storm since we got back home. I think she wants to impress you if she ever gets the chance to see you again."

"That sweet, sweet girl," Eli's mom replies, her voice filled with affection. "I sure hope we get to see each other again soon. How are the boys?"

I chuckle. "Pete is still glued to the screen, trying to conquer the video game he and Eli were obsessed with while we were there. He's determined to beat at least one more level before Eli calls next. And Eric . . . well, that boy is a mess. He's twice as rambunctious as the others were at his age, bouncing off the walls like he's filled with candy or something."

Anna laughs. "I remember Eli at that age, running around the house with a sheet tied like a cape, jumping off the furniture. He was a handful. Things do get easier though."

The mental image of a young Eli warms me. I cover my mouth to suppress my laughter.

"It was a sight to see," Ms. Emmy adds.

"I'm sure it was," I agree. "Eric did something similar about a week before our visit. He woke up, stripped down to his superhero underwear, tied a towel around his neck, and ran through the entire house. I had to threaten him with a month of no dessert before he finally stopped."

Eli chuckles in response. "Sounds like my kind of kid."

There's a knock at the door before Leah is pushing her way inside.

"I better get. People are starting to show up now. It was nice talking to y'all."

"You too, sweetie," Anna says.

"I'll text you later," Eli says as he ends the call.

Heather smiles knowingly. "I'd think twice about going out on another date if I were you. It seems like someone already holds the key to your heart."

Even though I'm not quite ready to get serious, I can't argue that Eli is wearing me down.

I guess it's a good thing I told Darren no to another date then.

Chapter Fifteen

I rise from my seat and make my way to the front of the family room. Tonight has been a fun-filled evening of laughter and chatter. We've finally settled on a game of charades. It's not my favorite, but it's fun with a group this size.

I reach into the hat, brushing my fingers against every slip of paper, finally clutching my chosen piece. My team, eager and ready, will have sixty seconds to figure out my silent performance. If they don't, the other teams will swoop in with thirty seconds and one guess each. The room is filled with noise as I get ready to act out whatever my paper says to do. I open it and take a look.

Washing Machine.

"How on earth am I supposed to do this?" I take a moment, but Cam isn't too patient tonight.

"Come on, Janie. We don't have all night, ya know."

"Oh, can it," I snap back.

Leah laughs, earning her side-eye from Cam.

Once the room quiets down, I dive into my performance. I stretch my arms wide, tracing an imaginary square around myself, mimicking the confines of a washing machine. Then, I lift my hand above my head, mimicking the motion of lifting a lid. I begin to twist and gyrate my body like the spin of an agitator churning clothes.

"The twist," Tom says.

I shake my head no.

As everyone else remains silent, I switch tactics, grabbing the fabric of my shirt and rubbing the ends togeter vigorously, simulating the action of scrubbing. Surely, someone will understand now.

"Scrubbing," Pat adds.

I shake my head vigorously, feeling the frustration build, and mime the circular motion of a washing machine churning clothes around me again. I even pretend to pour detergent into an invisible drawer, hoping they'll catch on.

"Time!" Cam shouts.

My shoulders slump, and I let out a sigh. That one should have been easy. I bet Mom would've guessed it right away.

"Thirty seconds on the clock," Tom announces, glancing at the stopwatch in his hand. "One guess each, team."

"Dryer!" Cam shouts, his voice echoing as he leans forward eagerly.

Leah playfully nudges him on the shoulder, shaking her head with amusement.

Mom chuckles softly from her seat across the room. "Dryers don't agitate or open on the top, son. That would be a washer," she explains, shaking her head with a knowing smile.

The lights begin to flicker as we get a power surge, followed closely by a booming thunderclap that rattles the windows and sends the kids into a fit of screams. My shoulders jerk involuntarily at the noise.

Once the power is steady again, Dad rises from his chair, clapping his hands loudly to gain our attention. "Alright, everyone, it's that time. Cam, you and Leah take the little ones and get them home safely. Don't forget to text us once you're inside. Pat, if you could start a fire before heading out. Tom, let's close off the upstairs, then you can leave. Make sure everyone updates the group chat once you're home."

"I've got this," I insist, though I know better than to argue with Dad. In our family, we always look out for one another.

Without another word, I grab Heather by the hand and lead her to the garage. Sage and Peter are already moving about, rearranging the furniture to make space. Heather and I begin hauling firewood inside, each stack of logs heavy and rough in our arms.

With everyone's help, the house is ready for the storm in under thirty minutes. Mom even pitches in by cleaning up the party trays, storing the food, and washing the dishes. I swear, I love my family.

I walk everyone to the door, where they pull on their coats and give hugs. "Let me know when you make it," I say.

Quickly, they make their way out the door and rush to their waiting cars, just as the thunder sleet begins to fall steadily.

I close my door and grab my phone from my pocket.

Cam: *We made it home safely. If you all need anything, don't hesitate to let us know. Love y'all.*
Me: *Everyone else just left. Same goes to y'all. Love you.*
Maddie: *We're pulling up to the house now.*

I make my way to the kitchen to get the kettle boiling. After that blast of cold, I'm in the mood for some hot cocoa.

Mom: *Boys, Dad said that there'll be cleanup when the storm passes. We haven't even made it yet and your father has had to get out twice to clear branches from the drive.*

Pat: *We just pulled up. Do you want me to turn around and come help?*

Mom: *No. We're about to pull into the garage now. We're okay. Y'all stay warm. Let us know if you need anything. Love you all.*

Once everyone has said their goodbyes via text, I gather enough mugs for everyone, arranging them on the counter while the water heats, then turn my attention to the microwave and make us all some popcorn. Moments later, Heather strolls in as I'm pouring water into each mug.

"Ready for some cocoa and popcorn?" I ask, glancing up at her with a smile.

"Sure. You ready for a movie?"

"Yeah. What are we watching?"

The grin spreading across her face tells me that she has something up her sleeve. "Tonight, I thought we'd switch things up a bit. The little ones are set up with my laptop, glued to some cartoon movie they've been dying to see." She picks up the tray carrying the buttery popcorn. "The older kids have the big screen for a film they picked out."

"What about us?" I balance the tray of cocoa mugs and join her as we make our way to where the kids are gathered.

"I figured we could watch that movie Eli mentioned, the one he wanted to see with his mom, and piggyback off their night," Heather suggests.

I pause, raising an eyebrow in her direction. "I'm not interrupting their night," I protest.

"It didn't sound like you'd be interrupting anything," she reassures me with a gentle smile. "He did say he'd message you later, so why not just turn it into a call instead?"

She's right; he did say that he'd message me, but that doesn't mean he planned to disrupt his time with his mom and grandma to do it. I just can't picture him doing that.

We continue walking to the family room, carefully stepping over the already-spread-out sleeping bags, and make our way to the coffee table. Once we set the trays down, we start passing out the snacks.

"Can I use your phone?" Heather asks. "Mine's on the charger."

I nod, fishing my phone from my pocket. "Yeah, sure." I hand it to her before handing out the rest of the cocoa.

Once everyone is settled in with their snacks, I gather the now-empty trays and head back to the kitchen. Just as I reach the counter, a loud crack of thunder rattles the house, and I let out a startled squeal.

Suddenly, the entire house is dark.

Thankfully, we anticipated this, and I won't have to rush around to keep the chill out. I crouch down and reach under the sink, pulling out a flashlight. Flicking it on, I find my way to the garage. Once there, I push the door open, the cold air hitting my face, and head to the corner where the generator waits. Maybe one of these days, I'll be able to afford a whole-house generator. That'd be a dream come true.

I yank on the pull cord, and the machine sputters to life, vibrating under my grip. I bounce from foot to foot, the concrete floor of the garage biting through my socks as I rub my arms vigorously to fend off the chill. I hadn't thought of grabbing a blanket to shield myself against the cold out here. I connect the gen-cord and then the fridge. Once the refrigerator's power is restored, I grab another extension cord and head back inside. With the door shut behind me, I cup my hands, blowing warm air into them to stave off the numbness.

Heather peers into the kitchen, catching sight of me leaning against the doorframe. "You good?"

I nod. "Did you get the lanterns and heaters set up?"

"I did."

The fireplace in the family room will spread warmth through there and most of the kitchen as well. But I remember the first winter in this house, when the bathroom became an icebox and the pipes burst from the cold. We learned real quick that setting up a heater in there was crucial to prevent that from happening again.

I walk into the kitchen and notice the orange extension cord stretched across the floor. I crouch down to connect it to the one I brought with me, making sure it's securely linked for the heaters and TVs. With some effort, I slide the fridge away from the wall, unplug it, and add it to the extension cord too. Luckily, the propane tank is full, which means we can cook on the stove, wash dishes, and take warm showers without any issues. I'm glad I opted for propane instead of relying entirely on electricity. That would have been a nightmare with all these kids around.

"Hey, J!" Heather hollers. "You have a call."

"Can you answer it? I'll be there in a minute."

"Sure."

I crouch down and rummage around under the sink, finally pulling out a roll of duct tape. Unrolling the tape, I press a large piece of it firmly along the length of the extension cord stretching across the floor, ensuring it stays put. Knowing it won't catch my foot and send me flying across the floor in the pitch black again is enough to make me be okay with scrubbing tape residue off my floor for a week afterward.

Once everything is taken care of, I head into the family room. Heather stands by the couch, holding out my phone.

I grab it from her and press it against my ear. "Hello?" I answer.

"Hey, Peach." Eli's voice crackles through the speaker. "I heard that the power went out. Are y'all okay?"

I glance at Heather, who gives me a knowing look from where she's settled into her sleeping bag. Her eyes twinkle with mischief.

"Yeah, it did," I reply, nodding even though I know he can't see me. "We're good, thanks. What's up? I thought you were watching a movie with your mom and grandma."

"We just started it not long before I got your text. I'm glad you decided to watch it with us. We're only ten minutes in. Mom said we can restart it."

Settling onto my sleeping bag nearby Heather's, I grab my pillow and playfully whack her on the head with it. She wobbles to the side, giggling, and raises her hands in mock surrender as she straightens up.

"I hate to say it, but I never texted," I confess. "That would've been my meddling friend. I was too busy freezing my butt off while getting the generator hooked up."

"Oh. Well, if you don't want to . . ." He trails off.

"I didn't say that," I quickly interject. "I'd love to join. I just didn't want you thinking I was barging in on your time with your mom and grandma."

"I don't think that at all. We're glad to have you join us."

Heather busies herself setting up the movie as I pick up my untouched popcorn and swap my now-cold cocoa for a bottle of water.

"Oh, I forgot to mention," Eli says, "I'll be there around the beginning of February, not the end, as I originally thought."

My stomach does a flip at the thought of seeing him again—and so soon.

"That's great! I can't believe February is just a week away. The weather is supposed to be nice, so maybe we can have a barbeque while you're here."

"That sounds good to me. Are we still planning to take the kids out?"

"As long as it doesn't coincide with their visitation. Mondays are their afternoons with Bryant."

The movie is ready to start, but instead of hitting play, Heather just smiles as she settles on her blanket. I know she's listening in, but I'd share with her anyway.

"I'll make sure it won't. I'll let you know the dates when I get my ticket." He pauses, and I hear Anna say she's ready before he comes back on the line. "Okay. Let's get the movie started."

Heather hits play on the movie and looks over at me instead of the screen in front. I hit the speaker button on my phone and set it aside. When she raises a brow at me, I shove a handful of popcorn into my mouth and focus on the screen in front of me. Maybe if I don't acknowledge her right now, I can get through this movie without hearing her say, "I told you so."

Chapter Sixteen

"What do you mean Bryant is seeking full custody?" I exclaim, my voice tinged with disbelief. "And *when* is the court date?" The questions spill out as I grip my phone tightly, trying to concentrate on my lawyer's voice.

I had missed three calls from him earlier while I was out on work calls. Concerned that something serious was going on, I returned his call immediately after clocking out, even if it meant missing my workout.

I stand outside work, pacing back and forth, thankful for the warmer weather. It's only been two days since the ice storm, but with sixty-degree weather, the ice and snow was gone quick.

"Bryant claims that he's in a stable relationship. He's been attending parenting and anger management classes. Additionally, he bought a home where each child can have their own room and plans to marry by the end of the year. He's fulfilled all the conditions set by the judge to qualify for at-home visitations at minimum." Mr. Darcy, my lawyer, clears his throat and sorts through some papers. "Court is set for February first at ten in the morning."

I pull my phone away from my ear, my heart racing with anxiety. I squint at the screen to see the date—January twenty-sixth. My heart sinks. "That's . . . that's in six days! How am I only hearing about this now?" I ask, my voice filled with frustration.

"The court he filed with had a sudden opening, and he seized the chance. I know it's unusual to have only a week's notice for something like this, but occasionally, these things do happen."

His words weigh heavily on my shoulders, causing me to sit down on the cement curb outside the station. "What do you think we're looking at here? I want to be prepared."

"For him, things look promising on paper this time around. He could get in-home visitations. I seriously doubt he'll get much more than that though."

Shock crashes over me, like a punch to the stomach. I double over, struggling to hold myself together. "What if my kids refuse to go? They saw him lay hands on me, and then he took them away, keeping them from me. Who in their right mind would give him a chance to do that again?"

"The two older kids might be able to speak up in court and tell the judge they don't want to go, but Janelle, your youngest is still too young to do that. It would put him in the position of going all by himself. I hate this as much as you do, believe me, but you need to brace yourself for what's coming." He clears his throat. "There's a new judge on the case this time. He's a father himself, someone who's endured his own custody battle. He might end up sympathizing with Bryant." He pauses a moment before he continues. "Like I said, on paper, Bryant is painting a pretty picture. You work a lot of hours, and as far as I know, you aren't even seeing anyone seriously. Meanwhile, Bryant can

offer them a stable home, one where they won't be shuffled around all the time. You cannot."

I can't hold back the tears streaming down my face.
Who would have thought that not being married—or
at least headed that way—could make you seem like an
inadequate parent?

"They aren't being shuffled around!" I cry, despera-
tion clawing at my throat. "My parents, the kids' grandparents, are the ones who care for them while I'm at
work. How can that be a bad thing? I don't understand—I just can't see the harm in that!"

"It's not bad," he reassures me. "But listen, in the
judge's eyes, all he'll see is that Bryant is offering a
stay-at-home stepmom, someone ready to raise the kids
while he's at work. They'll have security with him now.
This isn't like the last time—it's not so clear-cut. If you
were in a serious relationship, maybe even talking about
marriage, that would strengthen your case too."

Before I can stop myself, the words tumble out, driven
by a primal fear. "But I *am* in a committed relationship!
I just didn't feel the need to broadcast it."

Oh God, what am I saying?

"You are?" he asks, sounding surprised.

"Yes!" I insist, my heart pounding quickly. "He'll be
here in a week or two. When we went on that vacation,
it was to meet his family. Eli will be flying in soon."

I can't seem to make it stop. Eli would be furious with
me if he knew I was using him like this. Guilt stabs at me,
but the thought of losing my kids to their father tears at
my soul.

I can't lose them—I just can't.

"Janelle, I apologize, but I have to go. I'm due in court in thirty minutes. I'll have my secretary contact you tomorrow to set up a time to come in and discuss this further."

The conversation is over. There's nothing more I can do to change it.

When the call ends, I lower my phone and send a message to Katie.

Me: *Can we talk? It's an emergency. I'm on the edge of a breakdown.*

I bury my face in my palms, my fingers pressing against my temples as I sway gently, trying to pull air into my lungs. The seconds ticking by feels like an eternity, until my phone chimes with her response.

Katie: *Can you be here in twenty minutes?*
Me: *I'm on my way.*

I stand and head back toward the building. I jog in, past my coworkers, feeling their curious gazes following me, but I keep my focus ahead, ignoring their unspoken questions. Finally, I reach the lockers, my fingers fumbling with the lock until it clicks open. I retrieve my duffel bag and head back outside in a hurry.

Once at my car, I open the door, settle into the driver's seat, and toss my bag into the back. Inserting the key into the ignition, I start it and drive off without waiting for it to warm up. I'm certain there'll be questions when I return tomorrow, but that's for future me to worry about. Right now, I need to focus on getting to Katie's without injury.

As if the universe has finally decided to cut me some slack, every traffic light along my way glows green, allowing me to move through the streets without a single stop. In just under ten minutes, I find myself in the waiting room of Katie's office.

I sink into a big, plush chair, feeling it embrace me as I exhale deeply, finally able to release the tension that had been knotting my shoulders. I honestly feel like she keeps these chairs around because they genuinely feel like they're giving you a hug when you sit in them.

Katie emerges from the back, escorting another client to the door with a smile on her face. After locking the door, she turns to me. "Come on back."

I trail behind her to her office, and as soon as the door shuts behind us, I drop onto the couch opposite her and spill everything—well, everything except the part where I might have used Eli's name to help with my case. Once I've finished letting it all out, tears stream down my cheeks and my hands tremble. I understand this is just one more obstacle I must tackle with my ex, and I have faith that we'll come out on top in the end. However, lying about being in a relationship gnaws at me. I've managed to avoid sinking to Bryant's level all this time, yet here I am, resorting to lies the moment there's a real threat.

"I can see why you called for this session. How are you feeling now?"

"Like crap. I mean, how else should I feel? I have just one week to spend as much time as possible with my kids before their father drags me back to court again. They hardly see him, so how can he even consider fighting for full custody? It's just ridiculous!"

"Your feelings are completely valid. Do you have any idea how you'll handle this?"

I lean my head back against the couch and pinch the bridge of my nose. "I'm not entirely sure. I think I need to talk to the kids, though. Maybe I should arrange a family meeting too. If I don't tell my family, they'll be upset."

"Those are great starting points," Katie replies.

Telling the kids is going to tear me up inside. The thought of it twists my stomach into knots. My family can be a bunch of hotheads when it comes to Bryant. I just hope Heather will agree to take the kids for a while so I can tell them. That way, the kids won't have to hear their family's colorful words about their father.

But the real challenge will be figuring out how to tell Eli that I betrayed him. How do you explain to someone you care about that you threw them under the bus? Will he ever want to speak to me again? My God, I hope I didn't mess everything up.

Later that evening, I explain to the kids about the upcoming court date, and when my words finally trail off, the room is filled with soft sobs. Even Eric, who I thought might have been too young to recall the trauma, has tears streaming down his cheeks. My dad has mentioned that during their visits to see Bryant, Eric is the only one who truly engages

with him. That led me to believe that he'd be okay with
going. At least part time.

I guess not.

"I don't want to live with Dad," Eric murmurs. His
voice trembles, tearing at my heart.

"We won't. Don't worry," Peter reassures him. His
fists clench in defiance. "He doesn't really want us anyway; he's only doing this to hurt Mom."

"Peter," I scold. I try to maintain some semblance of
peace in the midst of this storm. "I know your father
has hurt each of us in his own way, but there's nothing
I can do to change this. I'm sorry this is happening, but
I don't want you to be mad on my account."

Sage turns to look at me, her eyes wide and filled with
a mix of fear and frustration. "How can we not be mad?"
she demands. "We have that right. I should've never had
to see my dad hit my mom and wonder if he might
hit us too. Do you even know how long it took me to
be able to sleep through the night without waking up
scared, terrified that he was coming back?" Her voice
cracks, the rawness of her words echoing what we're all
feeling. "And now he's trying to take us again. It's not
fair, Mom."

Peter stands so fast that his chair falls to the ground
before he storms up the stairs, slamming his bedroom
door behind him.

I'll give him a moment to sort through his feelings and
cool down before I go up and talk to him. I hate how
much this has affected him—all of them, really.

I pull Sage into my arms, feeling her tremble against me,
and hug her tightly. "I know, angel," I whisper softly. "It's
not fair at all, but there's nothing I can do right now except

go to court and fight for us. I promise I'll do everything in my power to make sure you don't have to leave."

As these words leave my mouth, the idea of Eli and I entering into a serious relationship to secure my kids' future is increasingly appealing. I won't manipulate him in any way, but once Heather comes to pick up the kids, I think I need to have an honest conversation with him. I'll lay out all the facts, and if he's willing to step into this role after hearing me out, then it looks like I'm diving headfirst into a committed relationship with him after all.

I push my laptop aside and slide under the covers. Eli gazes back at me as though I've dumped a bucket of ice water on him. When I texted him to ask about a video chat, he seemed eager to get it going as quickly as possible. But after I told him about the phone call from my lawyer this afternoon, the first thing Eli did was ask me how I was handling it and then asked if there was anything he could do to help. This led to me blurting out that I said that we were in a committed relationship. Since then, he's been quiet.

"Are you okay?" I ask.

"Huh? Yeah. It's just a lot to take in. So your lawyer says that being in a relationship will help your case?"

"Yes."

"And my name is the one you thought of first?"

"Yes."

"Alright, let me ask you something." He shifts on his bed to sit up and face the screen. "Before he called, how were you feeling? Were you getting closer to the idea of starting something with me?"

I clutch my pillow tightly and pour out my thoughts. "Yes and no. I'm still afraid of being in a committed relationship. Look at what happened to me the last time." I brush away a tear. "When I think about you, I feel deep down that it'd be more than just casual, and the thought of committing scares me. But, while on my date with Darren, I felt guilty for being there with him."

"Why did you feel guilty?" he asks.

I can feel my cheeks warming. It's embarrassing to admit that I felt like I was cheating on him when he isn't even really mine to begin with.

"Talk to me, Peach. If I agree to this, I need honesty. I need to know that if I say yes, we're aiming for something lasting."

I start fidgeting with the string on my pillowcase, suddenly finding it fascinating. "I felt guilty because I've been letting my guard down with you. I look forward to hearing your voice. It feels like more than just a friendship now. I can't date anyone else when it feels like I'm cheating on you." Now that I've said it out loud, it doesn't seem as intimidating. But I know I'll always have struggles. You can't just get over trauma, no matter how hard you try.

"That's all I needed to hear." Eli winks. "I like knowing that we're moving in the right direction."

Chapter Seventeen

Last night, my talk with Eli went well. He agreed to being my "boyfriend" in the eyes of the court, as long as I'm open to potentially viewing him that way in the future. Basically, he's giving me the label before we fully develop a relationship. Do I feel guilty about this? Definitely. But I'm prepared to do whatever is necessary to keep my children safe.

Knowing that Eli is on board to help do the same has me wanting to let him in further.

Heather took the kids overnight so that I could have the conversation with Eli, and now that it's morning, I can let my family know what's going on. Tonight, I'll be watching all the kids, including hers, in return.

As I step into the kitchen, the quietness envelops me like a warm blanket. It's been a long time since the house was this quiet. I feel a tug at my heart from the absence of my kids' chatter. My mom has always said that when your kids are always around, you can't wait for a break, but the moment they're gone, you miss them dearly. No saying has ever resonated with me more. I miss them a lot. It feels weird without them running around. I think if Thor hadn't hounded me to let him out, I may have gone stir crazy by now.

I tear up at the idea that this overwhelming feeling might remain in my home if Bryant wins in court. Whenever I start feeling the threat of defeat, I try to remember what Katie said during our meeting yesterday—*You can't let him have control over a situation that hasn't even happened yet. Allowing that is letting him win. You are stronger than that. He no longer has power over you, Janelle.*

"She's right," I say out loud to the empty kitchen. "I can't curl up and let him win. No matter how hard this is, I have to fight."

I move toward the coffee maker, fill a mug, and add a bit of cream and sugar. Taking my first sip, I savor the rich warmth spreading through me, then lean back against the counter and pull my phone from my pocket to send a message to the family chat.

Me: *Emergency family meeting. My house, twenty minutes.*

I expect a bit of a pushback from a couple of them, but I get none.

Mom: *We'll be there. See you soon.*
Cam: *Should Leah come too?*
Me: *You might want her here. It's up to you, though.*

Leah has a way of calming Cam that none of the rest of us have. I would never tell him to leave her behind. She might be helpful today.

Tom: *Mads and I will be there in ten.*
Kim: *Pat's in the shower, but we'll be there.*
Me: *See you all soon.*

I toss my phone onto the counter and open the fridge.
I don't usually have breakfast, but on mornings like this,
I crave comfort food. I really need to go grocery shopping
today; there's hardly anything left. My phone rings as I grab
a cold slice of cheese pizza and take a bite.

"Hello?"

"Hello, is this Janelle?"

"Yes, it is. How can I help you?"

"This is Gayla from Mr. Darcy's office. I'm calling to set
up a meeting for you to come in and go over the upcoming
court proceedings. We have an opening this afternoon at
two, or Monday at nine. Do either of those times suit you?"

I toss the rest of the pizza in the trash can and sit down
on the barstool, having lost my appetite. "I can make it this
afternoon."

"Great, I've penciled you in. We'll see you then."

After ending the call, I pull up Eli's number on my
phone.

Me: *Can this day be over with already?*
Eli: *Are you alright?*
Me: *My family will be here soon so I can update them on
everything, and then I have to meet my lawyer in a bit. I
haven't even had time to process the fact that I might be
losing my kids, and yet, I have to tell everyone else. It's just a
lot.*

Eli: *I wish I were there. I'm sorry you're going through all
of this. Remember, you are strong. He cannot take that
from you. You've raised three amazing kids who love you
fiercely.*

They're watching you to see how you handle this, so do it with your head held high. When you need a moment, step away and call me. I've got your back in this.

I wish he were here. He seems to know what I need, even before I do. I could use that now.

There's a knock at the door, followed by Tom and Maddie walking in.

Me: *Thank you. I really needed to hear that right now. Tom and Maddie just walked in. I better get going.*
Eli: *Anytime. Tell them I say hi. I'll call you later tonight.*
Me: *Make it after nine. Heather's kids will be here.*
Eli: *Done. Talk soon.*

"Hey, guys." I place my phone on the countertop as Tom and Maddie enter the kitchen.

Maddie pours coffee into a mug, then hands it over to Tom before she sets about brewing another pot. Tom leans in and kisses the side of her head before he settles against the island across from me, crossing his arms casually.

"So, what did Dipsh—"

"Thomas Cameron," Maddie interrupts. "Language, sir."

"Sorry, love." Tom shakes his head, but the grin on his face remains unyielding. "What did Bryant do?"

"Don't answer that, J," Maddie says. She slides in next to Tom, who is now scowling at her. "You know as well as I do that the others are on their way. If he really did something, there's no point in making her repeat herself more than once."

Tom begins to argue, but Maddie faces him and quiets him with a kiss.

Only Maddie could hush Tom in a way that he'd be okay with. I've seen him with other girls before. If they'd ever tried something like that, he'd have been frustrated. I love her even more for getting him to stop. She's right. I don't need to explain this more than once. Once is too many times as it is.

I grab my coffee and walk into the family room, perching on the edge of the couch. All I can do now is hope the conversation goes smoothly and my brothers don't end up wrecking my house by letting fists fly.

"Hasn't he already caused enough trouble for you and the kids?" Tom snaps. "That man is a menace. Honestly, he should still be locked up." He rakes his hand through his hair, pacing back-and-forth with agitation.

"I have to meet with my lawyer soon," I say. "He's going to explain what to expect, but from what he's said, Bryant stands a chance of getting at least in-home visits."

Pat pushes his chair back abruptly as he stands.

Kim quickly gets to her feet, as well, placing a reassuring hand on his arm.

"That jerk nearly killed you!" Pat exclaims. "There's no way in hell he's taking your kids out of their home. He'll have to go through me first."

"Babe," Kim pleads. Her tone softens as she looks at him earnestly. "*Please.*"

I watch them with a sinking feeling in my chest, realizing I should have warned them about the news I was about to deliver. Pat's episodes—migraines bad enough to make him lock himself away in a dark room, often alone—can be intense. And when he's triggered, it takes him days to recover. The thought of him spiraling again makes my stomach churn.

Mom rises from her chair and makes her way over to me, settling down in the seat beside mine and enveloping my hand in hers. Her voice is soft but firm as she starts. "We all need to calm down. Your sister needs your support more than she needs everyone getting worked up over this."

"Seriously, Mom? The man you're talking about almost killed your daughter!" Cam exclaims, his voice rising in disbelief.

I wince at his words and glance at Dad, who's already on his feet, looking at Cam, his face a mix of anger and concern.

Mom stands up and, with a swift movement, places her fingers in her mouth and blows an ear-piercing whistle that slices through the tension in the room. "That's enough!" she shouts. "If you hotheaded boys can't keep calm, I'll have your wives take you home. Got it?"

They all nod, looking thoroughly chastised, just like when we were kids.

"As I was saying, your sister needs you to manage your emotions and be there for her. The same goes for the children. You don't need to fly off the handle every time this man brings more drama." I hate that once again my family is going at each other over Bryant. "We've learned he'll do anything to hurt your sister. It's time we show him he can't mess with one Cameron without facing the entire family." She turns to me, extending her hand. "I want everyone to adjust their schedules. On February first, let's walk into that courthouse to support Janelle, and show the judge the strong family backing she and the kids have."

I wipe at my tears and pull Mom in for a tight hug. "Thank you," I whisper.

"Janie, baby. We're your family. We've always got your back. We might be loud and irritating sometimes, but we'll always be here for you. No matter what."

I feel another set of arms wrap around me, and I turn just in time to see Cam and Tom squeezing into the growing circle.

Cam's voice is warm and reassuring as he speaks. "Mom's right. No matter what, we've got you. I'm sorry for being a jerk."

I can't fault them for getting so worked up. It seems to be a Cameron trait.

A chuckle escapes me as Pat and Dad pile in. It's been ages since we had a Cameron huddle like this, and the nostalgia warms my heart.

"I feel left out now," Maddie whines playfully. "This kind of reminds me of my cheerleading days, except with a bunch of buff men instead of petite women."

Her comment sends a ripple of laughter through our huddle.

"Come on in, girls. You're Camerons too." Dad gestures for them to join the embrace.

Finally, Mom pulls back a little and cups my cheeks with her hands, her eyes soft and full of love. "We love you, Janie. Don't you ever forget that."

I nod, unable to speak, as tears threaten to fall.

Suddenly, the doorbell rings, jolting us from our cozy circle.

"Who could be at the door? We're all here," Tom says, scratching his head in confusion.

"I don't know. I'm not expecting anyone."

Before I can make a move, Dad is already heading toward the door.

I step back from Mom and my siblings and walk through the house after him. By the time I make it to the kitchen, he's coming back toward me, his expression soft. A beautiful bouquet of flowers is cradled in his arms.

He hands them to me, a playful smile tugging at his lips. "Looks like someone has a secret admirer."

As I stand there, inhaling the sweet fragrance, Tom sneaks up behind me. "Who's the guy, Janie?" he asks, a teasing grin spreading across his face.

"I don't know."

The flowers are breathtaking.

The bouquet is so large that I have to hold it with both hands, careful not to crush any petals against me. I walk over to the kitchen island, brushing my fingers against the granite as I set it down. The arrangement is filled with white roses, daisies, and lilies that fill the air with their sweet scent. Instead of the usual baby's breath, vibrant blue pops are scattered throughout. I can't help but smile as I admire it. When my eyes catch on a small envelope nestled among the flowers, I pluck the card from its hiding spot.

I hope this delivery brings a little light to your gloomy day. I rescheduled my meeting so I can be there with you tomorrow. I'll be staying until after the court proceedings, then I'll make a quick trip and be back. I hope that's alright. I want to be

I press the card against my heart and smile. I can't believe how lucky I am to have him in my life.

"I think our little Janie is in love," Mom announces.

Heat rushes to my cheeks as I swivel around to find my entire family standing there looking back at me. How could I have possibly forgotten they were here?

"Who's the guy?" Dad asks.

"Eli," I say with a shy smile.

I meet Maddie's gaze, and she gives me a bright smile before nudging Tom.

"He and I have grown close. Aside from Heather, Eli's my best friend," I add. "He's aware of what's going on and thought I needed a little pick-me-up."

"He found out before we did?" Tom asks in surprise, and I nod. "Wow, he works fast. It took me years to get Maddie to fall for me, and he won you over in, what, just a few weeks?"

"It's not like that," I argue. "I like him . . . a lot, but I haven't been able to let my walls down completely. We've only recently become a couple," I say, stretching the truth a bit.

Leah pushes her way through the mix and comes to give me a hug. "I, for one, am happy for you. It's about time you find happiness."

"Me too," Maddie says. "I'd be thrilled if you and Eli could make it work."

A large part of me agrees with her. He seems to fit perfectly.

However, there's a tiny seed of doubt that makes me hesitant. I knew Bryant for years, and I never would've predicted his violent behavior in the end.

Everyone gives their two cents before I start ushering them out the door. If I'm going to make it to my lawyer's office on time then get back here to clean the house before the kids get home, I need to head out. I just hope that now that I'm feeling better about my day, this visit with my lawyer doesn't take me down to my knees once again.

Chapter Eighteen

I toss my bag in the back seat, slide behind the wheel, and start the car, then fish my phone out, swipe to Mom's name, and dial as the Bluetooth connects. Last night, as promised, Eli called and gave me his flight information. He offered to rent a car, but since his flight lands after my shift, I told him I'd pick him up instead. The thought of seeing him again has my heart beating a little faster. I can't figure out if it's excitement or straight-up nerves. Maybe it's the way I've replayed his words on a constant loop in my head when he told me that he booked this trip so that he could be here for me. That thought spiraled into thoughts of what life would be like if we were more than just pretend.

Would he still be here for me if I wasn't his *fake girl-friend*?

The phone rings so many times I think I'm going to be sent to voicemail when Mom finally answers.

"Hello?"

"Hey, Mom. I just got off work and am heading to the airport now. Are you sure you're okay with watching the kids a bit longer?" I put my phone on the hands-free clip and turn on the heat. It's a bit chilly in here.

Mom chuckles. "Of course I am, Janie. In fact, Sage asked if they could stay the night. Why don't you and Eli sneak in a date while you're out? There's no sense in rushing. I'll take the kids and Thor over to my place."

I lean my head back against my head rest and close my eyes for a moment. "I can't ask you to do that, Mom. You've already had them all day, and you will tomorrow too. You're already doing so much."

She sighs. "I'm offering, honey. I know you're not asking. You're a great mom, but even you need a break sometimes. One night out with your long-distance boyfriend won't hurt."

I hate lying to everyone about Eli and me, but it's for a good cause. I'd do anything for my kids. I think that's why I feel so bad leaving them in Mom's care so often. Since Katie nudged me to start dating again, it feels like I barely see them anymore. But Mom did say the kids wanted to stay, plus Eli and I do have a lot to talk about.

"Okay. Thank you. Tell them I love them, and I'll call before bed," I reply.

"I will."

"Thanks, Mom. Love you. Call me if you need anything."

"Will do. Love you, too, honey."

I hang up, shift into reverse, and back out of my spot. Once on the main road, I head out toward the airport that is only minutes from my job. I scowl at the thought of navigating around the terminal. It's a miracle that I even volunteered to pick him up.

Pulling into the garage, I snag a ticket, then head in to find a spot. This is the same place where Leah was kidnapped and Cam was drugged on the way to their honeymoon. My pulse speeds at the thought. Since then, security has been upped around the parking garage—still, I grip the steering wheel until my knuckles ache. At level three, I finally find an open spot and park beneath a flickering light. I hop out of the car, put my key between my fingers, and grasp it tightly in case I need to defend myself, then hurry toward the elevators, while keeping an eye on my surroundings.

Once inside, I let myself relax and put my keys away. I pull out my phone to check my messages to help distract myself from the anxiety I'm feeling. Between the parking garage and seeing Eli again, this is a lot. There's a text from the pharmacy letting me know that my refill is ready, one from Katie's office confirming my appointment in two days, and one from Eli.

Eli: *I can hardly wait to see you. It might sound cheesy, but I cannot wait to wrap you in my arms.*

I lean back against the elevator wall, smiling at nothing in particular. I remember when I fell asleep on his couch and, after waking up, how I told him all about my past with Bryant. Eli was so caring. And then the *hug*, and the way he asked me if he could give me one before touching me . . . Heat floods my cheeks at the thought. I still can't believe he hasn't run for the hills with all my baggage.

The elevator doors ping open. I walk into the rush of the airport, and make my way down to baggage claim, where Eli and I agreed to meet. In a moment of bravery, with the carousel nearby, I lean back against the railing, phone in hand, and type my reply.

Me: *That doesn't sound cheesy at all. I'm here at baggage claim and can't wait to be in your arms again.*

Before I can back out, I send and instantly start doubting my decision. Eli is getting under my skin quicker than I ever expected anyone could. I have strong feelings for him, and despite my attempts to resist this attraction, I find myself struggling less and less each time we talk. When the three little dots appear, disappear, and then appear again, the nerves ramp up. I thought for sure he wouldn't see the text until much later.

Eli: *I'm glad you feel that way, Peach. We're deboarding now. I'll make sure to add a little more fuel to my step.*

He's here? Oh my God, Eli is actually here!

With shaky hands, I put my phone into my pocket and glance up just as the alarm for the conveyor belt blares. I rub my hands, damp from nervousness, on my jeans in an attempt to calm my racing heart. Why am I so nervous? I shake my hands out to release the tension and begin pacing back and forth.

I hear my name called from behind me.

I turn and spot him, about twenty feet away. Eli walks quickly toward me with a big grin stretching across his face. My feet move on their own, and I hurry to meet him halfway. I walk straight into his open arms, a sigh escaping my lips as he envelops me in a comforting embrace.

Oh man, this feels good. This is *exactly* what I needed.

I set my coffee cup back on the table and lean back in my seat, gazing over at Eli across from me. After picking him up, we decided to get him settled into his hotel just a few blocks away, then come out for dinner. So far, we haven't talked about our fake relationship like we planned. Instead, we've been getting to know each other better.

I learned that Eli has a passion for woodwork. He mentioned a small workshop in the Whitfields' garage, where he likes to lose himself in a new project when he gets the chance. His social circle is small, similar to mine, and his best friend is Johnny Whitfield, one of Maddie's brothers. It makes sense, given that Eli grew up alongside them. From what I understand, the twins also share Eli's background in the security field. At least, I think they do.

"You know about me and Bryant. Were you serious about anyone in your past?" I ask Eli.

The server interrupts, clearing away our empty dinner plates with a practiced smile. I return her gesture with a grateful nod.

Eli thinks it over for a moment. "I only ever had one serious girlfriend," he begins. "Lynn and I dated for most of high school. Out of the blue, just before she left for college, she broke things off with me. I'd thought that we'd get through college, get married, and have a brood of kids by the time we hit thirty." He glances over at me, a soft smile playing on his lips. "She was my heartbreak. But looking back, I'm glad she did it. Three years into college, she met her now-husband, and the rest is history." He pauses long enough to take a drink. "I have a few questions now, if you don't mind."

I nod. "Ask away."

Eli hesitates for a moment, then looks me straight in the eye. "It's about this fake dating thing. Like I said before, I'm only in this as long as you can see us heading toward actually becoming a couple at some point."

"Okay," I agree.

He shifts in his seat. "How will we approach the topic with your lawyer or the judge if they ask? I don't like lying."

I sigh, glancing out the window before meeting his gaze again. "Neither do I. I don't want us to lie more than we have to, but I also don't want to take the chance of losing my kids." I pause, choosing my words carefully. "It's more omission than an actual lie. I told my lawyer that we're in a relationship and that the kids and I met your mom on vacation. It was never asked of me to define my relationship. So in a way, we aren't lying."

If Eli doesn't like what I said, he doesn't show it. "One thing I ask is that you spend time with me, just like a girlfriend would. You don't have to kiss me, though I wouldn't mind." He smiles playfully. "And you don't have to hang off of me if you're not comfortable with all of that, but I do want to keep up pretenses." He leans forward, his expression softening. "Plus, there's no better way to move forward than by spending time together."

There's no use trying to come up with the words to answer him when all that's going through my mind right now is how much I want to lean forward and meld my lips with his once more.

I pop a gummy bear into my mouth as I push open the door to the gas station just around the corner from Eli's hotel. After dropping him off, I swung in here to top off my tank and grab something fruity to munch on. As I walk back to my car, I'm lost in my own little world, my steps in sync with the tune playing in my head.

I can't remember the last time I felt so light.

A woman at the car next to mine catches my eye. She's juggling a toddler on her hip while fumbling with her keys and ends up dropping her drink. The soda threatens to roll beneath her car. I jog over and snatch it up before it can disappear from sight.

"Here you go," I say, extending the rescued soda.

"Thank you," she replies, a sheepish smile playing on her lips. "It's been one of those days."

"No problem. I understand. Hopefully, your night gets better."

I turn back toward my car, but as I round the hood, my steps stop abruptly. The feeling of walking on cloud nine evaporates in an instant. Leaning against my car door is none other than Bryant himself.

"What do you want?" I demand, resuming my approach, making him shift out of my way.

"Would it kill you to be nice to me, Janelle?" he retorts.

"I don't have time for this. What do you need?" I reply, sliding into the driver's seat, starting the car, and turning on the heat.

"My lawyer tells me that you pulled a boyfriend out of thin air. You think you'll beat me by pulling a stunt like that? It'll take way more than some fake boyfriend to win one over on me this time."

I'm stunned, but quickly remind myself that nobody knows about Eli and me. So I push forward. "I'm not trying to *win* at anything. But I won't shy away from you anymore either. I'd rather die than let you have my kids."

A sinister smile stretches across his face, before he pushes off my car and saunters away. As he retreats, he turns to face me, walking backward with confidence. "That can be arranged," he says, his words lingering in the air.

I shut my door, trying to shake off his words, and head toward the house. But as I drive home, not even ten minutes into the journey, I'm forced off the road as another car swerves into my lane. The shoulder is narrow, and as the wheel is jerked out of my hands, there's nothing I can do as the car careens down the steep, grassy embankment on the other side. As it finally comes to a sudden stop at the bottom, all I can hear are his words echoing in my head.

That can be arranged.

Chapter Nineteen

After being run off the road last night, I had to call Tom out to trailer my car back home. Between him and Pat, they managed to get me out of the ditch in the matter of an hour. Luckily, I'm okay, and for the most part, so is my car. I have a banged-up bumper, and my front right tire is shot, but I'll take it. I was a little shaken and will have a nasty bruise from where the seat belt locked up on me, but I'm alive, and that's all that matters.

I hand my keys over to the tire technician and make my way to Maddie's car, where she's waiting for me. Leah and Kim are planning to join us for lunch at the nearby taco shop. With only two days left before court, I'm thankful for all the support they're giving me.

When I called Eli last night to fill him in on the accident, he was furious. Not with me, but with the fact that someone could be so careless and leave me there in the ditch after having run me off the road. I didn't share with him that I thought that it could've been my ex.

What good would it do really? I have no proof.

I get in the car and fasten my seat belt as Maddie drives off. Today, I'm spending time with all my sisters-in-laws. Eli offered to watch the kids so I could run some errands, and much to my own surprise, I agreed. After last night, I'm still rattled. I need some time to myself.

Within a few minutes, we pull up to Los Tacos and hop out of the car. I spot the ladies already waiting on us across the lot.

"Hope y'all are hungry," I say with a grin. "I'm ready to destroy some carne asada tacos."

"I was all set on carnitas until you mentioned that," Kim chimes in.

"How about we each get something different and share? Each plate has four tacos anyway," Maddie suggests.

Though I'm inclined to claim all four carne asada tacos for myself, I decide to go along with the others and share.

We exchange hugs and head inside to claim a table. The moment the server approaches, we place our orders for our food and beverages, not needing more time to decide.

"How are things going with the case?" Maddie asks.

The chip I'm holding pauses halfway to my mouth, and everyone turns to look at her.

"Seriously, Mads?" Leah says. "I thought we were here to distract her from the court stuff, not dive into it."

"My bad. I just figured we were here to support her, not avoid the topic."

I raise my hand to calm them. "It's okay. Maddie meant no harm. Court is unavoidable. Bryant's lawyer wants to prove that he's changed. His case claims that Milly's been a good influence, and Mr. Darcy says he trying to prove that he deserves a chance at being a good dad." I pause as our drinks arrive. "Thanks," I say, sipping my soda. "Mr. Darcy says I should be ready for the worst. The judge might sympathize with Bryant, as he's a dad who's navigated court for his own kids."

"Do you think it'll work?" Kim asks.

I glance over at her, noticing the tears forming in her eyes, and place my hand on hers. I know these women would do anything they could to support me and my children. You know the saying—*it takes a village*. This is mine.

"I'm not sure what will happen. I won't give up easily, that's for sure. But I have to keep in mind that the judge doesn't know us or our homes. He's going to base his decision on what he hears in court." It's not any easier to swallow, but it does give me hope that Bryant's record is a weakness. "Mr. Darcy mentioned he'll use that and all the records we've kept of things he's pulled to strengthen my case." I just wish I had proof that he took part in what happened to me last night.

"Well, he'd be a total idiot to hand them over to your ex, if you ask me," Maddie says.

"I couldn't agree more," Leah adds.

"Same here," Kim chimes in.

"Let's switch to something more cheerful," Leah suggests, turning to us with a smile. "Like how stuffed we're going to be after devouring all this food."

I laugh. If there's anyone at this table who loves food more than I do, it's Leah. Her love for food only grew after she had the twins.

The server arrives with our plates and a tray of salsa. We start swapping tacos and dive right in. I shove nearly half a taco into my mouth without hesitation. There's no one here to impress, and besides, who can resist tacos? As the flavor of pico de gallo hits my taste buds, I wish I'd taken the time to savor it.

I let out a satisfied moan.

"Good?" Leah asks, trying to suppress a laugh.

"They're amazing! Unlike guys, tacos never let you down." I chuckle, taking a bite and then wiping my mouth. "They're always satisfying."

"*J!*" Kim nearly spits out her food.

"What? Tacos are comforting. One good bite, and I'm a happy camper. There's no risk of getting hurt with them."

"Not unless you count the heartburn I'm gonna have later," Maddie chimes in.

I laugh at her remark, but Leah's not ready to put my comment to rest just yet.

"That's actually kind of sad. Why are you with Eli if that's how you feel?" Leah asks.

I chew thoughtfully before responding. "I'm trying. Eli and I had formed a solid friendship before we ever started dating. He, Katie, and Pat are the only ones who know the whole story. If anyone can break through my walls, it'll be him."

"You really told him everything?" Maddie asks. I nod and take another bite.

"I knew you two were getting close—I just didn't know how close. I bet Anna and Ms. Emmy are thrilled you two are together now. Ari says they haven't stopped talking about you and the kids since you left."

I feel my cheeks warm just thinking about Eli's mom and grandma. While I'm glad Eli's willing to help, I hate that we're deceiving everyone. This whole thing isn't fair.

I park my car outside of my house and turn it off. I've finally checked everything off my list, down to me getting a haircut! That's a rare treat for me. Since Eli's been at the house today, keeping an eye on the kids, he's also been tackling my never-ending list. He's even gone as far as cleaning out the garage. When he called me to ask if I had any caulking for the tub, he filled me in on that tidbit. I was a bit shocked but thanked him anyway. Tonight, Eli and I plan on having dinner with the kids so that we can fill them in on us "dating."

I exit the car, grab my bags from the trunk, and head up the path.

Eli slips out the door with a bright smile playing on his face.

"Hey," I say.

He pauses a few steps away. "Hey. How was your day?"

"It was productive. Thanks for watching the kids for me. I hope they behaved."

"They did." He reaches out, lightly touching the ends of my hair. "Your hair looks nice. Did you get it cut?"

"I did." I'm surprised he noticed. I didn't cut much.

"I like it," he says. He lowers his hand, takes the bags from me, and sets them on the ground. "We've got a surprise for you. I need you to close your eyes and trust me to lead you inside. Can you do that?"

I glance at the uneven path, concerned about stumbling if I can't see where I'm going. But I don't want to spoil the surprise, especially if the kids are part of it. "You won't let me fall, right?"

"I won't ever let you go, Janelle. I promise you're safe with me." When he talks to me like that, it does things to me that I haven't felt in a long time.

"But what about my bags?"

"I'll have Pete come and get them. Do you trust me?"

I nod. "I do."

Eli's lips curve into a reassuring smile, one that crinkles the corners of his eyes. "Okay, Peach. Put your hands in mine and close your eyes."

I place my hands in his, feeling his firm yet gentle grip. My eyes close, and the world fades, leaving only his steady presence. After a few steps, I stumble, my balance tipping forward until I land against Eli's firm chest. Despite him being lean, I can feel the chiseled definition of his abs beneath the thin fabric of his shirt. The cool breeze is a blessing—otherwise, I'd be fanning myself with my hand. I thought I was too young to have hot flashes.

I open my eyes and glance up, giving a shy smile. "Can't I walk on my own?"

"Nope. Keep those eyes closed. I promised to get you there safely, and I will." Eli bends down and lifts me effortlessly into his arms.

"Eli! Put me down before you hurt yourself."

"Not happening, Peach," he replies. "This is far safer than risking you tripping again. If you truly want me to put you down, I'll do it once we're safely on the porch."

"I'm too heavy for you to be carrying me," I protest. I feel panic threatening to settle in and I want to cry.

Eli gently sets me down but stays close, his presence un-wavering. He nudges my chin up to meet his gaze. "You're not heavy, Janelle," he insists. "You're beautiful, smart, funny, a wonderful mother, a loyal friend, and an overall amazing person. Whatever your ex did to make you doubt yourself makes me want to have a word with him. It hurts knowing you've suffered so much pain over someone who is unworthy of your time."

His words wash over me, acting as a comforting balm for the insecurities that have lingered in my heart for far too long.

I squeeze his hand softly. "Eli, I'm not used to this level of kindness. I'm so accustomed to being criticized that this feels overwhelming."

He cups my cheek, and I lean into his warmth, eyes closed. "You deserve the world, Janelle. You are worthy of being treated well. In the meantime, can you try to trust me? I wouldn't offer to carry you up those steps if I couldn't. Trust that you're not too heavy."

I glance up at his smiling face and grin back.

"You're beautiful," Eli adds.

My cheeks warm, and I begin to pull away.

"Don't, please. If it's too much, we can stop here, and I can head back to the hotel after we talk to the kids. Just don't pull away from me. Please."

I squeeze his hand tighter, making him chuckle. "Please don't leave me. I'm trying, Eli, I promise. Just be gentle with me, okay?"

"You've got my word. We'll move at your pace." He bends down to meet my gaze. "May I have the privilege of carrying you inside so the kids and I can surprise you the right way?"

Agreeing to this is a big step for me, but if I'm ever going to release my fears and learn to trust, now seems like the perfect moment to start.

"You may."

Eli leans forward, lifts me like a bride, and I wrap my arms around his neck, trying to relax. "I've got you, Peach. I promise, I'll never hurt you," he whispers. He kisses my head and starts walking. "Close your eyes, and remember, the kids worked hard on this."

Moments later, I hear the door creak open and sense Eli entering as he crosses the threshold.

"Are you guys all set?" he asks the children.

"Yes," Eric replies confidently.

"Good. Pete, can you run out and get your mom's bags, please?"

I inhale deeply, savoring the wonderful aroma. They must have prepared dinner for me. Right on cue, my stomach growls, making it clear just how hungry I am. You'd think that after the lunch I had earlier, I wouldn't be this hungry, but whatever they're cooking smells incredible.

Eli laughs softly and places me back on my feet. "I think Mom's hungry. Are we ready to let her see yet?"

"No!" Sage calls out. "One more minute."

Eli takes my hand, then leans in to whisper, "Come with me. And remember, this was all their idea. I just helped them put it together."

He leads me through the living room and in the direction of the dining room. He stops, just past where I believe the island starts, and removes his hand from mine. I feel him step away as the warmth from his body disappears.

"Can I open my eyes yet?"

"One second," Peter says.

In the next breath, my hand is being taken by a much smaller one—Eric's.

"Momma, you can open your eyes now."

I cautiously peek through my lashes, allowing a smile to grow across my face. As I open my eyes fully, the scene before me comes into focus. I have to fight back happy tears as I take it all in. My kitchen has been transformed into a heartwarming display. My children stand proudly in their Sunday best on either side of Eli, who is dressed in dark, well-fitted jeans and a maroon button-up shirt. In his hands, he cradles a stunning bouquet of vibrant flowers, similar to the one he sent me just days ago.

"You'll spoil me at this rate," I say, my voice coming out a bit shaky.

"I intend to," he replies with a charming grin.

"What is all this?" I ask. My gaze sweeps over the array of tea light candles scattered across the counter behind them. Each one flickers with a soft glow. Knowing Eli, they are likely battery-operated for safety. Flower petals are arranged around the candles, and to the side, the dining table is romantically set for two.

"We know you and Eli like each other," Sage says. "You don't have to be afraid of him, Mom. He's not like Dad; he won't hurt you. Plus, we *really* like him."

Tears start falling down my cheeks as I'm unable to hold them any longer. Tonight, we were supposed to tell the kids that we're dating, and yet instead, they had other plans.

"I made dinner with Eli's help," Sage proclaims.

"Pete and I decorated!" Eric exclaims excitedly.

"It's lovely, bud." I giggle at his childlike enthusiasm. "I can't believe you all did this. It's just so much. Thank you."

Eli places the flowers on the counter and approaches me before extending his hand, which I take. "Would you do me the honor of having dinner with me?"

"What about the kids?" I ask. "Weren't we going to talk to them?"

"Eli got us pizza and a new game," Sage says. "We're all set. Tonight, we're serving you. And we'll handle the cleanup too. You just need to enjoy your meal." She smiles over at her brothers. "Isn't that right, boys?"

"Right," Pete grumbles.

Eli winks before he leans in so only I can hear him. "Let's let them play matchmaker. Tomorrow, we'll tell them about us."

I nod and turn to the kids. "Y'all are the most wonderful children anyone could ever ask for." I then turn and follow Eli to the table and take a seat in the chair he pulls out for me.

Pete and Eric walk over, each balancing a plate of food in their hands. They set the plates down in front of us as best they can. Eli helps Eric so he doesn't spill it. Then Sage walks over and places a glass of tea in front of each of us. "On your plate tonight is alfredo, parmesan-covered green beans, and garlic toast," she announces.

"I helped make the toast," Eric exclaims.

I chuckle softly and catch Eli's gaze from across the table, his eyes sparkling.

"You did great, all of you did," Eli says.

"Taste it," Sage urges.

I lift my fork, twirling alfredo onto it, as the boys make their way toward the family room. I take a bite and can't help but hum in delight. "My goodness, Sage. You really outdid yourself tonight."

Her face lights up with a bright smile, cheeks slightly flushed, before she turns and runs off to join her brothers.

Looking back across the table, I feel a warmth spread in my chest. Eli reaches across the table, his fingers brushing against mine. I place my hand in his, feeling the comfort of his presence. I can't help but wonder if this is what life with Eli would be like, filled with moments like this. If so, sign me up. I'm done fighting it.

Chapter Twenty

I follow behind the gurney as Garrett navigates it through the chaos of the emergency room toward the exit. We've just finished transporting a gunshot wound victim. The scene we arrived at earlier was a chaotic mess, far from what I had prepared for. The brother of a single mom, in a moment of carelessness, had left a loaded firearm on the coffee table while he napped on the couch. Leaving it within reach of a toddler. The child, curious and unaware of the danger, grabbed it, resulting in the mother getting shot in the abdomen when the gun discharged as she tried to get it from her child.

"Cameron!" a voice calls from behind me. I stop and turn to see one of the nurses rushing my way. "You forgot to sign the report," she says as she steps closer.

I glance back at Garrett, who nods, before she continues toward our waiting ambulance. I pivot and follow the nurse back to the nurse's station.

"If you'll give me a second, I'll go grab the papers."

I wait as Jane rounds the corner to retrieve the papers I need to sign. The double doors to the right, further down the corridor, swing open with a loud clicking noise that grabs my attention. Over the counter, Jane hands me a clip-board with my report, and I put pen to paper and quickly sign across the bottom. As I glance up, my heart skips a beat. I could almost swear it's Milly walking in. But Jane's voice pulls me back.

"I'm sorry. What was it you said?" I ask, turning my eyes to her.

"Oh no, I was talking to someone else," she replies. I hand back the clipboard, and she gives it a quick look before smiling. "You're free to go now. Thank you for coming back with me."

I nod in acknowledgment and retrace my steps, my eyes darting toward the room where I thought I saw Milly dis-appear. But as I draw closer, a voice on my radio interrupts.

"This is Garrett with Rescue 14. We're five minutes out." My partner's voice is a reminder that I'm on the clock, and I quicken my steps on my way out. I make a mental note to check in later and make sure Milly's okay.

Bryant won't harm another the way he did me. Not if I have anything to do with it.

The end of my workday is finally here. I'm ready to wash off the day now that my muscles ache from a good workout. I dig into my locker, pull out my phone, and shoot a quick text to Eli.

Me: *I'll be ready in twenty if you want to head this way.*

Since picking him up at the airport and talking him out of renting a car, I let him use mine. It's a little inconvenient but not too bad. He's mostly out at my house anyway.

Eli: *I'm leaving now. See you soon.*

With a quick nod to myself, I grab my hygiene bag and head for the showers. I've worked my routine down to a fine art, managing to shower, shave, and get dressed in under ten minutes. When you're in the middle of a shower and get a call you have to rush to, or have three kids who start fighting, you learn to be quick. It doesn't really give me time to soak or figure out life's troubles, but it gets the job done. In record time, I'm out, toweling off my hair, and twisting it up into a bun just as Garrett walks in, her face lit up with a wide smile.

"What's got you smiling so big?" I ask, raising an eyebrow as I zip up my bag.

She clutches her phone to her chest and gasps. "Nothing."

"Mmhmm. Sure," I say with a knowing grin. Her eyes have that dreamy, faraway look, but I decide not to pry. This time. Swinging my bag over my shoulder, I open the door. "I'm out. See you Monday."

"Monday?" she echoes, a hint of confusion in her voice

"Yup. I've got court, remember?"

"Oh yeah. Let me know how that goes."

"Will do." I give her a quick wave and step out into the hallway, then walk down the stairs, saying bye to a few coworkers on my way out. By the time I reach the glass doors at the front of the building, I spot Eli pulling into the parking lot. Perfect timing. I push open the door and step outside, feeling the cool breeze on my face just as Eli steps out of the car with a smile.

"You can drive if you want," I offer. "I'd love to relax if you don't mind."

Eli walks over, taking my bag off my shoulder and placing it on his, then rests his hand gently on my lower back, steering me toward the passenger side. "I don't mind at all. Rough day?" he asks. Eli opens the car door, then waits for me to slide into the seat before handing me my seat belt with a smile.

I can't help but smile back, feeling a warmth spread through me. He's almost too good to be true. "No more than normal," I reply, settling into the seat. "But it is a Friday for me. I'm normally ready for a break by now."

Eli nods, shuts my door, and rounds the back of the car. He opens the rear passenger door, dropping my bag in before getting in behind the wheel of the car. He looks over at me and smiles. "How about I pick up dinner tonight?"

"You're always buying us dinner. I can't let you keep doing that," I protest.

"Sure, you can," he insists, his tone teasing. "You let me use your car all day. You have no idea how much I saved by not having to get a rental. Besides, it'd be the boyfriendly thing to do." He winks, a mischievous glint in his eyes, before turning the key in the ignition.

"But you're not really my boyfriend. At least let me pay for the kids," I argue, trying to maintain a semblance of fairness.

"Not yet, but I could be if you said yes." Eli pauses. "If I'm buying for you, I'd like to buy for them too. You're a package deal."

"Fine," I concede with a sigh. I'm too tired to argue.

"Fine to what? To being my girl for real or to dinner?" he asks.

I didn't know he was really asking. I pause, realizing I don't want to keep up the charade any longer. We shouldn't have ever started it anyway. Besides, last night I did say I'd stop fighting this. "Fine to both, I guess."

"See, was that so ha—" He stops midsentence, his eyes widening with surprise. Eli clears his throat, his voice a mix of disbelief and joy. "Did I hear you right? You said you'd be my girl."

"I did." I let out a soft chuckle, unable to hide my laughter.

If Eli were standing, I imagine he'd be doing a little victory dance. His eyes sparkle with excitement as he looks at me. "Seriously? This isn't too fast for you?"

"I'm serious. I don't want to keep fighting my feelings for you. You've somehow become my best friend. Don't tell Heather I said that. She might not like that too much." I laugh softly, imagining her acting as if she's mad at me even if she is really happy. "But, yeah. I'm your girl, if you still want me."

"Dang right, I want you," Eli says, his voice firm but filled with warmth. He calms himself, reaching over to take my hand gently. He places soft kisses on the back of it, his eyes meeting mine with an intensity. "Does this mean I can kiss you now?" he asks.

"Please do. I've thought about kissing you since Charleston."

As his lips find mine, all I can think is that I won't be running scared ever again. Not when I have someone who grounds me the way Eli does. With him, I finally feel safe.

"Oh, I got another one!" Eric announces, his voice rising with excitement. "Why did the cookie cry?"

Eli, sitting across from him, his elbows resting on the dinner table and a playful smile tugging at his lips, leans in closer. "I don't know. Why?"

"Because he felt crumbly!" Eric shouts triumphantly, his voice filled with delight. "Get it?"

I can't help but chuckle. "We get it, son. That was a good one. Did Grandpa teach it to you?"

"Nope, Uncle Tom did." Eric is grinning ear to ear, clearly proud of himself.

"They were going back and forth all morning," Sage says. "Grandma had to send them out to feed the cows. She said it was driving her nuts."

"At least you got to get away from them," Pete replies, his tone slightly grumpy. "I had to go and help them with the feed bags." He shifts in his chair, looking eager to leave. "May I be excused now?"

"Not yet," I say, glancing at Eli, who sits there with a gentle smile. "Eli and I need to talk to y'all."

"What about?" Sage asks.

"We wanted to let you know that we have decided to be a couple," I announce, feeling a flutter of nerves mixed with excitement. "Eli is now officially my boyfriend."

"Really?" Sage squeals.

I turn my gaze toward Pete, noticing his lips curve into a small smile as he looks at Eli.

"Does this mean you guys are okay with it?" I ask. I search their faces, holding my breath.

"Yeah. This is great," Sage says.

"It's cool," Pete adds. Even with the mask of indifference Peter is now wearing, I still see the slight lift of his lip.

"Does this mean you're going to be our new dad?" Eric asks.

My heart skips a beat, and I eagerly wait to see how Eli will answer this.

He looks at me as if he's questioning. When I nod, he shifts his focus to Eric. "Right now, your mom and I are just dating," Eli begins, his voice steady but gentle. "You have a father, and I would never dream of taking his place. But if your mom and I can make this work out between us, then maybe one day, with your permission of course, I could be your bonus dad." There's a pause as Eli glances at me. "But that is a ways off. Your mom and I will be taking this slow. So let's just have fun getting to know each other better for now. Okay?"

While a part of me wishes Eli hadn't given Eric hope that we might be heading in that direction, I can't help but feel grateful for his willingness to step in with my children. I glance at Eli, and my heart swells with appreciation. I'm so glad I finally quit fighting my feelings and allowed him into our lives on a new level.

Chapter Twenty-One

Early the next morning, there's a quick rap at my bedroom door before it swings open. Eric runs in, launching himself onto the bed with me, sending us both bouncing in every direction.

"You were supposed to be gentle with your mom," Eli calls from the hallway. "Mind if I come in?"

How did he get in here? I wonder. I sit up and pull the covers snugly around me while nudging Eric until he tumbles over onto the middle of the bed. "Come on in." I chuckle.

Eric's playful glare makes it look like he's ready to start a wrestling match. Honestly, it wouldn't surprise me if he was. Being a mom to two boys is a challenge sometimes. They're always so rough and tough.

"Good morning, Peach," Eli says. He steps in with a tray of breakfast goodies, closely followed by Pete with another tray and Sage, still in pajamas, clutching a cup of coffee.

"What's all this?" I ask.

Eli places the tray gently across my lap and takes the coffee from Sage, handing it over as well. Then he leans in and lays a quick kiss on my forehead. The kids climb onto the bed beside me, balancing their own tray. I give Eli a nod to join us at the foot of the bed, and he happily obliges.

"The kids and I had a talk about this last night. I'm taking all of you out for a day of pure fun and laughter. No chores, no stress about tomorrow—just smiles all around." He grabs my foot through the blanket and lightly squeezes. "Then when we get back, Sage already has a movie and snacks picked out for the evening."

I glance from the kids to Eli with a teasing lift of my eyebrow. "Oh really? And how did I miss all of this?"

Sage giggles. "You were on the phone, and we snuck Eli outside."

"Y'all are way sneaky." I chuckle. Glancing around, I notice that Thor is missing.

"He's already had his breakfast and is playing outside," Eli chimes in.

That's good—at least I don't have to worry about him getting into anything. "How did you manage all of this without me catching on?"

Eli gives a mischievous grin. "You left all your keys on the keychain when you let me take your car."

I nod in understanding, then take a slow sip of my coffee and smile. "This is so thoughtful. Thank you all."

"You're always so busy taking care of others that when they suggested doing something nice for you, I thought, why not? Like I've said before, you deserve the best."

"Eli said we could go to the cat café," Eric chimes in.

I glance at Eli with a knowing look. "I hope you're prepared to tell him he can't adopt every cat ready for a new home."

Eli looks at the kids as if they've played him. I'm sure they have. "I didn't consider that. All right, we can still visit, but no bringing home another pet unless your mom decides she wants one. Deal?"

"Aw, man," Eric grumbles. "I really want a cat too."

"You help Grandma feed the barn cat, and we already have Thor. I think that's enough for now. I don't have the time or money for another pet."

"Fine," he draws out.

"Eat up," Eli says. "We leave in an hour."

I toss a berry into my mouth and pass the bagel to Eli, who takes it gratefully.

This is nice—it almost feels like we're all a family. Sure, I'm scared of being hurt again, but as my mom often reminds me, nothing worthwhile in life comes without a little bit of fear.

Eli helps me into the passenger seat of my SUV while the kids climb into the back. "Thanks for driving us back. I can't believe I was so clumsy."

"No worries. I'm just sorry you fell. Are you sure you don't want me to take you to the doctor?"

"I'm sure. I just twisted my ankle. It'll be okay as long as I rest it for a while."

Earlier today, after we left the cat café, we headed to the mall so I could find a gift for Leah and Cam's twins. Their second birthday party is approaching, and I hadn't bought anything yet. We ended up with five gifts for each of them. I know that's a lot, but I couldn't resist. And now that most of my cards are paid off, there's a little more wiggle room.

Eli wasn't much help either. He mentioned it was his first time in the baby section of a store, and he was enjoying himself. Watching him try to figure out what the items were was adorable. I have to admit, it made me wonder what it would be like to see him as a father, specifically as a dad of a baby.

"I'm sure you know what's best, but if you don't sit down and ice that ankle when we get back, I'm driving you straight to the doctor." His voice is kind, even though it carries a warning. Eli's fingers caress my arm as he reaches across to fasten my seat belt. My heart skips a beat with him being so close.

"Are you going to kiss Momma?" Eric nearly shouts, his voice echoing through the car.

My cheeks feel like they're on fire, but all Eli does is throw a playful wink at me as he passes back over.

"I think I'll wait until we don't have an audience," Eli says with a grin. He takes my bag from my lap to prop under my ankle before he closes the door with a soft thud.

Before Eli can even get around the front of the car, the kids launch into their commentary.

"O-M-G, Mom! He almost kissed you!" Sage sighs dreamily.

"Seriously, Sage?" Peter grimaces. "I don't want to see Mom kissing *anyone*. That's disgusting."

As Eli approaches the driver's side door, I intervene. "That's enough. No more talk about us kissing. Got it?"

"Fine," Sage whines.

"Everyone ready to head out?" Eli slides into the driver's seat and pulls the door shut behind him. He takes my hand in his and kisses it, shooting me a wink, then the engine purrs to life, and he navigates the car out of the parking lot and down the road. The kids' voices start to rise as Eric mentions food. They would eat all day if I let them, but I guess it *is* getting close to dinnertime.

"What do you guys feel like eating?"

"Pizza!" Eric exclaims.

"We just had pizza," Peter argues. "How about chicken nuggets?"

Eric taps his chin with his index finger in thought. "I don't want nuggets," he whines, his voice a high-pitched protest echoing through the car. He throws his head back against his booster seat, pouting dramatically. "I want cheese pizza." He crosses his arms across his chest and gives Peter a look that shows his anger over the situation.

Eli adjusts his hand in mine, linking our fingers in a reassuring gesture. "What about you, Sage? What do you want?" he asks.

"She got to pick the snack. That's no fair." Eric continues his protest as his voice rises in volume. By this point, he's in full tantrum mode, his fists clenched in frustration.

I know Eli spends a lot of time with the Whitfield kids, but is he truly ready to take on all of this chaos? He's been a trooper so far, but come on. Is he really ready to step into a premade family, with all its drama?

"Eric Lane, that is enough," I say firmly. My voice cuts through the air with authority. "No more whining, or there will be no pizza votes the next three times we eat out." Eric has to learn that throwing a tantrum won't get him where he wants to go.

He huffs but doesn't argue.

"Can we get burritos? We haven't had that in a while," Sage says.

Eli glances over at me, his eyebrows raised slightly, awaiting my response.

I nod in agreement, a small smile playing at the corners of my lips.

"Sounds good to me. How about we stop on the way back out to the farm?" he suggests.

Eric starts to grumble, but one look over my shoulder in his direction silences him. He turns to gaze out the window, letting his anger deflate before we make it home. I hate that he's frustrated, but he can't act out every time things don't go his way.

Eli steers us through the drive-through, and once again, he insists on picking up the tab. It's been his routine all day, and at first, it rubbed me the wrong way. However, when I finally brought it up, his explanation left me without an argument—*I'm a gentleman, Janelle. When we take our woman out on a date, we open doors and cover all costs. You're my girlfriend—and you're a mom—so this is my way of showing you that I'm committed not just to you, but to the kids as well. In a sense, this is a group date. Please don't take that from me.*

I'm rarely at a loss for words, but I was utterly speechless.

With our food in hand, Eli navigates us toward the interstate. Between the kids' laughter and the sound of their movie playing in the back seat, I hardly notice the ride. Most of the time, I cannot wait to get home, but today, I don't mind the drive. In this moment, with Eli's hand in mine, I feel more whole than I have in years.

Minutes later, we're on the exit ramp, heading home.

As the house comes into sight, I reach over and grab the remote, pausing their movie. "Pete, as soon as we get parked, I'd like you to unlock the house and let Thor out. Sage, you grab our dinner and carry it inside. And Eric, I need you to make sure that Thor has food and water."

"If one of you could also grab the drinks from your mom and clear a path, I'd appreciate it." Eli looks back at the kids in the rearview mirror as he pulls into the driveway, then over at me. "Stay there. I'll come around and get you."

Before I have a chance to argue, Eli has turned off the engine and is hurriedly moving around the front of the car. The kids quickly follow suit. Sage helps Eric out of his booster then comes over to grab the bags of food, while Pete takes charge of the drinks, making a beeline for the door to unlock it. In the blink of an eye, Eli has my bag over his shoulder and has effortlessly lifted me into his arms once again.

"Eli!" I protest. "Set me down. I can manage the short walk."

"No arguing, please," he says. "In a matter of two days, you'll be back at work, and I'll be on a plane back home. Let me take care of you now so that you can take care of yourself when I'm gone."

I really need to learn how to stop fighting him on every little thing. If we're going to have any kind of future, I need to learn to let go.

I lean into him, feeling the warmth radiating from his body, and wrap my arms around his neck. Feeling compelled, I lean in and press a soft kiss against his neck, the faint scent of his cologne enveloping me. His scent is warm and welcoming, bringing back memories of a cozy evening by the fire, cuddled up with a good book and a steaming mug of cocoa—he smells like home. I nuzzle in closer, taking it all in.

Eli carries me inside and sets me down on the couch before smiling down at me. "Sit tight. I'll be back with an ice pack and dinner."

Thor, eager for attention after being alone all day, runs in from the kitchen.

"No, Thor!" I quickly curl up to protect my ankle from his full-force landing.

"Thor!" Eli booms.

Thor attempts to stop, sliding across the floor in the process. I turn back around in time to see Eli sitting down at the end of the couch. He grabs a couple of pillows and places them under my swollen foot, then takes off my shoe and sock. Reaching behind him, he picks up the wrapped ice pack and gently places it on my foot. As he stands, he takes Thor by the collar.

"Come on, boy, you've gotta let your momma rest. Let's go get you a bone." When he looks back at me, he has a smile on his face again. "The kids are already set up with dinner at the table. I'll be right back with yours. Do you want salsa?"

He really has thought of everything.

Even though he's only been here a few days, so much has already changed. What would it be like if he were here all the time?

No, I think. I can't let my mind go there just yet. There's still so much to learn about each other. I know that I trust Eli, truly, but do I trust myself?

Chapter Twenty-Two

Outside the courtroom, I pace back and forth along a narrow pathway. The tension feels like a heavy weight on my shoulders, increasing with every passing second. Silence hangs thick in the air as my family remains mute, watching as I struggle to maintain my composure. No one dares to intervene, likely afraid of provoking my temper. Given my past reaction, they might be right, but I still wish someone would at least make an attempt. It's unusual for them to be so quiet. Normally, they'd be all about telling me what to do.

This is driving me crazy; it's too quiet!

The judge has listened to both sides, then announced a recess to deliberate on the verdict. Beyond the wooden doors, time seems frozen, leaving me in a state of uncertainty. His decision will affect so many people's lives. Everyone in this hallway has a vested interest in the outcome. We're all suffering in some way, due to my ex.

I look over at Eli, catching his eye.

He pushes himself off the wall where he had been leaning and walks my way. Just a few steps away, he extends his hand, his fingers grazing my arm with a gentle touch, and I crumble. I step into him, feeling the solid reassurance of his presence as he envelops me in a strong embrace. It's exactly the support I need to finally let go. My tears break free, and Eli holds me close against his chest, his hand gently stroking the back of my head in soothing, rhythmic motions.

A clatter in the stairwell disturbs the peace, and Cam and Tom begin to stand. But it's only Leah, Maddie, and Kim walking up the stairs with hurried steps, a mix of relief and worry on their faces. They had left briefly to check in with the babysitters and ensure that Tom's car, parked at a metered spot, still had plenty of time.

I step back from Eli's embrace, using the back of my hand to dab away the tears.

"Mr. Darcy isn't far behind us," Kim says as she passes by.

Eli begins to move away, but I instinctively reach for his hand, clutching it tightly. He responds by weaving his fingers through mine, and a wave of gratitude washes over me, knowing that I have his support in this fight.

"Ms. Cameron," Mr. Darcy says as he reaches the top of the stairs. He moves my direction, stopping in front of me as my family begins to stand and come closer. "The judge has come to a decision."

Eli's hand starts to rub soothing circles on the side of my arm, his touch warm and reassuring. All the while, the fingers of his other hand remain interlocked with mine, providing a steady anchor.

"Remember, we hope for the outcome we want, but need to prepare for the worst. If this doesn't go our way, I'll ask for a temporary order so we can revisit this in three months."

Three months?

I nod, my throat tight and words refusing to form. My heart thunders in my chest like a relentless drum, each beat echoing my fear. The thought of losing my children claws at my insides, knowing they'd be in the hands of someone who thrives on inflicting pain, someone who would manipulate and toss them aside like forgotten toys. My only comfort is knowing that Bryant has never hit the kids. That doesn't mean that he hasn't left behind deep emotional scars, though.

"Breathe," Eli whispers softly in my ear. "You've got this. I'm right here with you."

I finally exhale, the breath rushing out of me like a gust of wind. I turn my gaze back at Mr. Darcy. "If things don't go our way, how soon can we appeal and try to overturn it?"

"My assistant is already on it. We're not wasting any time." He takes a step closer to the door, hand outstretched, and wraps it around the handle. "Ready?"

I manage a shaky smile and nod, though my stomach churns with anxiety. "I am," I reply.

Whether I'm ready is irrelevant. I need to know if I get to keep my kids or not.

Let's get this over with.

Eli and I have been cuddled up in my family room for the past hour. My family was here with us until a few minutes ago, when I asked them to leave. Heather will be bringing the kids back in a few hours, and I need some quiet time to sift through the tangled emotions and thoughts left by today's court proceedings.

The outcome wasn't the win I had been hoping for, but it wasn't entirely a loss either. I'm considering an appeal, though I can accept it as long as the children are safe. Mr. Darcy advised me to talk to the kids and get to know how they feel about the visits. If they're willing, seeing their father every other weekend might not be a bad idea, assuming he's genuinely changed. I'm still doubtful, but if the children want this, I'll put my feelings aside to allow them to bond with their father.

Besides the every-other-weekend visitation, Bryant is allowed to attend their school events and birthday parties if he's invited. Although he's still not permitted on the farm. I still have custody, but the judge mentioned that if everything goes smoothly, he'd be open to reconsidering our arrangement in three months when he revisits our case.

"How are you feeling?" Eli asks. "Is there anything I can do to help?"

I turn slightly to meet his gaze. "I don't think it's fully hit me yet. I doubt it will until I actually have to take the kids to Bryant's place and leave them there. That's going to require a lot of willpower on my part. Just the thought of leaving them there makes me sick."

"I don't know the guy, but after watching him in court today, I understand your concern. The way he looked at you when he thought nobody was looking made me want to wring his neck. It's surprising the judge didn't see through his facade. I certainly did." Eli gently twists a lock of my hair around his finger. "How about we get the kids cell phones before I head out tomorrow? I think it would be good for them to have them while they're with Bryant."

"I think I can manage that as long as I can keep their screen time in check. I don't want them to miss out on their childhood because of their devices." I need to address this with Pete, but thankfully, he's not too far gone. He's still willing to set down the controller and play outside.

"Ari installed a program on her kids' phones that limits their screen time and sets specific hours for usage—something like four to nine, if I recall correctly. You could do the same. Outside those hours, the phones are essentially useless, but they can still dial 911 in emergencies."

"That's a great idea. Can you get me the name of the app?"

"Of course," he replies.

I lean back in his embrace and try to soak it all in while I can. The thought of Eli leaving fills me with dread. His unwavering support in court today has shown me that I can truly rely on him. The way he stood by my side has sparked hope in my heart. I know this journey won't be easy, but starting today, I'm determined to break down the walls I've built around myself for far too long.

Eli and I deserve a real chance at happiness.

We sit in comfortable silence for several minutes before he softly breaks it. "I sure am going to miss you and the kids," he says. "Being here with you has been so much more than I could have ever imagined."

I survey the family room. The chaotic play corner has remained untouched by anyone other than the kids for days. The toys have slowly started spreading throughout the room. "You still feel that way, even with the tantrums and extra work you've taken on? Honestly, I'm surprised we haven't scared you away yet."

Eli shifts, sitting up slightly from our embrace, turning to face me with a sober expression. "Do you remember what I said before we began this relationship?" he asks, his eyes searching mine.

I shake my head, puzzled by his question.

"You're a mom first and foremost," he reminds me. "I would've never come into this expecting anything different. You're not alone in this anymore, Peach. I'm here for you. We've only just started dating, but I'm not going anywhere. A cluttered family room and a little extra work won't run me off. I'm happy to help." He looks at my lips, his eyes caressing them softly before his hand cups my chin, lifting my face until our eyes meet once again. "May I kiss you?" he asks gently, his voice a soft murmur that envelops me in a comforting embrace, sending a thrill through my chest.

I nod, my smile growing with warmth and eager anticipation. "Always."

As he leans in, his lips softly meet mine, and it feels as though an electric current surges through me, awakening every nerve with a newfound vitality. The sensation I feel is entirely new to me; it's an awakening I never experienced in all my years of marriage.

Eli's hand moves to the back of my head, his fingers weaving through my hair as he deepens the kiss. In that moment, I am completely and blissfully lost to all things Eli.

When the need for air becomes too great, he breaks the kiss but doesn't retreat. Instead, his lips trace a delicate line down the curve of my neck, eventually lingering at the tender spot just behind my ear. A shiver courses through me, electric and undeniable, as his lips brush over the shell of my ear.

"I hope you realize," he murmurs, his voice a deep, comforting whisper, "that after a kiss like that, I'm completely hooked."

Pulling back just enough to meet his gaze, I search his eyes for understanding. "I'm scared, and I don't know if that fear will ever completely go away." Eli takes my hand in his as I continue. "I knew Bryant for most of my life, trusted him, and yet he still became someone who hurt me deeply in the end. But I want to open up to you and give us a real chance. I'm trying to take down these walls and let you in, but you need to be easy with me. I never want to experience that kind of pain again, and, most importantly, my kids need to see what a healthy relationship looks like."

If Eli and I hadn't known each other before we started dating, I would've never had my kids around him so quickly.

"Would it help if we, in the future, maybe after a few months of dating, consider going to couples counseling? I want you to feel safe, and I know you already have a therapist. Maybe it'll provide a safe place for you to express your feelings, and we can learn how to move forward together."

I nod, unable to hold back a tear that slips down my cheek. Bryant had been opposed to therapy, dismissing it no matter how much I pleaded. The thought of being with someone who values communication and healing makes it hard not to give my heart to him entirely. He already holds a significant place in it.

Unable to speak through my emotions any further, I place my hands gently on either side of Eli's face and pull him closer for a kiss that I hope allows him to know exactly how I feel.

No matter how much I've fought it, I am falling for this man.

"Hand me that roll of wrapping paper, will you?" I ask Eli. I nod toward one of the many nearly empty rolls of birthday wrapping paper lying just out of reach.

We're sitting cross-legged on the family room floor, surrounded by the twins' gifts—toys, books, and stuffed animals. I carefully fold the paper over the present, smoothing out the edges, while Eli attempts to help. Earlier, he wrapped a box so haphazardly that I had to undo his work and start over, the paper crumpled and tape stuck at odd angles. It drove me crazy looking at it. I couldn't help laughing.

When Heather texted me earlier to say she was taking the kids to dinner and they'd be back in about two hours, Eli and I pulled ourselves away from our cozy spot on the couch where we had been wrapped up in each other and decided it was time to tackle the gift-wrapping. Still, Eli leans in now and then, brushing his lips against mine, a playful grin spreading across his face, before we return to the task at hand. It's almost like we're teens who can't get enough of each other. I chuckle to myself. It's kind of fun.

By the time I finish wrapping four out of five gifts, I end up with five empty wrapping paper rolls. One roll had so little paper left, it was comical. After completing the last gift, I stand up and place the empty rolls on the table in the corner. As I'm heading back, Eli playfully taps me on the rear with an empty tube.

Thor, who's been lounging comfortably in his bed in the corner, perks up with interest.

I burst into laughter. "Get him, boy! Did you see that? Eli just hit me!"

"You gonna sic your dog on me now?" Eli teases with a grin.

"You bet I am." I chuckle as I bend down to grab my own tube from the floor and give him a playful whack on the shoulder.

By now, Thor has joined the game, bouncing around us with excitement.

Eli and I adopt a mock sword-fighting stance, exchanging playful blows. Laughter spills out of me uncontrollably as Eli sneaks up and wraps his arms around me from behind.

"Got you," he whispers lovingly.

"That you do." I twist in his embrace, allowing the tube to slip from my fingers and fall to the floor. My arms snake around his neck as I rise onto the balls of my feet, drawing closer. Our lips meet in a warm, seamless kiss that makes everything else fade away.

A soft cough echoes from somewhere behind us, causing me to pull away from Eli, who grins down at me. I rest my forehead against his chest, working to steady my breathing and calm my burning cheeks.

"What are you two up to in here?" Heather's voice breaks the moment, her tone playful.

"We're having a wrapping tube fight," Eli explains. He steps away from our embrace and crouches down to retrieve the cardboard tubes scattered on the floor. With a swift motion, he tosses them to my kids, who have just come into the room.

Their laughter fills the space as they resume the game we started earlier, waving the tubes around like makeshift swords. I should be joining in, but my mind is elsewhere. The weight of what I need to share with them hangs heavy. Now that they're home, I have to tell them about their father's new visitation schedule. My heart beats a little faster at the thought.

I can only hope they won't resent me for being the messenger.

Chapter Twenty-Three

I park the car outside Bryant's house, unbuckle, and turn back to look at the kids. Today marks the beginning of Bryant's first weekend with the kids.

"Do you all have your phones and chargers with you?" Eli inquires, his voice crackling through the car's speaker. He wanted to be here for this moment but couldn't reschedule his meeting again. It's been six days since he left, and his presence is missed. Our calls are just not the same.

The kids nod, murmuring their agreements.

"How are you feeling?" Eli continues.

"Not good," Sage replies. She stares out the window, her expression a mixture of reluctance and resignation. "I don't want to be here, but Mom says she can get in trouble if she doesn't bring us." Her words hang in the air, tinged with helplessness, tearing at my heart. I wish I could change this for them.

"What about you, Pete?" Eli asks.

Peter crosses his arms defiantly and scowls, looking out the opposite window as if he could will himself away from here. "I wish he never got out of jail. He's not any father of mine. A dad is supposed to treat you with love, not use you as a pawn."

"Just don't let your dislike for your father turn you bitter. We've come too far for that," I say, hoping my words sink in.

As I speak, something catches my eye near the hood of my car. It's Bryant, standing there with his arms crossed over his chest, a deep scowl etched across his face. I raise a finger to signal him to wait.

"We're going to have to cut this call short. Bryant is waiting for the kids."

"What time are you supposed to have them there?" Eli inquires.

I glance at my watch, noting the time. "We still have twenty minutes."

"I wouldn't let him push you if you all need to take a moment to get your bearings. But I can understand wanting to keep things civil."

He's right. The kids should be able to take all the time they need right now.

As I sit here, Milly steps off the porch and joins Bryant at the hood of my car. Instantly, his whole demeanor changes. The tension in his shoulders melts away, and his face softens with a warm, affectionate smile. He actually looks like a doting father who can't wait to spend time with his kids. This is the same version of him he showed the judge.

"Did you see that?" Pete asks.

"See what?" I say, trying to sound casual while hoping he didn't notice what I did.

"When she walked over, he smiled," Pete points out. "He doesn't look mad, like he did a minute ago."

"Yeah, I saw that," Sage says.

"I did too," I say softly.

There's a brief pause in the conversation as we all take it in.

"Maybe he'll be on his best behavior since Milly's here," Sage says.

"I sure hope so," Eli replies.

"Here's what I want you to do," I state. "Go in and get this visit started. Be the kids that I know you to be and try to have some fun. If there's a chance that your father has changed, then now is the time to find out. Every night, check in with me and let me know you're okay. Make sure that you guys write in your journals too. I'm only a phone call away if you need me."

A sharp rap on the window interrupts us. I turn to see Bryant outside, tapping impatiently at his wristwatch, a reminder that time is ticking. He must have moved there while I was focused on the kids.

"We better get going," I state.

"Love you, Eli," Eric says.

"Me too," Sage echoes, smiling warmly.

Peter gives a slight nod, his lips sealed but his eyes conveying agreement.

"I love you too. Make sure you call me when you get back home. I want to hear all about your weekend." Eli waits for their agreement before continuing. "Hey, Peach?"

"Yeah?" I respond.

"Call me when you get back in the car. I'd like to chat a minute."

"Done," I assure him.

Once Eli hangs up, I push open the car door and walk to the back to unbuckle Eric from his booster seat. Before I lift him out, I glance over at Bryant. "Did you manage to get a booster seat?" Noting the slight crease forming between his brows, I continue. "I'll let you use mine for today, but if these visits are going to continue, you'll need to buy one for yourself. Eric can't ride without it."

Milly approaches, her engagement ring glinting in the sunlight as she rests her hand on his shoulder. Her smile is warm and inviting. "No worries. We plan to take the kids shopping while they're here. They've got rooms to decorate and stock. We'll grab a booster seat while we're out."

I turn back to the car, getting Eric out as Sage and Peter come around to join us.

Eric wraps his arms tightly around my neck, reluctant to let go, while Sage and Peter hang back, showing no eagerness to approach their father either.

"Hey, guys," Bryant says with a forced cheerfulness. "How about a hug?"

Sage and Pete exchange uncertain glances, their eyes searching mine for guidance.

I glance over at Bryant, offering him a soft, reassuring smile. "It might be best to start out slow," I suggest. "It's a lot on them, going from a few hours a week to a full weekend."

Bryant's expression hardens. "Maybe if you let me see my own kids more, they wouldn't be so standoffish," he retorts sharply.

I catch Milly's eye, noticing her surprise at his abruptness.

"I didn't come to argue with you, Bryant," I reply softly, trying to defuse the tension. "I'm here because of a court order. If you want to build a relationship with the kids, this is your chance to let go of the past and try to be the father they deserve."

Bryant extends a hand toward Eric, who clings to me with even more determination.

I gently rub his back, coaxing him to meet my gaze. "Hey, bud," I say soothingly. "Remember what I told you? I'll be back to get you in two days. I promise."

"Pinkie promise?" Eric asks.

I nod and extend my pinkie finger, locking it with his.

"Let me have him. It's getting late," Bryant says.

Once again, Eric pulls back, slipping from Bryant's grip.

Milly takes a step forward, her expression gentle. "Can I try?" she asks, her voice soft.

Despite the knot of jealousy tightening in my chest at the idea of another woman stepping into a motherly role for my child, I give a reluctant nod. I much prefer Milly's gentle demeanor over Bryant's stern approach.

She bends a little to Eric's level, her eyes warm and inviting. "Hey there, sweet boy. Do you remember me from the visit before you went on vacation?"

Eric looks at her as if he's trying to place her and shakes his head.

"You told me all about your robot dog. He sounded so cool I wanted one for my house. I still can't find one though." She sticks out her bottom lip and mock pouts, causing Eric to chuckle. "Anyway, I'm your daddy's fiancée. Do you know what that means?"

Eric nods, his expression thoughtful. "That means you two are getting married."

"That's right," she confirms. "It also means that I'm going to be your bonus mom soon. Is that okay with you?"

Eric shifts his gaze to me, seeking answers.

I offer a supportive shrug, knowing this decision is his to make, despite my internal conflict.

"Are you nice like my momma or mean like Dad?" His eyebrows furrow with concern.

Milly glances back at Bryant in confusion, as if trying to piece together the image he might have painted of me. I can only imagine the stories he's spun.

"I'd like to think I'm pretty nice," she says. With a warm smile, her eyes crinkle slightly as she looks over at me. "Do you mind?" she asks, gesturing toward my son.

I shake my head, and she gently reaches out to take Eric into her arms. He clings to me, his small hands gripping my shirt with surprising strength, and she takes a step back.

"How about this," she suggests. "If your momma is okay with it, she can come inside with us and see your room. She can help you get settled before she leaves."

Bryant crosses his arms and grumbles under his breath, "I didn't say anything about Janelle coming into the house."

Milly turns sharply, placing her hand on her hip with a determined look. "No, you didn't," she replies. "But this poor child is scared out of his mind for some reason. If his mom comes in, then maybe he'll see that it's okay to stay. Unless you have a better idea, I'm inviting her inside."

"Can you come in, please?" Sage asks me.

I glance at her and nod, my expression softening. "Okay." I turn back to Milly, flashing a warm smile. "Lead the way."

As soon as I step over the threshold into their home, a small, fluffy dog with a tinkling collar comes running toward us, its tail wagging furiously.

"Jingles, go lie down," Milly commands. "These are your new brothers and sisters. You're going to have to get used to them." She shifts her gaze to me and offers an apologetic smile. "Sorry about that. She's been my baby for so long, so she's not used to kids just yet. But she's a good dog."

"I have a big dog at home," Eric whispers. "Thor's bigger than me but he's my best friend. I wish he could come with me. Then I wouldn't be scared."

As we move through the living area, Bryant veers off toward the kitchen, leaving Milly, the children, and me together.

"I'm sure we can arrange for that," Milly says to Eric.

"That'll never happen," Peter states. "He hates our father. Thor tried to bite him when Dad raised a hand at Mom once."

Milly's brow arches, but I keep my mouth shut. I'm not about to stir up trouble between them before leaving my kids here for the weekend. Yet, judging by her reaction, I suspect there'll be plenty for them to discuss.

As we make our way to the bedrooms, we stop at Pete's room first. It has a queen-sized bed and dresser, the walls painted a dull beige, and no bedding in sight. The room feels bare.

"Your father didn't know how to decorate your rooms," she explains, a hint of apology in her voice. "But I'll be taking you shopping so we can set up the rooms however you like."

"He didn't know because he doesn't even know us," Peter mutters. "It's fine though. All I need is some bedding. I'll just bring what I have from Mom's when I come over."

Milly nods, her lips curving into a tight smile, but I catch a flicker of sadness in her eyes.

I make a mental note to talk to Pete about his tone later. Addressing it now would only deepen his frustration.

We continue to Sage's room, which mirrors Pete's in its bareness, and then to Eric's. At least his room has a toy box and a bookshelf that brings a bit of life into the space.

"I'll leave you guys to settle in," Milly says. "You can find me in the living room when you're done."

I step into the room, setting Eric down on the plush carpet. His eyes dart around, taking in the unfamiliar surroundings. I take his backpack and carry it over to the dresser. As I begin to unpack his clothes and put them away, Pete and Sage shuffle in, their footsteps soft against the floor. With a sigh, Pete flops back onto the bed while Sage and Eric climb on beside him.

Once I've tucked the last pair of socks into the drawer, I turn to face them. "Listen, I don't want you guys giving Milly a hard time, okay? She seems like a nice woman, and I really doubt she knows much about what's happened with your father. Give her a break. I think she's really trying to make things work."

Sage nods, and Eric mimics her gesture. Peter, with his brows furrowed, remains silent, a hint of skepticism in his eyes. I understand his hesitation; trust needs to be earned.

"Come here, you guys," I say. I kneel down and open my arms wide. "I should probably get going before I overstay my welcome. Remember to call or text me every day, okay?"

They rush to me, wrapping their arms around me in a hug.

As I start to leave the room, the kids fall into step beside me, ready to see me off. We make our way to the living area where Milly stands, a welcoming smile on her face.

"Did you all get settled in?" she asks.

"They did," I reply. "I'm going to head out now. Please call me if there are any issues."

Bryant, sitting in a recliner with a whiskey glass in hand, interjects. "You can go now. They're my kids, too, Janelle. I think I know how to handle them." He downs the amber liquid in one swift motion, the clink of the glass against the table echoing softly as he stands and walks away.

I turn back to Milly, hesitant but determined. "I don't want to cause trouble, but just in case they need me, or you do, for anything, call me."

She nods.

I kneel down once more, pulling the kids into another hug and kissing their cheeks softly. "You guys be good for Milly and your father, please. I love you and will be back on Sunday at four p.m. sharp. If you need me, you know how to get hold of me."

Sage and Eric's eyes glisten with tears, their cheeks flushed. Pete turns away, retreating to the room they gave him, his shoulders tense.

I swallow hard, blinking back my own tears. *This isn't how things should be*, I think, as my heart aches.

Chapter Twenty-Four

I sink into the worn cushions of my family room couch, a cold beer clutched in my hand. The TV is playing one of the kids' shows on repeat. I rarely indulge in drinking, but this weekend has been different; I've had a few. The house feels eerily still—almost like it's been frozen in time. The absence of my children's laughter and footsteps bouncing off the walls leaves a void I don't know how to fill.

Thor has been just as restless as I've been, pacing around as if he's looking for the kids, finally settling at the foot of Eric's bed. His soft whines echoed through the house all night, a plea for his buddy to come home. I won't deny it; the first night after dropping the kids off, I found myself lying beside Thor, wrapping my arms around him as we shared a cry.

Though tomorrow promises relief. I get to go to their father's place to bring my kids back home. And it won't be a moment too soon. It's been a long, agonizing weekend without them, every minute dragging on endlessly.

My phone rings, vibrating on the coffee table. I reach for it, my eyes fixed on the TV, and answer without even glancing at the screen to see who's calling. "Hello?"

"Peach? Are you okay?" Eli's voice comes through the speaker, sounding concerned.

My shoulders instantly sag as tears start to flow again. I've shed more tears over the past few days than I have in years.

"Janelle?"

"I'm here." I try to steady my voice as I sniffle.

"Are you crying? Is everything okay?" Eli's concern is palpable.

"I'm fine," I try to assure him, though my voice wavers. "I just miss my kids. The house feels so empty without them here."

"Aw, baby. I'm sorry. They'll be back home and in your arms tomorrow. Do you have anything planned for when they return?"

"No, nothing special. I have work during the day, and then I'll be picking them up afterward. We'll probably stop for dinner on the way home, but it'll be a quick one. They need to get to bed early since they start back to in-person school first thing Monday morning." The decision for the kids to return to classes came after the court case was over and the school felt it was now safe.

"How about we take them out for a movie and dinner?" Eli suggests.

"*We?*" I ask, surprised. "Aren't you in Wyoming?"

"I am, but only for the next hour. I got the job with Damon and I'm flying in tonight so I can sign the paperwork tomorrow. I'll be moving to Oklahoma within a month."

"You will?" I sit up so abruptly that I knock over my half-empty beer, wincing as the liquid spills onto the carpet, knowing I'll have to steam-clean it later.

"I am. Are you okay with that?" Eli asks.

"I'm more than okay with it," I respond, a smile breaking through my tears. "I'm thrilled, and I'm sure the kids will be too. Would you like to come with me to pick them up tomorrow?"

"I'd love to be there, as long as you don't think it'll cause an issue."

I shake my head, forgetting that he can't see me. "It won't. Where will you be staying?"

Thor starts whining impatiently at the door, so I get up and slide it open to let him out.

"I got a room near the airport for a couple of days," he explains. "I'll be in town for five days, and then I'm heading back to finish up here and pack for the move." He pauses. "Do you have a Valentine's date yet?"

I chuckle and lean against the doorframe, feeling the cool breeze on my arms. "You're my only date, sir. Why? Do you have plans?"

"If you can find a sitter, I'd love to take you out on an official date," he says. "But I'd also like to set something up special for the kids so they feel included, if possible."

Thor comes running back up the porch steps and darts into the house, and I close the door behind him with a soft click, then turn the lock.

"We might be a bit stretched for time," I reply. "They have school, and I have to work. Maybe we can have a date night the night before? It'd be easier to find a sitter then, and we could plan something fun at home with the kids the next night. Unless you have another idea in mind."

"No, that sounds good. We'll just have to stop off at the store to pick up some supplies for them while we're out. Do you mind picking me up from Damon's office after work?

If it's out of the way, just let me know and I'll rent a car instead."

I pull my phone away from my ear and open the GPS app, scanning the map to see how far his warehouse is. The screen shows it's only seven miles from the fire station, a quick drive in traffic. "I've got you covered," I say. "I'll text you when I'm leaving work tomorrow."

"Sounds good. I can hardly wait to see you." Eli's voice is warm, carrying a hint of excitement.

"I can hardly believe it's only been eight days and you're already coming back. The kids are going to be over the moon when they see you!" I couldn't stop the smile on my face if I tried.

I hear Eli chuckle softly through the phone. "Are they the only ones who'll be happy to see me?" he teases.

"No. I can hardly wait to see you, myself. I almost hate to admit it, but I've missed you a lot more than I thought I would have."

The clunk of a car door shutting on his end echoes through the line. "Now *that* is something I'd like to unwrap, but it'll have to wait. I have to get in there and catch my flight," he replies.

"Will you message me when you land?"

"It'll be late," he cautions. The hum of announcements are barely audible in the background, letting me know that he's now inside the airport.

"I don't care what time it is. I'd still like to know you made it safely."

"Okay, I'll message as soon as I land in OKC. I really do have to go now. I'll see you tomorrow."

"See you then."

When the line goes dead, I take my now-empty beer can and toss it in the recycle bin, then fish out my carpet cleaner.

With a sigh, I pull out my phone again and scroll through my contacts until I find Heather's number. My fingers fly across the screen as I type out a message, the words spilling out like a confession.

Me: *SOS. I'm in deep with Eli. I just made him promise to message me when his flight lands tonight. You know that's the Okie equivalent of telling someone that you love them.*

I don't expect her to message me back for a few hours since she's at work, but when I notice the three dots appearing and disappearing on the screen, signaling she's typing, I abandon the carpet cleaner and settle onto the stool at the kitchen island while I wait for her reply.

Heather: *Girl, you owe me a bestie night. I'll be there with dinner in hand in a few hours. You had better have all the supplies ready for a spa night. I'm talking full-on pampering. I just lined up a sitter. How dare you hold out on me.*

Me: *I'll run down to the dollar store and grab everything we need. But if I'm spilling my guts, I want chips and lots of queso. I mean the big cup, not that tiny one you brought last time.*

Heather: *Okay, fine. I'll bring the big cup, but you'll be spilling all the details for that price. Gotta go; we just got a call. LUV YA.*

I suppose I should clean this carpet and make a trip to the store. What was supposed to be a quiet night in, crying my eyes out, has become a time for me to sort through my feelings. Truthfully, though, there's nothing to figure out—I'm in love with Eli.

Heather knocks on the door, then walks in without waiting for a response, her arms filled with two large takeout bags. She walks past me standing by the kitchen island and makes a beeline for the family room. "Grab the wine and come on," she calls over her shoulder. "There's no time to waste. I need details."

I chuckle, setting down the dish towel I was holding. "What's the rush?" I reach for the wine that's been resting on the counter and snag two glasses from the cabinet before following her into the family room, where she's already sitting on the couch.

"Seriously?" She gives me a knowing look. "*What's the rush?* Have you forgotten that we're single moms? At any moment, we could be summoned away by a phone call. There's no time to waste. Spill it, sis." She leans forward, anticipation shining in her eyes, as I settle in beside her and pour the wine.

"I'm not sure where to begin."

"I know you both finally decided to make your relationship official, and he supported you in court. Then life got busy and we haven't had much chance to talk. I can see a lot has happened since then, especially since you're now talking about love." She accepts the wineglass I offer her, takes a sip, and smiles. "Why don't you pick up from where we left off last time?"

I take a slow sip of my wine and grin as the image of me being wrapped in Eli's arms, and the thought of his lips on mine, crosses my mind.

"Come on, you *have* to spill what you were just thinking about. You lit up in a way I've never seen before."

I take a moment to open the queso and chips, then glance back at Heather with a smile. "Maybe it's because I've never been treated like this before. Eli has a protective nature, yet he's gentle and loving. And, oh my God, he's so much fun."

Heather places her hand over her heart, as if she's falling too.

I recount what happened after the court session and how he asked for permission before kissing me even though we had kissed prior. I still can't believe he actually asked—who does that these days? Especially since we were already dating.

"Since he's been gone, we've spoken every day. He makes sure to call during the day to chat with the kids. Eli even took a break from work to join us on the phone when I dropped the kids off at Bryant's the other day. You should have heard him talking to them—he told them he loves them! I swear, Heather, they look up to him and hang off every word he says. He's *so* good for them."

"I think he's good for you too. Do you truly think you're in love with him?"

I nod as I swallow the chip I just ate. "I don't just think it anymore; I know I am. Did I mention he's moving out here?"

"No! When did this happen?"

I update her on the conversation Eli and I had earlier and the fact that, soon, he'll be living in Oklahoma for real.

"So he's relocating not for you and the kids, but for a job?"

"Exactly. I think if it was for us, at this point, I'd be worried that things were moving too fast, and I might want to pull back. But I know Eli's not trying to rush me into anything. He's been clear that I'm the one in control of the speed of our relationship, and I believe him, which has helped me let my guard down a bit."

Heather sets her wineglass down on the coffee table and picks up her dinner tray. "I'm glad he's willing to do that for you. Where will he be staying when he moves here? Not with you . . . right?"

"I don't know yet. I might love him, but that doesn't mean he's moving in with us. I need to be sure that this relationship is truly heading in the right direction before I'm willing to go there."

"Oh, sweetheart. There's never going to be a way to know with absolute certainty. All you can do is give your all and pray for the best." She leans over and touches my knee, her eyes filled with reassurance. "You said that he's a momma's boy, right? That he's good to her?"

"Yeah. He's great to her, actually." I smile and remember a story that he told me. "Eli mentioned that after his dad stepped out on them when he was a little younger than Pete, he became the man of the house at a young age. Between Mr. Whitfield and his mom, Eli learned how to be a gentleman early on."

"See? That speaks volumes for him already." Her smile becomes somber, and she hesitates a bit. "Jacob was a momma's boy. That wonderful man set the bar so high that I don't think I'll ever find another like him. If Eli's anything like my Jacob was, that's something special." Heather wipes at her fallen tears, then smiles. "Sorry. I just miss him something fierce sometimes."

I feel for Heather. Her love for Jacob was so intense, and when he passed away, he left her with a broken heart and a promise to fulfill—to one day find love again. I can't fathom experiencing such a profound love and then attempting to date someone new. Even though I've only been with Eli for a short while, I can't picture myself moving on after him. No one could ever compare to the impact he's made on my life already.

Chapter Twenty-Five

It's later than usual when I finally get around to taking inventory and restocking the rig. Our schedule was thrown off thanks to the horrible twelve-car pileup at the junction where I-35 intersects with 240. Twisted metal and shattered glass were scattered everywhere. I'm surprised that only one person was transported from the scene in critical condition.

"Hey, Cameron!" Garrett shouts from across the bay. "Val just came in saying there's a guy outside waiting for you."

"Thanks, I'll check it out."

I'm not expecting anyone, so I close the hatch and rush out the bay door, heading towards the front to make sure I don't miss whoever it is. As I turn the corner, I see him—Eli. He's facing away from me, but I can still tell he looks great. He always does. I want to run into his arms, but I know I'm a mess right now.

"What are you doing here?" I ask when I'm only a few feet away. "I thought I was supposed to pick you up." I look at my watch to make sure I'm not that late. Nope, it's only now three.

Eli turns around and gives me a big smile. His eyes scan me from head to toe, and his grin widens further. "You were, but we finished early. Damon gave me a lift. Hope you don't mind me dropping by like this."

Lieutenant Hugh passes by and gives me a smile. "Cameron."

"Lieutenant." I nod my head and want to grumble.

"Why don't you invite your boyfriend inside? He can wait in the mess hall while you wrap things up." The suggestion comes with a nod toward the open door leading us back inside.

"Will do." I turn to Eli, arching an eyebrow. "I hope you know that you've just opened a can of worms. These guys are going to tease me relentlessly for weeks about my *boyfriend* dropping by unannounced." I take his hand in mine, linking our fingers together as I lead him inside and down the hall toward the mess hall. A mischievous thought bubbles up, and I let out a chuckle. "I might have to return the favor once you're settled in at work. I bet Megan would love to help me plan something special for you and Damon." The fact that I know the wife of the owner of his new workplace is a bonus.

Eli throws his head back with laughter, the sound echoing through the hallway. "As long as I'm allowed to stake my claim and show those guys that you're mine, you can stop by all you want."

I stumble a bit, surprised by his confident reaction.

We make it to the mess hall—well really, it's more of an all-in-one room. Along the back wall is a fully stocked, open kitchen that overlooks a long dining table, a few couches, a big TV, and a pool table. Each of us takes a turn at cooking, and more often than not, we sit around the table and share that meal together.

Garrett's voice cuts through the moment. "Cameron!" she hollers from the hallway, where she's standing with one hand on her hip, a playful smile tugging at her lips.

I glance back at Eli. "I'll be back in a bit. Just hang out here. There are some cold drinks in the fridge if you want one." Leaning in, I press a soft kiss to his cheek. "Duty calls." With a quick turn, I jog toward Garrett, her eyes glinting with curiosity.

"Is that the new guy?" she asks, tilting her head toward Eli. She drapes an arm around my shoulder, guiding me toward our rig. "He's cute."

"He's more than cute, and yes," I reply, a smile spreading across my face. "He and I are officially a couple." I glance at her, a sense of urgency creeping in. "Can we try and wrap this up quickly? I need to rush and pick up the kids."

"Oh, that's right," she says, tapping her forehead as if to jog her memory. "I forgot it's their first weekend with your ex. Let's get this done so you can get out of here. We'll catch up tomorrow."

One good thing about working here is that we may tease each other relentlessly, but we always have each other's back. We're like family—ready to do anything necessary to make sure we're all okay.

Garrett and I efficiently run through our checklist, inspecting the equipment and moving in a synchronized dance of familiarity. Just as we're finishing up, a call blares over the loudspeaker. Val and Johnston take their places and wave as they back out of the garage.

I run up the stairs two at a time, eager to shower off the day's grime. The water is scorching but refreshing. I towel off quickly, ready to head out and collect my kids. Even though it means skipping my usual workout, the thought of spending time with them and Eli makes it an easy decision.

I'm more than happy to call it a day.

By the time I make my way back to Eli, I find him at the corner table, focused on a game of cards with the lieutenant. Hugh's eyes find mine as I approach.

I offer a quick nod. "Sorry to rush," I say, as I glance at the clock on the wall, "but if we're going to make it to Bryant's by four, we have to run."

Eli pushes back his chair with a scrape and stands, tossing his cards down onto the table. He shakes the lieutenant's hand and thanks him for the game.

"Anytime. It was nice to meet you." Then Lieutenant Hugh's eyes turn to me. "You're going to your ex's?"

"Yeah, I thought you would've already heard the news. This was his first weekend visit with the kids."

Lieutenant Hugh mutters a few choice words under his breath, his face a mix of empathy and frustration, then shakes his head. "Go on. Tell the kids hello for me. If you want to bring them by later, I'll pull out the truck so they can honk the horn again."

"Will do. Thanks again," I say, grateful for his kindness. I reach for Eli's hand, intertwining our fingers as we head toward the exit.

I toss my bag in the back seat of my car, then slide into the car. Leaning over the console, I give Eli a quick kiss, then buckle up.

"I gather your coworkers aren't fond of your ex either," Eli says.

"No, they're not fans. Lieutenant Hugh was covering a shift at another station the night Bryant landed me in the hospital, of all nights, and ended up being the one who responded to our call for help."

I shift the car into reverse and carefully back out of the parking space. Once we're headed down the road toward Bryant's, I reach over and intertwine my fingers with Eli's. If picking the kids up is anything like dropping them off, I'm going to need his support.

"Oh, wow. Is that how you got your job here?"

"Yes and no." I release his hand momentarily, focusing on the road as I make a left turn. "My family comes from a long line of police officers. While I admire their dedication, I always knew that path wasn't meant for me. I wanted to help people on a deeper level. When I was in the hospital, Hugh visited me nearly every day. During one of our conversations, he suggested that once I felt ready, I should think about becoming an EMT. That sparked something in me. However, I decided to push further and became a rescue paramedic. Working as an EMT was fulfilling, but the salary just didn't stretch far enough to provide for three kids and a dog without relying on government assistance. And before you ask, no, Bryant hasn't ever paid child support, even though he was ordered to. Hugh was the support system I never realized I needed. I hold a deep respect for him."

"I knew I liked him the minute I saw him," Eli replies.

I chuckle softly, feeling the warmth of his hand in mine before I release it again, this time with a gentle squeeze. "This is it." I nod towards the house with the red door as I slow down in front of it. "As long as Milly is around, all should be okay. Try not to let Bryant get to you." I pull the car into the driveway, then turn to face Eli, offering a reassuring smile. "You ready?"

"Whenever you are." He leans in, and I catch the faint scent of his cologne as his lips brush mine in a quick, affectionate peck before he pulls back.

"Let's go get the kids."

Together, we step out of the car and make our way to the front door.

Before I can even knock, the door swings open, and Peter barrels into me, nearly knocking me over, his arms latching tightly around my waist. His eyes are wide as he tilts his head up. "Can we go now, please?" he pleads.

I wasn't expecting that kind of reaction from Pete, but I suppose he missed me. I chuckle. "I've missed you, too, Pete. Of course we can. But you need to go grab your bag and your siblings first. And don't forget to tell Milly that you're leaving, alright?"

With a quick nod, Peter spins around and spots Eli standing nearby. Launching himself into Eli's welcoming embrace, Peter laughs as Eli lifts him off the ground for a moment. Once his feet touch back down, Peter dashes inside, his footsteps echoing through the house. The way he's reacting to Eli and I being here reminds me of how he was before all the issues with his father started.

Bryant walks around the corner at the back of the living area, and when he spots me standing at the front door, he moves toward me with a determined look in his eyes. My muscles tighten and my heart races until Eli steps up beside me, draping a comforting arm over my shoulder. Bryant halts a few feet away, his face shifting into the familiar mask of a doting father, a smile spreading across his lips that never quite reaches his eyes.

He extends his hand to Eli, gripping his hand in a handshake. "You must be the Eli guy that my kids have told me all about," he snarls. Seeing how Bryant pretty much turned his back on us at court, I wouldn't imagine he knew Eli's name until this weekend. "You certainly seem to have made quite the impression on them." Bryant's confident smile falters for a moment, revealing a flicker of scrutiny in his eyes. He scans Eli from head to toe, as if assessing every detail. It's evident that Bryant is weighing Eli, trying to decide how serious this is.

"I'm glad, because they've certainly left a mark on my heart too," Eli says. "They're really good kids." Eli stands his ground, meeting Bryant's scrutinizing gaze without wavering. His posture is relaxed yet confident, as if he's silently asserting his commitment to me and the children.

"Momma!" Eric's voice echoes through the house as he yells, his footsteps pounding against the floors. Just like Pete did earlier, he comes charging toward me, his arms wide open and eyes gleaming with excitement. When he crashes into me, I scoop him up with a swift motion, wrapping him in my arms. Unlike with Pete, I shower Eric with exaggerated kisses all over his cheeks, making a smacking sound with each one. "Eww," he giggles, squirming in my hold as he scrunches up his face.

I chuckle, my heart swelling with affection. "I've just missed my baby boy so much." I nuzzle his cheek with my nose as he wriggles in my arms.

"Good Lord, Janelle. Let the boy breathe. He's not a baby anymore," Bryant growls.

Eli takes a step closer to Bryant, his eyes flickering with determination.

I turn to stop Eli by gently placing Eric into his arms. "Hold him for a minute, will ya?"

I move past Bryant and enter the house when I notice Milly and Sage at the entrance to the hallway, each struggling to juggle the bags they're carrying. I step up and grab Eric's bag from Sage and shoulder it, then take the bag out of Milly's hand, leaving one for Sage to carry.

"Thank you. It didn't look that bulky when you carried it in," Milly states.

I shrug. "I'm used to it. I'm a paramedic. If I can't lift my own body weight and then some, I wouldn't be able to do my job very well."

She nods appreciatively, brushing a stray hair from her face. "Still, thank you. I thought their father was going to come and help with the bags, but when he never came back, we figured we'd just get them ourselves."

I nod in understanding, glancing towards the hallway. "Is Pete ready?"

"He's nearly finished," Milly replies, checking her watch. "I'll send him out in a minute."

"Thank you. If you can get me Eric's booster, I'll get them loaded up."

She walks me to the door but stops to lean into Bryant. "Will you go out to my car and get Eric's booster seat for them, please?"

Bryant nods, taking the keys, and heads toward the car.

I walk out to the rear of my vehicle, loading the bags into the trunk. I pop open the back door for the kids, and Sage climbs in without so much as a backward glance or a goodbye. Bryant approaches with the booster seat, and I take it from him, fitting it securely into place.

Just as I'm about to lift Eric into the car, I catch sight of Pete making his way out of the house. "Would you mind strapping Eric in?" I ask Eli before I move to help Pete.

As I approach, I see Bryant reach out to grip Peter's arm. "Next time you come over, you best have learned some respect."

Peter's eyes flash with defiance. "Respect is earned, and you haven't earned mine," he retorts.

I step in swiftly, my hand softly on Peter's opposite arm, letting him know I've got him. "You need to remove your hand from my son's arm," I say, my tone steady and unwavering. "If you have an issue, we can talk it out, but there will be no touching. Especially where threats are given." My gaze shifts to Peter, who stands rigid, his jaw set. "Go and get in the car. I'll be there in a minute."

He nods and heads toward the car with his siblings.

"Who do you think you are to undermine me like that?" Bryant's voice is sharp and threatening. It sends a shiver down my spine, but I won't back down. Not this time.

"I'm his mother," I reply. "If you want the kids to respect you, then you'll have to put in the work. You can't expect them to fall at your feet after everything you've done. Their memories of you are clouded by the pain you've caused."

Bryant takes a step closer, so close that I have to tilt my head back to meet his eyes. But no matter how close he gets, I refuse to let fear show on my face. His voice drops to a low rumble. "You get that boy to respect me in my home or—"

"Or what?" Eli interjects. His presence is a welcome barrier, causing Bryant to retreat a couple steps. Eli now stands a step ahead of me, in a protective stance. Yet when his hand finds mine, there is a quiet invitation for me to step up beside him if I choose to do so. "What are you planning to do to them? I'd like to hear this." Eli's voice is calm, but there's an edge to it, a challenge that hangs in the air between us all.

"Who exactly do you think you are?" Bryant's voice is sharp, his eyes narrowing as he glares at Eli. "These are *my* kids, and Janelle is *my* ex-wife. You have no business sticking your nose into our affairs."

Eli stands his ground. "In just a few days, she'll be *my* wife, and those kids will be my stepchildren," he replies. "I think that gives me the right to be involved, especially when it sounds like you're threatening my family."

My mind struggles to process Eli's words. My wife? How did we jump from casually dating and taking things slow to planning a wedding in a matter of days? No, not even planning, but getting married.

I squeeze Eli's hand to gain his attention—this has already gotten out of hand—but he continues. "It'll be a cold day in hell before I ever let you hurt them again."

Oh Lord, help me resist the urge to strangle the man I love.

Chapter Twenty-Six

Eli stays downstairs with the two older kids and Thor while I head upstairs, kneeling by the bathtub to give Eric a bath. The ride home was suffocatingly quiet, minus the few words exchanged between me and the kids. When we pulled into the driveway, Eli offered to grab the bags. I nodded, grateful for the chance to escape, using the excuse of getting Eric cleaned up and ready for bed, even though it's not all that late yet. I needed a moment alone to sort through the thoughts crashing through my mind.

I love Eli, that big ole dolt, but was he serious about us getting married? Surely not. Either way, I can't believe he let Bryant get to him like that!

I know the moment we pulled out of his driveway, he was already dialing his lawyer, concocting a way to paint himself in a better light at the next court hearing. How can I back out now? It would make us appear dishonest if we don't follow through. Why couldn't Eli have simply said that we were engaged?

Or better yet . . . kept his mouth shut.

"Momma, are you mad?" Eric's voice cuts through my thoughts.

"Hmm?" I ask. "What was that, bud?"

"Are you mad? You only make us go to bed early when we're being bad."

I lean down, pressing a kiss against his damp hair. The scent of his bubble bath lingers in the air. "No, bud, Momma's not mad. I just needed a minute to think. I'm sorry if I made you think I was upset. After your bath, you can go downstairs and play. But no getting dirty, okay? You have school tomorrow."

"But I want to stay home and play with Eli," he whines.

"I know you do, bud, but you have school. You can't miss your first day back," I reply, trying to sound cheerful. "Besides, Eli is here for a few more days. I'm sure you'll be seeing him a lot."

Even though I assure Eric, inside, a knot tightens in my stomach as I think about the conversation Eli and I need to have. We have to figure out how to tell the kids about the changes ahead. I don't see any other way around this situation. I could call everything off, but that would mean ending my relationship with Eli, too, wouldn't it? Just because I'm not ready to be married yet doesn't mean I can't ever imagine it happening. I've only just accepted the fact that I love the man. I thought I'd have more time to process the thought of getting married again.

I mean, *seriously*, he didn't even ask me!

In a million years, I never would have imagined Eli would surprise me with something as monumental as an engagement like this. In my mind, I pictured him down on one knee, his hand outstretched with a ring, in some kind of a grand, heartfelt gesture that would bring tears to my eyes. Not springing it on me—in front of my ex, no less. I feel cheated out of what should've been a magical day for the two of us.

I shake my head, battling the sting of unshed tears that blur my vision. "I'll be right back, bud." I feel the heat rising to the tips of my ears as I stand and make my way to the hallway. The moment I'm out of sight, I lean my back against the wall, close my eyes and inhale deeply, trying to steady the whirlwind of emotions threatening to spill over. I refuse to let my kids witness me unravel this way.

I have to wonder, though, is it Eli's sudden proposal that has made me so upset, or the fact that I feel cheated out of what should've been a special moment between us?

What is wrong with me?

Why can't I get past this?

"Mom!" Sage hollers. "Dinner's ready."

"We'll be down in a minute."

I dry my face and step back into the bathroom, where Eric stands, ready to get out of the tub, shivering slightly, water droplets sliding down his skin. I reach for his towel hanging on the hook by the door. After ruffling his hair to ensure all the soap is rinsed out, I lift him out of the tub, wrap him in the towel, and begin patting him down. His giggles punctuate the air as I tickle his sides, making sure he's thoroughly dry. Once satisfied, I help him wiggle into his soft doggy jammies. Anything that reminds him of Thor, this boy will throw a fit for.

"Alright, bud, it's time to get down to the table. Sage said dinner's ready." I scoop up his dirty clothes and the damp towel from the bathroom floor and toss them into the hamper before leading him down the stairs.

As I walk through the living room, the sight before me brings a smile to my face. In the dining room, Eli has gathered the kids, who are now seated around the table, each with a plate in front of them. Even though I'm still irked with him, I can't help but feel as if a piece of me that's been missing for so long has been put back in place.

Eli makes this family whole again.

Noticing my approach, he flashes me a soft smile as he steps over to my chair and pulls it out for me. "I hope you don't mind—I borrowed your car and went over to Wagon Springs to pick up some burgers."

I lower myself into the seat, returning his smile. "Not at all. Thank you for dinner."

Eli makes his way to the kitchen, grabs both of us a plate, and brings them back, setting mine down in front of me, then joins us at the table. As he settles in, he leads us in saying grace, a ritual I've noticed he does before every meal. Once finished, we dig in and listen as the kids tell us all about their visit with Bryant.

It seems like Milly was a hit with everyone. She took the kids out on a shopping trip and treated them to a lunch at an Italian restaurant they'd never been to before. All while Bryant stayed behind in his home office, saying that he had to work. One of the few times they had to face Bryant alone was when Milly left to pick up dinner and run to the store. Pete said that with Milly gone, Bryant's mood changed. He became a bear to deal with, so they stayed in their rooms.

I don't understand why he's fighting for them if he wants nothing to do with them. Unless it's to punish me.

Moments later, the chatter around the table dwindles into silence. I glance up and catch Eli's gaze. His eyes are filled with a mix of concern and apology that tugs painfully at my chest. The moment he blurted those words out in front of Bryant, it was clear that my ex knew exactly how to push his buttons. Yet here, at home, Eli shows us nothing but love and kindness. Still, he has to learn to keep his calm around Bryant or we'll all be caught in a storm we can't escape.

I offer Eli a soft, reassuring smile. No matter what comes our way, I'm not giving him up. Even if I want to wring his neck.

As soon as my feet hit the bottom step, I go in search of Eli. I make my way to the kitchen, seeing that he's already tidied up for the night. Thankfully, that's one less task for me to do before I can finally rest.

With the kids in bed now, the house is quiet. It's the perfect time to talk.

I open the fridge and grab a bottle of water just as the garage door swings open. I turn in time to see Eli standing there with a soft smile. Despite my urge to fall into his arms and lose myself in his kisses, I know we need to have a conversation. It can't wait any longer.

"Can we talk?" Eli asks.

I nod and gesture towards the family room. He follows and sits beside me on the couch.

Facing me, he takes my hand. "I know I messed up. I'm incredibly sorry for making a decision that should have been ours together. If you want to break up with me,

I'd understand, but . . ." He glances at our intertwined hands, shaking his head. "There's nothing you can say that I haven't already thought about myself. I hurt you, despite promising never to do that. You can't imagine how disappointed I am in myself right now."

I can't stand seeing my kindhearted man in such pain. Yet again, Eli's behavior is completely different from how Bryant would've responded in this situation. Bryant never hesitated to make decisions for both of us, and I can't recall a single time he ever apologized.

I gently pull one of my hands from Eli's grip and place it on his cheek. When his eyes finally meet mine, I give him a brief kiss. "What you did was careless and done without thought, and it hurt me. But not for the reasons you might think." I reclaim his hand in mine. "You know how much I've struggled with our relationship. It's not just about *us*, but the idea of being in a long-term commitment with *anyone* has terrified me for a long time now." I pause to gather my thoughts. "I was with Bryant for most of my life. I believed I knew him and trusted him. Everyone always said what a good man he was and how fortunate I was to be with him. Even when I considered leaving, those constant reminders echoed in my mind, making me feel like I was the one at fault. So, I stayed."

Eli squeezes my hand gently, offering support.

"Being with you meant I was finally letting someone in. You're my fresh start, my chance at something real. I started to dream again. It's not that I can't imagine marrying you someday—it's just that I'm scared of what comes with it. I thought I had time to work up to it. You promised me that. And then . . ." A tear escapes, and Eli wipes it away. "And then you made a decision for the both of us without a care in the world. You didn't even give me a choice. No proper proposal, no loving words, no 'I love you's' exchanged. It was used to put my ex in his place." I try to steady my breathing as I pour my heart out. "I was just beginning to get used to the idea of loving you, and you shattered my heart by taking away my chance at a beautiful love story. I won't even have a tale to share when the kids ask how you proposed. Every woman —even us tomboys—wants a genuine proposal, Eli."

Eli flinches as if my words have struck him. "I can't change what I've done, but I can promise that if you can accept my apology, I'll never take away your choices again. As soon as I said those words, I regretted them." Eli appears remorseful as he wipes away the tears that have been streaming down my cheeks since I opened up to him. "I hate that I made you cry. It hurts to know I did this to you. Can you forgive me for being so foolish?"

"I'm working on it."

"Do you still want to be with me?"

"God help me. I do."

Eli smiles and kneels before me. "I know I handled everything wrong, and I'm incredibly sorry for that. I promise that if you don't want to go through with this, we won't. I'll admit that I was running my mouth." Eli lifts my hand to his mouth and kisses it when I don't respond. "Let me at least try to make up for my mistakes." Eli takes the necklace from around his neck and removes his grandma's ring, holding it between his fingers. My heart races. "I know this is all new, and there's no way you'd say yes so quickly under normal circumstances. I promise that I'll keep dating you until you will, and one day, I'll give you that grand gesture you want and deserve. But for now, I hope this can help make up for the pain I caused. Janelle, I love you. I've loved you since you fell asleep on my couch, if not before. I always knew you'd be the woman I'd kneel for. This ring is the same one my grandad proposed to my grandma with. I admired their marriage my whole life." He smiles softly. "I only planned on doing this and the wedding once, but seeing as how I messed up so badly, I'll do it again and again until I get it right, as long as it's with you." Eli takes my left hand in his and readies the ring to slide onto my finger. "Janelle Cameron, will you do me the honor of becoming my wife?"

Tears are flowing freely once more—this time, for a whole new reason. I had hoped he'd hear me out, but I never thought he'd actually propose to me. At least not yet. And with his grandma's ring?

"I will." He slides the ring onto my finger, and I pull him in for a kiss. "I love you, Eli. Everything is happening so fast, but I genuinely love you and want to make this work."

After the proposal, especially knowing how much I wanted one, I want nothing more than to leap into his arms and kiss him . . . but I stop myself.

This is still a marriage in name only, I remind myself. He said he'll still be dating me.

If things don't work out, it won't just be me losing a spouse; the kids would lose another father figure too. Oh Lord, I hope I'm not making a mistake.

Chapter Twenty-Seven

When I hear the door to my room creak open, I prop myself up on my elbows to see what's going on. Standing in my doorway is Eric, his hair a tousled mess and his doggy pajamas slightly askew.

"Momma, it's school today," he says.

The room is still dark, with only the faint glow of light from the hallway shining in. Last night, after the heart-to-heart with Eli, we stayed up way too late, making up and figuring out how to navigate these next steps. Our number-one priority is making sure the kids and our families remain unaffected by our half-truth. Eli and I truly do love each other, even if we're not entirely ready for such an important step. Yet. Essentially, we've only hit fast-forward on our timeline. Eventually, we hope to get there, and when we do—*if* we do—no harm done.

I roll over and squint my eyes at the screen of my phone to check the time.

2:15 a.m.

There are still thirty minutes until my alarm goes off, and I'm not ready to get out of bed just yet. "It's way too early to be up, bud. How about you come and keep Momma company until my alarm goes off?" I pat the empty space beside me on the bed. Once he falls asleep, he'll be out of it until my mom wakes him up later. I'll just let her know he's in my bed instead of his.

"But it's schooltime. You said I get to go to class today," Eric insists.

I sit up fully and pat the bed again, offering him a warm smile. "I did, and you will when it's time. There are still hours until you have to even get up and get ready. Plus, Eli has my car right now, so we have to wait for him anyway. Come keep Momma warm. It's too cold to get out of bed yet." I try to coax him in, feeling the chill of the early-morning air even through the thick comforter.

Eric runs over, his feet thumping across floor, and leaps onto the bed with a bounce. I wince, wishing I had reminded him to be gentle. "Will Eli take me to school today?" he asks.

"I'm sure if you ask him nicely, he will." I wrap an arm around him to pull him closer for a morning cuddle. Just as I settle him against me, my arm grazes his pajamas, and the unmistakable dampness makes me inwardly cringe. "Bud, did you have a potty accident?" I ask gently.

Eric nods.

"Why didn't you say something? I don't want you staying in these dirty jammies. Let's get you cleaned up, and then we'll change your bedding."

Eric hasn't had an accident in over a year. I wonder what caused this one.

I guide him to the bathroom and help him into a warm bath. The sound of water rushing into the tub fills the room as I toss his damp pajamas into the laundry basket. After shutting off the water, I head across the hall to remove the bedding from his bed next.

Just as I start stripping the mattress, Eric shouts from the bathroom, "Momma! Come back in here!" His voice is laced with panic, sending my heart racing.

I rush into the bathroom and scan the room, half expecting to find some kind of spider or scorpion or something in the tub. But there's nothing.

"What's wrong, son?" I try to keep my voice steady, trying to calm both him and myself.

"I don't want the potty monster to get me. Can you stay with me?" His eyes are wide with fear.

I frown, trying to comprehend. "Of course I'll stay, but there's no such thing as a potty monster, bud. Who told you that?" I crouch down to his level, noticing his lower lip quivering slightly. I gently brush a damp curl from his forehead and give him a quick kiss.

"Dad said that when big boys wet their beds, the potty monster will come for them," he sobs. "I didn't mean to wet my new bed. I was just too scared to get up without Thor. Can I take him next time, so I'm not scared anymore?"

Every part of me wants to drive over to Bryant's house and give him a piece of my mind for being so thoughtless. Who says something like that to a five-year-old? I suppose it's a good thing Eli has my car right now.

This is not acceptable!

"You were in a new place; it's understandable that it would happen. But about Thor, I'm sorry, he can't go. He doesn't like your father, remember? Maybe you can ask Milly if Jingles can sleep with you when you visit." I raise both brows a couple times, causing him to chuckle. "No matter what she says, I want you to remember that there is no such thing as a potty monster. Your father is wrong about that. Nothing will come after you for being scared and having a small accident."

"Peter said there wasn't one, too, but Dad told me that Pete was just being nice and didn't want to scare me." His lower lip trembles as he looks at me. "I didn't mean to make Dad and Pete argue again, Momma." Eric picks up his rubber duck and puts it in the toy net. "I wish Dad wouldn't always yell at us."

That's it.

I'm determined to get full custody of the children and ensure that Bryant loses his rights. There's no way he should be allowed to see the kids if all he's going to do is upset them like this.

"I know, bud. I'll see what I can do to make it stop, okay?" I clap my hands and reach behind me for a towel. "Let's get you out of this tub before you end up with more wrinkles than Grandpa."

After switching out the bedding for both Eric and myself, and getting him tucked back in bed with Thor at his feet, I head downstairs to start the laundry. Seeing that it's so close to time for my alarm to go off anyway, I might as well stay up.

When I hear a knock at the front door, I glance at the microwave clock. 2:45. I still have about forty minutes before I need to leave, so I doubt it's Eli. Then again, he does have my car, so it very well could be him. Sure enough, upon opening the door, I see him standing there, coffee in hand, offering one to me.

I raise my hands, halting him. "Let me wash my hands first."

Eli steps inside, closing the door behind him, and follows me to the kitchen. I give him a quick rundown of my morning and what Eric said before I put him back to bed.

"Bryant doesn't deserve them," he responds.

"He definitely doesn't." Passing by Eli, I lean in to give him a brief kiss. "I need to run upstairs and get changed real quick. Mom's going to be here at any moment. Make yourself comfortable. I'll be back down soon."

In just fifteen minutes, I'm dressed and ready to head out the door for work. I quietly step out of my room, padding softly down the hallway, and peek my head into each of my kids' bedrooms. Satisfied that they're all still sleeping, I make my way downstairs. As I reach the bottom step, I spot Mom shrugging off her coat. "Good morning," I say.

"Morning, Janie," she replies. Her eyes drift toward the kitchen, where Eli sits at the island, coffee in hand. She raises a brow at me, her expression questioning, as if asking for an explanation.

"Do you have a moment to talk?" I ask, glancing at the clock. I have about twenty minutes before I absolutely have to leave for work. It's not enough time to discuss everything, but it's all I've got.

"Yeah, of course. What's up?" Mom responds.

We wander into the kitchen, and after pouring two cups of coffee—my first long gone by now—we join Eli at the counter. As we sip our coffee, I fill Mom in on the morning I had with Eric.

"Bryant is a real piece of work," she says, shaking her head. "He doesn't deserve to be called a father."

"Agreed," Eli affirms.

I walk over and settle onto a stool next to Eli at the bar. Taking a deep breath, I let the cat out of the bag, so to speak. "In other big news . . . this might come as a shock to you, but before you freak out, know that I've thought it through and am happy." I take Eli's hand in mine for support. "Tomorrow, Eli and I will be getting married. We would like to keep it small, just us and the kids. Of course, we'll have our two witnesses—which we'll figure out later, but for now, this is what we want."

"Haven't the two of you only just started dating? What's the rush? You're not . . ." Mom's gaze drops to my stomach, her eyes widening with concern.

"Oh God, no, Mom!" I nearly spill my coffee in my urgency to reassure her. "I'm not pregnant."

"Then why the rush?" Her brow furrows as she searches my face for answers.

"That would be on me," Eli declares. He gently takes my hand, his fingers warm and reassuring, and brings it to his lips, pressing a tender kiss onto my skin. "I'm in love with your daughter. I know that I want to spend the rest of my life with her." He pauses, glancing at me with a soft smile before turning back to my mom. "Sure, we've only just started dating, but we've been talking for a while now. Sometimes when you love someone, it doesn't matter how long you've been together—you just know. If Janelle were to tell me right now that she needed time, it might hurt, but I'd wait however long she needed. But I really would love to start my life with her and the kids. They're my family, and I can't wait to make it official."

Mom raises an eyebrow, clearly still puzzled. "But I thought you were so dead set against marriage, Janie. It wasn't that long ago that you told me you could never see yourself doing it again. What changed?" she asks.

"I did. I started letting my walls down and let Eli in. I realized that I could trust him. I know that this is rushed, but this is what I want. Can you please support that?"

Mom narrows her eyes at Eli, her voice firm. "You better not mess this up." Her finger taps the edge of her coffee cup. "After what she faced with her ex, if you don't treat her right, I won't stop my husband and boys from dragging you out back."

"Mom!" I fuss, my cheeks flushing with embarrassment. "That was way out of line."

Eli places his hand on my leg, offering a gentle squeeze of reassurance. "I disagree." He meets my mom's gaze. "You have every right to feel that way. I know you don't know me as well as your kids do. If I were in your position, I might not be so nice."

Mom's stern expression softens, a hint of admiration in her eyes.

I take a deep breath before explaining the need to keep it small. "With everything that's happening with Bryant right now, we want to keep this low key. We're planning a bigger wedding in the future once things settle down. No rush, but in time, we'll get there." We're sticking as close to the truth as we can.

Mom nods, taking a thoughtful sip of her coffee. "I guess that makes sense," she concedes. "So, who all knows about this quickie wedding?"

I glance at Eli, seeking confirmation. "As far as I know, just you," I reply. "We plan on telling the kids and his mom and grandma over dinner tonight."

"What about your father and siblings?" she presses.

"We'll tell Dad tonight," I assure her, "but the others will have to wait until after we say 'I do' tomorrow. You know how they are—they'd find a way to crash the courthouse, no matter what I say." My phone's alarm jolts me, signaling that it's time to head out. That's when it hits me. "I nearly forgot. Eric mentioned wanting you to take him to school this morning," I tell Eli.

He chuckles, a warm smile spreading across his face. "I'd love to, but since you're dropping me back off at the hotel, I won't have any way to get back here afterward. I don't have my car here yet."

"How about this? You drive me to work first, then come back here and take the kids to school. You can even swing by the donut shop on the way back. It'd be a nice way to make their first day back a little more special."

"Sounds good to me," he replies.

I rise from my chair and walk around the island, placing my mug in the sink before leaning in to plant a kiss on my mom's cheek. "Love you, Mom. We might be a bit late getting home tonight because we need to pick up our marriage license before the courthouse closes. Would you mind staying with the kids a little longer than normal today?"

She smiles, the corners of her eyes crinkling. "Not as long as you're prepared to break the news to your dad when you get back."

I nod, glancing at Eli, who's leaning against the counter, his eyes meeting mine. "We will," I assure her.

"Then the two of you better get out of here," Mom says. "I'd hate for you to be late to work. And Eli?" she adds with a playful grin. "I wouldn't mind having an apple fritter the size of my head."

"You got it," Eli replies.

"You better get yourself something too. Unless you have something pressing to get to, I'd like to get to know my son-in-law."

I can only hope that everyone else reacts to the news as well as Mom did.

Chapter Twenty-Eight

By the end of day, I have a few things worked out for tomorrow. Val is willing to swap days off with me, so I now have tomorrow and Valentine's Day free, and I'll be working Saturday and Sunday instead. As much as I hate giving up my weekend off with the kids, this will work best with everything that's going on right now.

The one thing that I'm dreading is that next weekend, when I'm off, Eli will be back in Charleston, packing up for his move, and the kids will be with Bryant. The thought of spending the weekend without them again is depressing. Heather told me that her sister is planning a visit around that time, and if the dates align, she'd be happy to come and hang out for a while. I considered messaging the girls about a get-together, but I'm sure I'd just bring everyone down. I don't understand why I'm so sad when they go for their visits. Usually, when the kids spend the weekend with my family or Heather, I manage just fine. But it feels different when I send them to Bryant's. It's got to be because I know they're with him. It's the only explanation that makes sense.

As I'm lost in thought, Val walks into the locker room and smiles. "Hey, Cameron, your fiancé's here." She sits down next to me on the bench as I put on my shoes. "When were you going to tell me? I didn't know you guys were that serious already."

"Yeah, it happened fast, but you can't control it when you fall in love."

I hate deceiving everyone. I'm not lying about my feelings for the man, but I wish I didn't have to fib the details either.

With my shoes laced and my duffel bag slung over my shoulder, I wave to Val, who gives me a nod in return. Then I set off to find Eli.

The alarm echoes through the station, signaling a call for those on duty.

Lieutenant Hugh passes by and gives me a slap on the back. "Congratulations on the wedding," he says. "I want to hear all about it next time I see you." He smiles brightly and then continues down the corridor.

As everyone begins to leave, I find Eli waiting by the mess hall door.

"Are you all set?" he asks.

"Whenever you are."

As we head out to get our marriage license, I can't help but hope that I'm not making a big mistake. Again.

I peek through the blinds in the living room, my foot tapping a restless rhythm against the floor as I anxiously wait for Dad and Eli to come back inside. Moments after we got home, Mom and I got busy in the kitchen preparing things for a lasagna dinner while the kids finished up their homework for the day. Meanwhile, Eli quietly slipped outside with Dad and Thor. With dinner now baking in the oven, I finally have a chance to check on them.

Eli is throwing the ball across the yard for Thor to fetch before he resumes the chat with my dad. They're both standing in the center of my enclosed front yard, engaged in a serious discussion. A blend of nervousness and relief stirs within me—I'm uncertain about my feelings regarding him taking charge like this. I know he means well, but shouldn't I be out there in case things go south?

"They'll be okay, Janie. Give them a minute to talk." Mom's voice makes me jump as she approaches from behind. "I like that young man of yours. I'm sure your dad will too. He has a good heart, and the kids adore him. You should've seen them light up this morning when they found him waiting for them at the breakfast table. The donuts he brought along were just an added bonus."

I turn around to face her, letting a smile spread across my face. "They really do love him." It feels good knowing that they'll be thrilled to know that Eli is here to stay.

"They do," Mom replies softly. She reaches out and gently brushes my hair off my shoulder. "And you do too. I can tell. I'm happy for you guys," she continues, her voice a mix of joy and concern. "I just wish that you'd wait and have a real wedding."

The front door swings open, making me instinctively step back. Eli stands there, his gaze shifting from me to the blinds, a knowing smile lighting up his face. Warmth floods my cheeks as I lock eyes with him, the realization hitting me that I've just been caught in the act.

Right behind him, Dad chuckles. "Janie, baby, if you were curious enough to spy on us, you could've joined us," he says. Dad walks in past Eli, giving me a peck on the cheek. "Your mom and I are heading out so you and Eli can have that important talk with the kids."

"I thought you guys were having dinner with us," I protest.

"Not tonight. I've got a hot date lined up with your mother," he teases. I love that my parents are still as in love as ever after all these years. Dad gently tugs Mom over, enveloping her in a hug. Then he leans in to plant a kiss on her neck. A playful giggle escapes her lips.

"Thank you both for stopping by, but I think it's time to get going now," I say. If I let them, they'd have no problem making out right here in my entryway. *No thank you.* I saw enough of that growing up in their home.

"Aww, come on, Janie," Mom protests playfully.

"Kids, come give Grandma and Grandpa hugs."

They come running in from the family room and wrap my parents in their arms.

Once the kids have run back out of the room, Dad turns his attention to Eli. "I expect to see you the next time all of us guys get together." His gaze shifts between us, settling on Eli with a serious expression. "I'm trusting you with my daughter. You best do right by her and those kids. They've already seen way too much pain in their lives."

Eli extends his hand, meeting Dad's grip with a confident shake. "You have my word, sir," he replies.

A smile spreads across Dad's face. "No need for that 'sir' business. You'll be my son tomorrow. You can call me Dad, or Butch if you're not comfortable with that."

With tears burning the back of my eyes, I step into my dad's embrace as Eli moves on to Mom. "Thank you, Dad."

"As long as you're happy, I'm happy." He pulls back and smiles.

"I am." I say my goodbye, then give them both a quick kiss on their cheeks. "Excuse me, I need to check on dinner." If I stay any longer, the tears I've been fighting are liable to fall.

I make my way to the kitchen and notice the timer on the oven shows that there are fifteen minutes remaining. I swing open the fridge door and gather the makings for a side salad. Seeing that we still have half a lemon pie from the other night, I take it out as well. Setting them on the counter, I put a tray of garlic bread in the oven to toast up and then turn on the burner under a pot of green beans. With all this out, the meal is coming together nicely, causing my mouth to water.

"Do you need a hand?" Eli asks, entering the kitchen after seeing my parents off.

I pull the bread out of the oven and get to work on the salad next. "Not really, but why don't you bring the kids in here so we can talk to them?"

He steps out of the kitchen, returning shortly with the kids trailing behind him. He directs them to each take a seat at the island. When they're in place, he faces them and clasps his hands in front of him. "Your mom and I have something to tell you."

I dry my hands with a dishrag just in time for the oven timer to ring. Eli pulls out the lasagna, then turns back to face the kids. I join him, holding his hand.

"Eli and I are going to get married. Tomorrow." I pause to let the surprise register.

Peter's brow furrows, as if he thinks we might be pranking him. Eric looks back and forth between his siblings, his eyes searching their faces for clues on how he should react. But Sage, though she's not frowning, doesn't show any signs of being happy either.

Have I somehow misjudged how much the kids love Eli?

Are they not okay with this?

Eli must notice, so he carries on. "If it's alright with you, we'd like to take you out of school so you can be there with us."

"Are you guys really getting married?" Peter asks. He glances between Eli and me as if he's missed something. His gaze settles on Eli. "So you're moving in here, and what? Are you going to be, like, our dad now?"

"Yeah, kind of. I'll never replace your father, but I'd love to be a bonus dad, if you're okay with it."

"Eli's going to be my dad!" Eric shouts excitedly. "Yes!"

"That's awesome," Peter says. He nods as a smile spreads across his face.

Sage is the only one who hasn't reacted yet. I turn to her, unsure if she's pleased or not. "Angel?" I ask. "What do you think about this?"

"I'm happy, but I thought if you got married again, I'd get to wear a pretty dress and help you with yours. If the wedding's tomorrow, there won't be time for us to even go dress shopping. That makes me a little sad."

Eli gives my hand a reassuring squeeze. "If your mom agrees, how about we wake up early and head into town? We can spend the day at the mall and pick out something special to wear. I already have a hotel room nearby, and I can book another one if they have it so we can get ready in our own spaces."

"What about the cake and dancing?" Sage asks.

"We'll plan a reception after Eli moves in. How does that sound?" I ask.

"Why not tomorrow?" she complains.

"Because Eli and I will be going out on our own after the wedding. The following day, we've planned something special for you all here at the house before he flies back to Charleston."

That final comment triggers a flood of questions.

Why can't we join him?

Why does he have to leave again?

Can't he just stay here with us?

Rather than responding myself, I let Eli handle the questions while I start serving our dinner before it gets cold. We still have a call with his mom and grandma later; I can't help but feel anxious about it. I can only imagine how well they'll take not being able to be here. I mean, Eli is Anna's only child. I'm not really starting this marriage off on the right foot.

Eli holds my hand as the screen lights up, revealing Anna and Ms. Emmy smiling at us. Eli begins by updating them about his new job and how the kids are doing. Finally, the moment arrives, and I feel my stomach tighten with nerves.

"We have something to share with you both," Eli says. "I asked Janelle to marry me."

Anna's eyes widen, and Ms. Emmy simply beams. "You did?" Anna asks.

"I did," Eli confirms, glancing at me with a smile. "And she said yes."

Anna looks at me, placing her hand over her heart. I nod in confirmation.

"We're going to have a small ceremony with the kids tomorrow, and once the case is settled with her ex, we'll plan a bigger celebration."

"Wow, that's a lot to take in. I'm thrilled, but why the rush?" Anna questions.

Ms. Emmy playfully taps her arm and grins. "When you know you know."

Most of the rest of the call goes smoothly. The only issue raised is that we're doing this so soon and without either of them present. The guilt from lying to everyone gnaws at me as we continue the charade. *But is it truly a lie?* I wonder.

Our love is genuine.

We will be legally wed.

He did eventually propose.

I suppose the only lie is that we want it all at this very moment. Do we both picture a future together in marriage? Absolutely.

Yet, I can't help but wish for more time.

I lean my head against Eli's shoulder and sigh deeply. I really hope we're making the right choice.

Chapter Twenty-Nine

I step out of the steamy bathroom with a towel wrapped around my hair and another around my body. I feel so much better after indulging in an everything shower that lasted much longer than usual. Eli is already downstairs, keeping an eye on the kids, giving me a moment to myself. I still can hardly believe that today is my wedding day.

As I let that thought settle in my mind, it feels more and more comforting. Eli is nothing like Bryant; his kindness and patience are a breath of fresh air. After my morning session with Katie, where we dissected my reluctance to let Eli fully into my life, I wonder if it's my own insecurities holding me back, rather than a fear of history repeating itself.

I pat myself dry before slipping into the pale-pink sundress that I bought last Easter. It's made from light, airy fabric that flutters around my knees, and the delicate floral pattern makes it the prettiest thing I own. Though we're about to head out for dress shopping, I wanted to wear this just in case I don't find something that fits me perfectly.

As I glance in the mirror, smoothing the fabric over my hips, I find myself questioning what Eli sees in me. When

I linger on that thought, a familiar urge to flee creeps in, but I try to push it aside. I've spent too many years running scared, and today, I choose not to run anymore.

Now that I'm dressed, I return to the bathroom and stand in front of the mirror, my blow-dryer in hand, ready to tame my hair into something fitting of a bride. Then I move on to my makeup, only adding a touch of blush and a sweep of mascara. That's rare for me anymore. Once satisfied, I nod. I look nice.

I slide into my closet and reach for my trench coat and a pair of closed-toe heels. It's February in Oklahoma, after all. The weather here can be unpredictable. Even if it's been nice as of late, there is a storm in the forecast.

I step out of my room, smoothing the fabric of my dress as I head down the stairs. I drape my coat over the back of the couch on my way to search for my family. The sound of laughter filters through the hallway, and before I can even enter the family room, Thor runs over, his tail wagging furiously as he barks to announce my presence.

Eli turns at the sound, his eyes meeting mine before they travel over me from head to toe. I realize this might be the first time he's seen me dressed like this. He saw me in a dress for the gala, but it was far more glamorous than this.

"Wow." Eli approaches with a smile, his eyes sparkling as he reaches for my hand. His touch is warm and reassuring as he lifts it to his lips for a soft, lingering kiss. "You're stunning," he murmurs. "Do a turn and let me take you all in."

With a gentle lift of my hand, he encourages me to spin. I twirl slowly, feeling the fabric of my dress flutter around my legs.

Eli lets out a low, appreciative whistle. "I'm one lucky man. You're beautiful on any given day, but when you have the time to pamper yourself, you make my heart race," he says. His gaze sweeps over me once more with genuine affection.

"You're laying it on kind of thick, don't you think?"

"Not at all." He grins. "A beauty like yours deserves to be appreciated."

"Wow, Momma. You look pretty," Eric chimes in.

I glance over to Eli's left and see the kids standing there, ready to go.

"Thank you, bud. You look handsome too. Did you comb your hair this morning?"

He nods his head vigorously, a proud grin spreading across his face. "Eli helped me. He brought over some mouse and perfume. Wanna smell?"

I chuckle, catching Eli's eye as I lean in to smell. A warm blend of citrus and spice wafts up, mingling with the faint aroma of hair product. "Wow, bud. Your *perfume* is really nice."

"It's mousse, bud," Eli corrects. "And remember what I said? Cologne is like perfume but in a masculine scent. It's a little different."

"Can we go dress shopping now?" Sage interrupts.

I nod and gather the kids, guiding them toward the door. Eli grabs our marriage license from the kitchen counter, and we all pile into my Suburban. Eli slides into the driver's seat, the engine purring to life as he turns the key, and we head out of Baycliff Valley, merging onto the interstate heading toward the city.

Eli pulls his phone from his pocket and hands it back to Sage. "Can you let your grandma know that we're on the way?" he asks, glancing at her in the rearview mirror.

I turn to him, puzzled. "On the way?" I echo, my eyebrows knitting in confusion. Heather is supposed to meet us in the city to be a witness for our wedding, and I thought we'd find a second at the courthouse. Why is he asking Sage to call my mom?

Eli nods, his face softening. "I know this is rushed, but it's still our wedding day. The idea of our parents not sharing it with us was bothering me. Your mom and dad will be there, and I'll ask someone to hold my phone so my mom and grandma can watch too."

My heart swells, touched that he's ensuring our parents can be part of today. It means everything to me.

Eli reaches over, gently takes my hand, and kisses it. "If you want your brothers there, you can make the call. I'll leave that decision to you."

"As much as it pains me to say it, I still don't want them there," I admit sadly. "They'd only try to talk me out of marrying you. I don't need all of that." The thought of excluding them stings, but knowing my brothers, one of them would probably throw me over their shoulder and carry me away, creating a huge scene. I love them, and hate not having them here, but not today. Today is not their day, it's ours—Eli's and mine.

Eli intertwines our fingers, and I feel certain that regardless of what comes our way, we'll be facing it together.

After an exhausting day filled with shopping and pampering, my mom, Sage, Heather, and I are finally ready to meet up with the guys. Mom and Sage stepped out a moment ago to check in on them.

The quest for the perfect dress took almost two hours. Our first stop was a seasonal prom dress shop that always appears around this time of year. They had a limited selection in my size, and nothing felt right; every dress seemed to reveal more skin than I was comfortable with. We traipsed from one store to another, while Eli texted that he and the boys had already found their suits. Sage found a beautiful blue dress that complements her eyes perfectly. At last, in the final store, I found a dress that felt like it was made for me. Mom snatched it up, paying the bill before I could talk myself out of buying it. Now, I'm standing here in an off-the-shoulder, cap-sleeve dress in a very subtle shade of pale blue. The high-low maxi dress fits just right, and the back of the skirt dips low, grazing the floor slightly due to my height, giving it an elegant, almost-bridal feel.

Heather runs to the door as a few quick knocks echo through the room. She cracks it open just enough to reach her hand through, grabbing a package from the unseen person on the other side, before snapping the door shut with a soft click. A grin lighting up her face, she walks over carrying a large bag. "Every bride deserves to feel like a princess, no matter how rushed the day might be."

Carefully, she opens the bag and lifts out a small box, handing it to me with a shine in her eyes. I open it, my breath catching as I reveal a delicate white floral garter, adorned with tiny pearls.

"This is beautiful. Thank you."

"This is your something borrowed. I wore this very garter belt on the day I married my Jacob." She wipes away a tear before reaching back into the bag. "You already have your something blue in your dress, so I skipped that part. But here's your something old." She reveals a simple yet beautiful rhine-stone necklace with matching earrings. "These are the same jewels I wore to my prom. If I had more time, I could've done better. And here is your something new." She hands me a bouquet of white roses. "This is the closest thing I could find to a bridal bouquet."

"This is all so thoughtful. Really, I can't thank you enough."

"No need to thank me. You're my best friend, and I'd do anything for you." She leans in and gives me a quick hug. "Now, how about we head out before your mom starts looking for us?"

We quickly gather our belongings and make our way out of the room, taking the elevator down. As soon as the doors slide open, I see my family waiting across the lobby. But it's the man in the sharp navy-blue suit, beaming with the widest smile, who catches my attention first.

Eli.

He strides across the lobby with purpose as I step past the open doors.

"You take my breath away, Peach," he says as he comes to stand right in front of me. "Will you do me the honor of marrying me?"

"I will," I reply. A smile finds my lips just before his meet mine.

"Oh my God, you two. Get a room," Heather comments. "No, wait, we've got to get you to the courthouse first. Let's move it or you'll be late."

Eli, the kids, and I pile into the car, with Eli driving. Mom, Dad, and Heather are right behind us. Since the building is only ten minutes away, I think we'll be on time, but I don't want to risk it. We've come this far, and I don't want something as small as time to ruin it.

I glance back at the kids. "Make sure you behave for Grandma and Grandpa tonight, alright?"

"We will," Eric says. "Grandma said that we can pick up Thor and take him to their house."

Thanks to my parents, our date night has unexpectedly become a little getaway. They booked us a honeymoon suite across town and offered to look after the kids all night.

"That's nice of her. I wouldn't want Thor to be home alone all night."

Eli signals and turns into the courthouse parking lot. Before we know it, we're parked and heading inside, making our way up to the court clerk's office to check in. There's a couple ahead of us, so we're asked to wait in the hall while they finish up.

"Are you ready for this?" Mom asks.

I look over at Eli, who's propped up the wall across from me talking to Pete, and smile. Believe it or not, I actually am. I don't know when it happened, but I'm actually looking forward to becoming Mrs. Eli Boyd.

The door to the courtroom opens and a happy-looking couple steps out. They smile and share a quick kiss before heading back toward the court clerk's office.

"Janelle and Eli?" a woman says from the doorway.

"That's us," Eli replies. He extends his arm for me to join him. I grasp his hand, and we follow her inside. Just inside the doorway, he leans close, whispering so that only I can hear him. "I love you, Janelle. If at any point you want to back out, it won't change my feelings for you."

"Eli, I love you, too, and I'm done running. You're stuck with me," I assure him.

We proceed to the front of the courtroom, standing where she directs us, close to the judge's bench. Our family doesn't take seats; instead, Mom and Sage stand beside me, while Dad and the boys stand with Eli. Heather has Eli's phone with Anna and Ms. Emmy on video.

The beginning of the ceremony is a blur. I can't stop my hands from fidgeting. When the clerk finally asks if we have rings, I shake my head no, but Eli grins and pulls a pair from his pocket.

"We do," he confirms.

I raise a brow in question, and he winks in reply.

"Eli and Janelle, please hold hands. You mentioned you've prepared some vows for this moment—please share them now."

At the last minute, we decided to forgo the traditional vows, looking up some alternatives online and making them personal to us.

Eli pulls a piece of paper out of his blazer and takes my hand. "Janelle, I love you. You have quickly become my closest friend. Today, I give myself to you in marriage. I promise to encourage, inspire, and boast about your beauty inside and out every chance I get. To laugh with you and to comfort you in times of sorrow. I promise to love you in good times and in bad, when life seems to throw things at us, and when it becomes a challenge, I promise to dig in and fight for us. I promise to cherish you and the beautiful family that we build together. I'll work by your side in creating a beautiful life." He slips the ring onto my finger before he looks up at me with a smile. "With this ring, I thee wed." He reaches up and wipes away a fallen tear from my face with his thumb.

"Janelle, please share your vows."

"Eli, I love you. I fought our relationship from the first moment you showed interest in me, but you broke down my barriers and captured my heart—not only mine, but the kids' as well." I glance at them and smile. "You've breathed new life into this family after so many challenging years. My mom used to say that when I met the one, he'd find me amid the chaos and help carry the weight. I never believed it, not until now." I share a look with Mom as she laughs through her tears. "Today, I offer my heart and soul to you in marriage. I vow to encourage you every day, to try and find joy in your quirks, even when they drive me crazy, and to hold on to you in moments of sadness. I pledge my love to you today, tomorrow, and for all the days of our lives. When life gets hard, I promise not to run away anymore. With you by my side, we can get through anything. I vow to cherish you and our family until my last breath." I slip his ring onto his finger. "With this ring, I thee wed."

"Eli and Janelle, by the authority vested in me by the state of Oklahoma, I now pronounce you husband and wife. You may kiss your bride."

Chapter Thirty

I lie back against the couch and snuggle into Eli's warm embrace as the credits roll on the movie we just finished watching. It's hard to believe that just two days ago, we became husband and wife. Seriously, I wonder why I fought him for so long. He's perfect for me . . . and the kids. I still wish we'd gone the conventional route of taking our time in dating and then getting engaged, having a big wedding and all, but there's not a single thing I regret.

Yesterday was Valentine's Day. While the kids were at school, Eli and I went out on a nice lunch date. He even stopped and got me flowers. I'm still taken aback by the kindness he shows me.

After school, we baked heart-shaped cookies with the kids, then cuddled up on the couch to watch a family movie, played board games, and surprised them with Valentine's gifts. Eli even got Sage her own bouquet of flowers! It was the best Valentine's Day I've ever had.

Tonight, my family is coming over for "game night." Really, it's so we can share the big news about our marriage with them. I'm not looking forward to that part. I have a feeling my brothers, protective as they are, will have plenty to say. But in the end, I'm sure they'll be happy for us.

As Eli shifts to get up, he pauses just long enough to lean down and plant a soft kiss on my lips.

"Where are you going? I was comfortable," I whine, pouting slightly as I reach out to pull him back.

He chuckles. "The movie's finished. Plus, it's almost time to go pick up the kids from school."

"Nope," I reply with a grin. "Kim said she's taking care of that today. She wants to take them to dinner before game night."

"Well then." Eli drops back onto the couch with a playful bounce, causing me to tip over into the cushions. He leans over me, a mischievous glint in his eye, and a slow smile spreads across his face. "Looks like I've got just enough time to shower my beautiful wife with the kind of love she deserves."

I giggle. What is it with this man and making me feel so girly?

As Eli's lips find mine, my eyes flutter shut as if on cue. In this moment, the world around us disappears and it's now just the two of us. The scent of his woodsy bodywash mingles with the rich aroma of the coffee he just drank. He deepens the kiss, stealing my breath and making my heart race.

Eli pulls back slightly, and my eyes slowly open, finding his gaze inches from mine. His eyes, full of warmth and affection, crinkle at the corners as he smiles. "You have no idea how happy I am," he murmurs. "It's because of you that I have a family I adore. You gave me a life I could've only dreamed of. Janelle, you're the woman I'd choose over and over again. I promise I'll do this right one day, but until then, I'm happy just as we are. Mrs. Janelle Boyd, you are the love of my life." He leans in, pressing a kiss to the tip of my nose. "I have no idea how I'm supposed to leave you behind while I go back and pack."

A single tear escapes me, sliding down my cheek, landing in my hair. Eli's eyes follow its path before gently wiping it away.

"I love you," I whisper, lifting to put a kiss on his chin. "No more marriage by name. Eli, I'm yours. You hold the key to my heart."

This kind and loving man of mine holds my gaze, his eyes shimmering with emotion as a beaming smile lights up his face. In this moment, I know that our marriage, which didn't start as it should have, will now have a fighting chance.

I'm all in.

That evening, as Eli and I are getting the snacks ready for game night, I'm floating on cloud nine. The day spent at home, just me and my husband, was glorious. I'm fully aware that this is the honeymoon phase, but I also know that even in the high moments with Bryant, I never felt such peace. That alone gives me hope that this relationship is truly different.

"I'm going to go let Thor out before everyone gets here," Eli says. He walks over to me, his eyes filled with love, and pulls me into him, planting a quick kiss on my lips before he heads toward the back door. Even that brief kiss, the way he draws me to him, sends a shiver down my spine, making my toes curl.

How is that even fair?

If I had known things with him would be this good back when I first met him, I might've accepted that coffee date offer without hesitation. Who am I kidding? No, I wouldn't have. Regardless of what I know now, nothing would've changed. I wasn't in a good place. But now, I'd like to think I'm in a much better place in life.

The main stressor is still my ex, who has been awfully quiet these last few days.

Suddenly, the front door swings open with such force it slams against the wall, jolting me from my thoughts. "Momma!" Eric shouts as he bursts into the room, his feet pounding against the floor as he races toward the kitchen with wide eyes.

"What is it, bud?" I kneel and catch Eric in my arms as he barrels toward me.

"Aunt Kim and Uncle Pat took us to Aunt Leah's restaurant for dinner. It was yummmmy! But a mean man was picking on Aunt Kim," Eric explains. "She said we had to come home before Uncle Pat got in trouble for hurting someone."

A while back, Leah mentioned a guy who'd been working at Uncle Joe's for several years having a problem with Kim. I wonder if it's the same guy. That seems like a long time to hold a grudge in my opinion. Surely it's not him.

"I'm sure Leah's Uncle Joe will handle it. Uncle Pat won't get into any trouble. Thank you for telling me, bud."

Eric loves his uncles and would hate to see them in any kind of danger.

I hear the back door open and shut, just before Thor runs into the room with his tail wagging furiously. I'm all but forgotten. Eric runs off to hug Thor and Eli.

A moment later, as I rise to my feet, Eli walks into the kitchen, his brow furrowed with concern. "Everything okay?" he asks.

"It is," I state. I fill him in on what Eric just told me. "I'm sure Pat will talk to Joe and put a stop to it. I can't imagine him letting anyone treat his wife badly." Eli pulls me in and nuzzles my neck. "I know I wouldn't let anyone mess with you."

When he says things like this, I swear, I fall a little more each time.

"Knock, knock," Leah says from the door.

"Come in," I say.

Eli takes a step back and grabs the potholders before moving to the oven to take out the wings he put in there to reheat. My family trickles in and makes plates before heading into the family room. Eli keeps himself busy by slipping into the garage, mentioning something about grabbing more beer. When it takes him longer than usual, I find my way out there to check on him. I scan the space, expecting to find him at one of the two fridges, but instead, my eyes land on Eli sitting on the ice chest at the back of the garage, his head cradled in his hands. My heart sinks at the sight.

I make my way over and stand in front of him, lowering myself into a crouch so he can see me fully. "What's going on? Are you okay?"

He raises his head, and the worry etched into his features causes me to gasp.

"What happened? If one of my brothers—"

He chuckles softly and reaches out, pulling me onto his lap, then lays his head onto my shoulder. "I'm okay. You don't need to go to battle for me. I just needed a moment. Telling your brothers about us isn't going to be easy, you know. What if they don't like the idea and they try to convince you to—"

"Don't you dare," I interrupt. I pull back just enough to look him in the eyes. "I made a commitment to you. No matter what my brothers say, I chose you. Did I not make that clear enough earlier?" I smile and raise my brow.

"You did." He returns my smile before leaning in and giving me a quick kiss. "I guess I just got in my head."

"I already do that enough for the both of us," I tease. I cradle his face in my hands, feeling the warmth of his skin beneath my fingertips, and lean in for a kiss that makes my heart race and leaves me breathless. As I pull back, I intertwine my fingers with his, feeling the familiar comfort of his grip. "How about we get in there and rip off the bandage before one of the kids spills the beans?"

He brings my hand to his lips, placing a gentle kiss on the back of it, and flashes me a smile. "I'd much rather face the Whitfield brothers than the Camerons right now." He chuckles, a hint of nervousness in it.

We begin our walk out of the garage, pausing only to grab another case of beer. "You know, they aren't really that scary. They're more bark than bite," I say, trying to ease the tension.

"Says the one raised a Cameron," he replies.

I stop just before we reach the door, turning to look at Eli. "I don't want you to fear them. You're part of this family now. I'm sure when we tell them, they'll get loud, but no matter what happens, in the end, they'll be the ones leaving tonight. You'll be the one in our home, our bed, and in my heart for the rest of my life. Their opinion is just that—an opinion. Besides," I add with a mischievous grin as I grab the door handle and swing it open wide, "if they so much as tick me off, I'll sic their women on them."

Eli laughs. "Oh, that's mean."

"You've seen how much bigger my brothers are than me. I've gotta use whatever I can. Now . . . let's get this over with so I can kick them out and spend the rest of the night in your arms."

"What do you mean you two got married?" Tom's voice cracks as he stands up from the couch in a hurry. "And why wasn't I invited?"

Eli wraps me in his arms, pulling me in a little closer. Just minutes ago, he and I stood here, at the front of the room, and filled my family in on our wedding. Thank God Mom has the kids with her or this outburst would really tick me off.

"You're not the only one," Cam says, folding his arms across his chest. "I didn't get one either."

"None of us did," Pat adds, cheeks flushed. "After everything with your ex, you'd think you'd give us a heads-up."

"That was a low blow, Patrick," Kim says. "I understand you're upset, but that's a bit much, don't you think?"

"I agree. Ya'll know Eli," Maddie states. "Especially you, Thomas. You know he's a good man."

Leah may be quiet but she's looking at the guys as if she's upset with them.

Regardless of the ladies' help, Pat's words hit their mark.

No matter that Maddie just got onto Tom, he carries on. "I can't believe you did this, Janelle. We're family. I'm . . . disappointed in you."

Tears begin to fall. In all my years, no one in my family has ever said they were disappointed in me before. It hurts almost as bad if I'd been hit.

Eli unwinds his arm from around me, threads our fingers together, and takes the slightest step forward. "If you need someone to be disappointed in, let it be me," he says, voice low but firm. "You've been landing verbal punches on my wife since we opened our mouths." He squeezes my hand the slightest bit. "I love Janelle and the kids with everything in me. Tom, you know I'm nothing like her ex. I'd rather die than hurt her. Janelle and I are two consenting adults in love, who chose to marry in private. She's never told any of you how to live your lives, so why are you telling her how to live hers?"

The room goes quiet. I know my brothers are upset, but they never even gave me the chance to explain anything. Once they heard we got married, they went on the attack.

Dad stands, ready to jump in, but when I shake my head, he stays quiet.

I glance at Eli, then toward my brothers. I wipe the tears from my cheeks and take a steadying breath. "This night is over. I'd appreciate it if everyone left. I love you all, but I need some space."

Tom opens his mouth to protest, but Maddie puts her hand on his arm, stopping him.

"You heard your sister. It's time to go," Dad's voice booms. As my siblings start gathering their things, Dad walks our way. "Your mom sent me a text saying that she'd like to keep the kids tonight. We can bring them to the city tomorrow after you get off work."

I nod. "Thanks, Dad." As much as I hate the thought of them being gone tonight, I also know that I need a moment.

He looks between Eli and me. "Take care of each other. We'll see you tomorrow."

My stomach flops at the thought. I'll be dropping the kids off at their father's and then driving Eli to the airport after I get off.

Dad shakes Eli's hand. "Hurry home, son. We'll see you when you get back." Then he guides everyone out. Once the front door clicks shut, the house is finally quiet.

Eli exhales. "That could've gone better."

I lay my head against his chest as he wraps both arms around me and holds me close, his chest rising and falling against mine. "I just want to stay here with you forever and forget about tomorrow."

Without a word, he lifts me into his arms. My legs instantly wrap around his waist and my arms around his neck. I bury my face in his shoulder as he carries me toward the stairs. Each step he takes puts a distance between us and tonight's chaos, and yet gets us closer to a goodbye I'm not ready to have.

Chapter Thirty-One

Yesterday, after dropping the kids off with Bryant and Milly, I drove Eli to the airport, sending him back to Charleston to pack up his things and get himself ready for the move. It wasn't until I was home and tucked into bed that the weight of the day caught up to me.

I have been married for all of three days and was just beginning to enjoy having Eli here in my home—well, *ours* now—full time, and now he's gone. Although I know he's coming back, the house feels unusually large and quiet in his and the children's absence.

Earlier today, my phone alerted me to a text from Sage. She told me that Bryant had confiscated Peter's game console and phone because he had been glued to them since they got there. I could picture Peter oblivious to the world around him. If I let him have his devices all the time, I'm sure he'd be the same way here. I understand why Bryant did it; I would've done the same. Peter knows the rules about screen time. But when Sage mentioned that Bryant had decided Peter wouldn't be getting them back at all, I knew it was time for me to intervene. I just haven't done so yet.

Now that I have a moment to deal with him, I reach for my phone and pull up Bryant's name.

Me: *Hey, how's everything with the kids?*

Bryant: *Hey! It's Milly. Bryant left his phone in the living room and is in his office. The kids are doing well. Although Peter's a bit upset with Bryant, which is kind of the usual. Bryant took away his devices, said he's keeping them. But don't worry, I'll hand them over to you when you come to pick the kids up.*

Me: *Thanks, Milly. I really appreciate you helping smooth things out between those two. How's Eric doing? Any more potty accidents?*

Bryant: *Nope, all good. I've been checking him and his bed every morning, and I even do a night check when they're here just to be sure. That whole potty monster story didn't help much, but Bryant insists he didn't mean to scare him. Oh, Bryant just walked in asking about dinner, so I gotta run. We'll chat more when you come by to get the kids.*

Thankful that Milly answered instead of Bryant, I let out a deep sigh of relief, feeling the tension ease from my shoulders. Glancing at the clock on the wall, I see that it's barely five. On my way home from work, I swung by my favorite fast-food joint and picked up a greasy burger and fries for dinner. There's no point in cooking just for me. Thor is outside in the yard, and the girls aren't due to arrive for another hour. It's a rare occasion when we manage to get our schedules together for an evening gathering instead of our usual lunch meetups. Tonight, I need my girls way more than I need another family game night.

My brother's reaction to the news of my wedding was far from supportive. And, honestly, I don't even want to see them right now. I get that they're mad that they didn't get to be there, but couldn't they have at least been supportive of my decision? Now, I'm just annoyed, and so, in a fit of pettiness, I decided I'll be giving them the silent treatment.

My phone vibrates on the couch beside me, the screen lighting up with Eli's name. I swipe to answer and lift it to my ear.

"Hello?"

"Hey, Peach. How are you holding up? Are the girls there yet?"

"Hey there, Romeo." I can't help but chuckle. I've never been one for pet names, but when Eli told me that he played the role of Romeo in high school, the nickname just seemed to fit. "I'm hanging in there, though I swear I've memorized every bump on this ceiling out of sheer boredom. The ladies should be here within the hour. How are things on your end? Have you managed to get everything packed up yet?"

Eli's scheduled to return home in two weekends. He's hoping to make it back earlier, but that's the plan for now.

"I've sorted through most things in my storage unit and packed up what I want to bring. I drove a truckload over to the donation center. Moving into a home that's already furnished lets me part with a lot of my old stuff."

I hate that he thinks that he has to get rid of his things.

"This may have been rushed, Eli, but you're still my husband, and this is your home too. Most of this stuff is what I had with Bryant. I've wanted to redo it since he moved out. So bring whatever you want. Who knows, maybe this spring, we can revitalize this place together and truly make it *our* home."

"I don't mind what we have now. Most of the stuff I'm donating has been in storage for several years anyway. Since I moved back in with Mom after college, I haven't used any of it. A springtime renewal sounds good. I have a bit in savings we can use." After college, Eli got the job he's currently leaving and began traveling so much that it didn't make sense for him to get his own place. With the Whitfields paying most of the bills, he was able to save a lot of his pay. With this new job, he won't be traveling nearly as much, and since our home is paid off and I'm nearly debt free now, a spring renewal could work.

"Great. Once we're done with this court stuff with Bryant and the kids are on break, I say we get started."

There's a brief lull in the conversation before Eli finally breaks the silence. "If that's what you want, then we'll make it happen."

I stand from the couch, and head toward the door to let Thor back in, his tail wagging furiously.

"I miss you," Eli says. "I even miss Eric's tantrums. Never in my wildest dreams did I think I'd miss those, but I do. As much as I know I'm going to miss Mom and Grandma when I get back, I'm ready to be home with you."

The doorbell chimes, interrupting our chat and drawing my attention that way.

I turn and head toward the front. "I guess I should get going. That would be the ladies." I twist the knob and pull the door open, stepping aside to let Maddie and Kim in. As they shrug off their coats and hang them on the nearby rack, I turn my attention back to Eli, who's still on the phone. "I love you and miss you like crazy," I say softly.

"I'll send you a message before I go to bed tonight."

"Alright. I love you too. Make sure to enjoy yourself. You deserve it."

After the call ends, I turn back to the girls, who smile softly.

"You know, this silent treatment is driving Tom crazy. He almost didn't let me leave the house without him tonight," Maddie begins.

"Right? Pat hasn't quit talking about it either," Kim chimes in.

"They'll just have to deal with it. I'm not speaking to any of them right now. I'm allowed to live my life, and I know they would've tried to talk me out of marrying Eli if they had known. It's not like he and I aren't planning a big wedding later anyway. They can attend that as long as they come to their senses by then."

We start heading toward the kitchen when there's a knock at the door, followed by Heather walking in. Before she can even shut the door, Leah, her sister Kayla, and Mom are coming in too.

"The party has arrived!" Kayla says. Above her head, she holds a bottle of sparkling cider. Not that long ago, she found out that she and Mike are having another baby, so it's no booze for her for the foreseeable future.

"Hey, ladies," I say. I open the cabinet and drag out my blender, then move to get the key for the cabinet where I keep the liquor. "Who's up for margaritas?"

Heather, Mom, Maddie, and I are the only ones who want one.

I look from Kim to Leah and raise a brow. "Are we doing virgin drinks for a reason, ladies?"

Leah nods vigorously. "Cam and I have decided to start trying for another baby. I don't want to take any chances."

"Kim?" I ask. The smile on my face grows wider, as I can only hope for the answer I think is coming.

"We haven't started trying just yet, but we plan to this summer. But I've been cutting out alcohol and changing my habits out for healthier ones. I don't want anything getting in the way of us having one when we start trying."

"Oh my gosh. That makes me want to get married now so that Tom and I can start trying! We've already said that we won't try to stop it. If it happens, it happens. We both want a lot of kids." Maddie and Tom are now engaged—he finally popped the question just the other day. I'm thrilled to finally be able to claim her as family in name and not just heart.

"I guess that just leaves Janie and Heather," Mom says. "Do the two of you think you'll be having more kids in the future?"

"I'm good with my two," Heather says. She raises her hands in mock surrender, then steps over to the counter, taking control of the blender.

"What about you, Janie?" Maddie asks, her eyes twinkling with curiosity. "Will you be giving Eli any babies?"

I hesitate, choosing my words carefully. "We haven't really decided yet. He mentioned wanting to have a kid at one point, but I wasn't too sure if I wanted another."

Maddie leans in, her interest piqued. "How do you feel about it now? Like, what would you say if he were to seriously ask you to have his baby?"

Surprisingly, the question isn't difficult for me to answer. "Before Bryant came into the picture, I dreamed of having as many children as I could. But when he wanted to stop at two, I agreed. Then when I found out I was pregnant with Eric, I was thrilled at the thought of expanding our family further. Now, with my age getting up there and with having older kids, it might feel a bit odd. But it's not entirely off the table for the future, if we can figure everything out. My job demands a lot of my time and energy. I don't even know if I can continue working there if I get pregnant."

Would I have to quit my job? If so, would I be willing to give it up to stay at home with the baby while they're little again? I've already done that once and look where that led me.

But Eli isn't Bryant, and I know he'd be a great father—heck, he already is.

"Sounds like you've got a lot to think about," Maddie says.

That I do.

As the sound of the blender fills the kitchen, I reach up to retrieve a few champagne flutes from the cupboard and pass them to Leah to be filled with cider.

Heather finishes mixing the drinks and pours the margaritas into a few glasses before handing them out with a smile. "Cheers to new beginnings," she announces. "With so many weddings, babies, and new dating prospects, it looks like all of us Cameron-ish women have something to look forward to."

I glance over, curiosity piqued, my brow arching in silent inquiry, but Mom beats me to the punch. "Who's this new dating prospect?"

Heather grins. "You know my neighbor, right?"

"Ben?" Kayla asks excitedly. He's this easygoing guy who once lived in the same New York City apartment building as Kayla. He eventually returned to Oklahoma, staying with a friend named Shannon until she got serious with her now-boyfriend, Zeke.

Last summer while we were out on Heather's porch, a moving truck began backing into the driveway next door. When Ben hopped out of the driver's side, I was shocked to see him. Kayla started bringing him and Shannon around the farm a bit so even though I don't know him well, I know of him.

"Exactly. Well, he has a friend moving in this weekend," Heather continues. Her smile is so bright, it's blinding. "I only met Blaze briefly when I went next door to get the ball Chris knocked over the fence. But when our hands brushed, just for a moment—I don't know, there was something electric about it."

"I thought you were into Ben," Kayla says.

A chuckle escapes my lips. Honestly, any woman with eyes would find Ben attractive.

"Who isn't?" Heather replies. "He's a great guy. But according to Shannon, he's got his eye on a woman who works at Joe's restaurant."

"Who?" Leah asks. "Do you know her name?"

"No, but from what Shannon said, he's got it pretty bad."

Love is in the air, and if Ben and Heather find it—even if not with each other—I'm happy for them. A month ago, I might've shrugged it off, but now that I've found love again, I can genuinely be happy for my friends. I just wish that I hadn't fought it for so long.

Chapter Thirty-Two

I stand in the kitchen, my hands submerged in a large ceramic mixing bowl. I have been kneading together the makings for a batch of cowboy cookies big enough to keep us happy for the entire week. That is, until Thor started scratching and whining at the door, eager to be let outside. Sage is tucked away in her room on the phone with Grace, while Eli and Eric are in the garage, leaving just me and Peter available. With my hands coated in dough, I call out to Pete, who is lying on the couch playing one of his games, and ask him to let Thor out.

"How about you let your own dog out? I'm not your servant."

Stunned, I stare at him, my jaw slack with disbelief. He's never spoken to me that way before.

It's been just over two weeks since Bryant took his electronics, and ever since I supported that decision—not the part of keeping them, but of taking them away—Peter has been acting out. Now, I'm wondering if I should've kept them longer myself.

"Pete, you really need to apologize to your mother," Eli interjects. I startle at the sound of his voice. I didn't know he'd come back inside yet. "She didn't do anything to deserve you talking to her like that." He moves to the door to let Thor out, then walks back over to the island and leans his backside against the counter.

Eric walks in from the garage and heads to the fridge to grab a drink.

"I'm not saying sorry when it would be a lie." Pete stands from the couch, setting down his system and crossing his arms defiantly over his chest, locking eyes with Eli, who stands at the edge of the island, his hands resting by his sides. Eli poses no threat, but he remains unwavering in his position.

"Peter!" I shout. I know my voice is laced with frustration, so I try to calm it. I move to wipe the dough off my hands in case I need to step in. "Watch it, son. You're treading on thin ice here. If there's something bothering you, I'm here to talk. You know that. But I won't tolerate you sitting here disrespecting me . . . or Eli." I lock eyes with Peter, searching for any hint of regret or understanding, but he stubbornly keeps his focus on Eli. I can't fathom where all this animosity is coming from. Peter has been Eli's biggest fan since long before there was an "us."

"Come on, Pete," Eric urges. He moves over to grab Peter's arm in an attempt to guide him away. "Let's go play."

Sage walks into the room, her gaze shifting between Peter and Eli before landing on Eric. "What's happening?" she asks.

"I heard Pete shouting at Mom when Eli opened the door, so I came inside. Then Peter was being mean to Eli, so Mom yelled." Eric shrugs his shoulders. "I tried to get Pete to come play with me like you taught me, but he won't listen."

"It's okay. At least you tried."

Eric head off toward the play area.

I turn on the faucet and start washing my hands. I've noticed the kids have become a lot closer since the visits at Bryant's have started. It's kind of nice to see them looking out for each other like this. At least I know they'll be okay when they aren't with me.

Maybe if I give them a moment, they can reach Pete without this escalating further.

Sage's expression is filled with determination as she turns to look at her other brother. "You really need to stop, Pete," she urges. "If you'd just tell Mom what's making you so mad all the time, she can fix it."

Peter's eyes snap toward her, the intensity of his gaze making me want to reach out and pull him in for a hug. I know my kids are hurting—it makes me feel like a horrible mom—but the visits are court ordered, so there's nothing I can do to stop it.

"Nobody can fix this, Sage," he responds. "No matter what we say, the court will just keep making us go over to that jerk's house." He looks my way, his eyes filled with anger. "If she hadn't made babies with him, then none of this would be happening right now."

In a sudden, explosive motion, faster than any of us can react, Peter hurls his metal water bottle against the wall. It hits with a resounding thud, splattering water across the room, followed closely by a shattering sound as a frame and the bottle hit the floor. Peter storms out, leaving a unsettling silence in his wake. The sound of his bedroom door slamming shut makes my shoulders tense.

I drop the towel I'm holding and start to follow him upstairs, but Eli stops me by placing a hand on my arm.

"Kids, why don't you put on your coats and go outside with Thor for a bit? Your mom and I will clean this up," Eli suggests. Grabbing a trash can and a dish towel, he watches the kids head outside, then turns to me. "Give Peter some time to cool off. If you go up there now, you'll both end up saying things you'll regret." He pulls me into a firm hug and gently runs a hand through my hair. When I step back, he smiles softly. "I'd like to talk to him later if that's okay with you. He needs a man in his life he can vent to without fear of retaliation."

"Pete can't just act like that without facing any consequences. That would teach the others that it's okay to explode in anger and break things. It's not okay, Eli."

"No, it's not. And after he's calm and he and I have a talk, he'll face those consequences. Whether we like it or not, Peter is becoming a young man before our very eyes. He feels the weight of taking care of this family on his shoulders." He takes my hand and guides me to the living room. There's a small indention in the wall, and shards of glass lie scattered around the broken picture frame from where the bottle knocked it off the wall. "If Mr. Whitfield hadn't stepped in when my father walked out, I might've ended up in a very different place. He confronted that angry young man I was and allowed me to vent all my frustrations. Then he wrapped me in a love I'd never felt from my own father. He showed me what it truly meant to be a man, how to treat a woman with respect and kindness, and how to control my temper when it threatened to boil over. If you'll allow me, I'd be honored to do the same for Peter."

Eli places the trash can down, and I wrap my arms around the back of his neck, leaning in to kiss him softly.

"Have I mentioned today how much I love you?"

He smiles at me and pecks the tip of my nose. "Not today."

"Eli, you're truly a good man. I've been so used to handling everything on my own that it's hard to let others help. But now you're their stepdad, and I need to step back and allow you to help. This is new to me, but I'll get there."

Speaking this aloud lifts a huge weight off my shoulders. I have support, a genuine partner in life, and that realization fills me with hope.

Later that evening, I'm tucked into Eli's side on the family room couch. The situation from earlier has settled down enough for us to enjoy a movie night. Eli had a talk with Peter, and even though Pete didn't want to go into detail, he filled us in on his frustrations with his father. Apparently, Bryant has been harder on Pete than anything. It's not that Peter really blames it on me, but in the moment, he lashed out at me because he knew I was safe.

I've decided to contact the kids' therapist on Monday to increase their monthly visits to weekly.

Peter wasn't pleased when I gave him his punishment, but he needs to understand that actions have consequences. He'll be doing odd jobs around the farm for his aunts and uncles until he earns enough money to replace the broken frame and water bottle. I know Eli and I could replace the items ourselves, but making Pete earn it will give him time to think about his actions. Additionally, he will have no electronic devices for the rest of the weekend.

I explained that I want him to learn to communicate his feelings with words rather than resorting to violence. From now on, his punishments will match his actions. If he can express his anger verbally and respectfully, the punishment will be minimal or possibly not necessary at all. I can handle a healthy debate. Yes, I'm a mom, but I'm human too. He has every right to tell me if something I'm doing hurts him in any way.

"Eww." Eric elongates the word. "Why do parents always have to kiss?"

I look up at the TV just in time to catch the mom and dad in the show we've been watching kiss one another.

"Because kissing is fun when you're in love," Eli replies. He turns to me and gently lifts my chin so our lips meet. I chuckle as we kiss, while the boys groan in the background.

"I think it's sweet," Sage chimes in. "I love it when our new dad kisses Mom. I'd rather not watch, but it makes me happy to know he loves us enough to show it."

I blink back tears of joy as Eli pulls away, smiling. "New dad, huh?"

Sage nods. "Yeah. You are our new dad. Do I have to keep calling you Eli? I kind of like calling you Dad."

Eli turns to look back at me, a shimmer of unshed tears in his eyes, and raises a questioning eyebrow. "What do you think?" he asks softly.

I lean close, letting my lips brush his for one more brief kiss. "I think this is a decision for you and the kids to make together. To me, if they choose to call you Dad, it's because you've truly earned that title. I'm perfectly okay with whatever y'all decide."

He turns back to the kids. "If you want to call me Dad, then I'd be honored to have that title." He reaches up a hand to wipe away the few tears that have managed to escape down his cheeks.

"Who votes to call Eli Dad?" Sage asks. She raises her hand as high as she can without standing, her eyes sparkling with excitement.

"I do!" Eric declares. "I already told my friends that I have a nice dad now," he adds. He looks over at Eli with a wide grin.

At that moment, I, too, lose the fight against my own tears. Eli's hand finds its way to my knee, offering a gentle squeeze that shows support and understanding.

"I'm fine with it too," Pete adds, "but I'd be happier if you could be our real dad. That way, we wouldn't have to ever go back to *Bryant's* house."

I almost say something about his disrespect, but Eli quietly signals me not to. After his discussion with Pete, Eli let me know that he would keep the rest of their conversation confidential unless absolutely necessary. Although it frustrates me, I appreciate it at the same time. Peter needs that connection with a father figure. I'll try my hardest not to interfere, even when I feel compelled to correct him.

"Alright, it's time to clean up and get ready for bed."

After Eli and I decide to split bedtime tasks so we won't end up going to bed past midnight, I step into our bedroom and stop in surprise. Before me is a scene unlike any I've ever seen. The floor is covered with pale-pink rose petals and battery-operated candles. Above, matching pink balloons hang with their strings cascading throughout the room. I glance at the bed, noticing petals scattered across it, too, and a bunch of roses in the center, along with a shopping bag.

How did he . . . ? I shake my head. I don't care how.

This man has turned me into a crier. I wipe the tears from my cheek as Eli clears his throat, drawing my attention to him. There he stands, my handsome husband, leaning against the bathroom doorway with a smile and an out-stretched hand. "Come," he says. "I ran a bath for you. After you finish soaking, I have everything ready to give you a massage. I noticed you've been favoring your back lately."

I take his hand and follow him into the bathroom, where the scene mirrors the bedroom. Rose petals are strewn all around. The bathtub is filled with bubbles, and candles are arranged along the edge.

I pause and have Eli turn to face me. "This is the nicest thing anyone has ever done for me. But there is one thing that I can think of that would make all this better."

"What's that?" Eli asks. He gently moves my hair from my shoulder.

"I'd like for you to join me, Romeo."

"Are you sure?" he asks.

"I am."

The man before me, whose hand now gently cups my cheek, holds the key to my heart.

Chapter
Thirty-Three

As I step out of the steaming-hot shower, I wrap a towel around myself and head toward my dresser. This week has been a whirlwind, between juggling long hours at work, managing the kids, and supporting Eli through all the changes he's made to his life lately. He's been working so hard, while trying to take on the roles of husband and father, along with having a new job and being in a new state. It's a lot on a person.

Last night, after we cleared the dinner plates, I could tell he was tired, even though he never complained. Knowing that my brothers were about to get together, I encouraged him to go over to Pat's and hang out with them while the kids and I took care of the rest. I've finally forgiven my brothers—for the most part anyway. It took a week, but their persistent efforts made it impossible to stay angry. They ended up devising a plan, coordinating so that one of them was always reaching out—whether by a call, text, surprise visit, or delivered gift. This has been their routine since we were kids—whenever they pulled off a bone-headed stunt and I got mad, they always knew how to draw me back in. I guess that's what has kept us so close.

We can never stay mad at each other for long.

After drying off, I slip into a T-shirt and slide back under the covers, nuzzling in beside Eli, who was sleeping peacefully moments ago. The sharp intake of air when my feet find his lets me know that he's now awake.

"I don't think I'll ever get used to how cold your feet get." Eli pulls me closer until there's no space between us, our bodies perfectly pressed together. His embrace is warm and comforting, like a protective cocoon. "You smell so good." His voice is still a gentle rumble from sleep, sending a shiver down my spine.

"I just got out of the shower," I reply. Tilting my head back, I plant a kiss on his chin, which is a bit rough with stubble. Ever since I casually mentioned how much I liked the neatly trimmed beard look on him, he's been letting it grow out. Now, when we kiss, I can feel the soft bristle of his beard against my skin. It's just long enough for my fingers to run through and playfully tug, yet short enough that it doesn't irritate my skin.

"What time is it?"

"It's just barely six," I whisper against his neck as I leave a kiss there. "Go back to sleep. I didn't mean to wake you."

His lips gently brush the top of my head, pressing a soft kiss that sends a wave of warmth through me, making me sigh with contentment. These moments, when the world fades away and it's just the two of us in the quiet cocoon of our bedroom, are rare. I savor them whenever they come our way.

Falling for Eli has been a long journey, filled with its ups and downs, but now that we're here, I can't help but want him all to myself sometimes.

"It's impossible to go back to sleep when my beautiful wife smells this good and is pressed up against me like this." His arms wrap around me tighter. "If you don't quit kissing my neck like that, I don't think either of us will be going back to sleep anytime soon."

As his fingers lightly graze up and down my side, I try to hold back and be in the moment with him. But when he hits a sensitive spot, a snort erupts from me—a laugh so loud and unexpected that it echoes around the room. My body jerks instinctively away from his touch, unable to resist the tickling sensation any longer. Despite my best attempts to stifle the laughter, it bursts out of me in waves.

I'm halfway across the bed when Eli follows, playfully grabbing my legs and pulling me beneath him until he's hovering over me. "How did I not know you were this ticklish? That snort was the most adorable thing ever."

I cover my face with my hands, shaking my head. "You need your hearing checked, because there's nothing cute about snorting."

"My hearing is just fine, thank you very much." Eli slowly leans in, his eyes holding mine with an intensity that makes my heart race. His lips brush against mine softly at first, capturing me in a kiss that seems to make the room around us disappear. A shiver runs down my spine, leaving goose pimples in its path. His hand cups my cheek, pulling me closer until our noses almost touch and our breaths mingle. Our lips move together in a delicate rhythm. It's as if time has stopped, a moment where nothing else matters but the connection between us.

There's a knock at the door, followed by Thor barking, which causes me to jump.

Eli pulls back slightly and buries his nose into the curve of my neck, his breath warm against my skin.

"Mom. Dad. I'm hungry. You said we could have pancakes this morning." The hint of impatience in Eric's voice makes me chuckle.

"Note to self, avoid promising pancakes the night before," Eli murmurs. He matches my chuckle with his own.

I give him a reassuring pat on the chest. "Welcome to parenthood." I lean in for a quick kiss. "Coming, bud! Go and get dressed. I'll be down in a minute."

Eli flops onto his back, his arm draped over his eyes in mock exasperation. "I love that boy to death, but he sure does have horrible timing," he grumbles playfully.

I chuckle again, shifting so I'm now hovering over him, my hair brushing against his face. "Why don't you hop in the shower while I get breakfast started? You can join us downstairs when you're done." I lean in and give him one more heated kiss before pulling away.

As I begin to crawl off the bed, Eli playfully swats me on the rear, making me glance back with a smile. "Have I told you how much I love you?"

"Not today."

A smile spreads across my face as I feel that flutter of joy inside. It's been far too long since I've experienced this kind of happiness in my life. I truly hope this lasts forever.

I lie back on the couch, a sleeping Noah in my arms, my feet in Eli's lap, as I laugh at Pete and Pat. "What on earth are you supposed to be?" I ask.

Eli takes my foot in his hand and squeezes lightly, while smiling.

Tonight, the family has gathered for a game night at Tom and Maddie's place, and just like last time, charades is on the menu. Pat, however, has enlisted some help from Pete for his performance. Pat has Pete so that his hands are on the floor and his feet are in Pat's hands. I knew the moment it started that he was acting out a wheelbarrow, but the look of disgust in Pat's eyes when Cam yelled out "stroller" and Tom guessed "shopping cart" had me adding to it.

Eli leans in closer to me, his eyes darting back to the timer on the coffee table. His voice drops to a whisper. "Do you really not know what they are?"

"Wheelbarrow!" I shout, just as the final grains of sand slip through the hourglass, signaling that time's up. "I knew it all along. I just wanted to make Pat sweat a bit," I tease.

Eli grins as he straightens up, shaking his head. "I hope I never get on your bad side."

"Really, Janelle?" Pat complains. He crosses his arms in a huff. "You didn't have to wait until the last second to make that guess."

"Oh, I definitely did," I reply with a smirk. "Maybe next time you guys want to act like jerks to my husband, you'll think twice." Though I've mostly forgiven my brothers, being the only sister gives me the right to hold on to a little bit of pettiness for a few more days.

Eli rests his hand on my knee, giving it a gentle squeeze. I cover his hand with mine, reassuring him with a soft smile that everything's alright.

"I thought you said you weren't mad at us anymore," Tom chimes in. "We like Eli just fine. Us being that way had nothing to do with him. It was all about the quickie wedding we weren't invited to. I thought you knew that."

Eric runs over and leaps into Eli's lap, his arms wrapping tightly around Eli's neck. "Quit being mean to my dad."

I hand Noah off to Maddie and turn to Eric as I sit up. I slide closer so that Eric can see me clearly. "I'm sorry, bud." I brush my hand gently through his hair. "Your uncles aren't being mean. They were just being protective brothers, like you and Pete are with Sage. Momma was just being a bit of a butthead because that's what sisters do when their brothers make them mad."

He glances over at my brothers with a furrowed brow. "So you guys don't hate him like my other dad does?" His eyes are searching, and I can tell he's genuinely concerned.

I never intended for my teasing to hurt him—this feels like a parenting fail on my part. I've always exchanged playful jabs with my brothers, but it never crossed my mind that it might impact the children.

Eli places a reassuring hand on Eric's shoulder, pulling him back so he can look at him. "I appreciate you looking out for me, but this is a safe place. Okay? You'll never need to protect me from this family. Or from anyone, for that matter. It should be the other way around. *I'm* the one who needs to protect *you*."

As Eli speaks to Eric, I scan the room, finally settling on Dad, who meets my eyes with a small, sad smile that says he understands.

I hate to admit it, but I messed up.

I get up and head to the kitchen to grab a drink and try to compose myself. Hurting my kids, even unintentionally, always weighs heavily on me.

Dad enters the kitchen behind me and pulls me into a hug. "Oh, sweetheart. Everyone knows you didn't mean anything by it. The fact that you're in here upset over it shows just how big your heart is."

"Thanks, Dad. I really needed that. I honestly didn't mean to hurt anyone; I was just teasing the boys like I always do."

"I know that, and I'm sure they do too. But the kids are having these visits with Bryant now, which I've heard aren't going too well. And they've gained a new dad in Eli, whom they adore, so their emotions are bound to get tangled somewhere."

Eli walks up behind my dad and gives him a friendly pat on the shoulder. "I think it's time to call it a night. The kids are getting their coats, and Maddie said not to worry about the cleanup."

Dad turns to Eli, shaking his hand firmly before excusing himself.

"Are you upset with me?" I ask.

"No, not at all. Why would I be? You were just having fun with your brothers. I understand you didn't mean any harm. Honestly, if Eric hadn't been so upset about it, I'd have appreciated how he stood up for me. I didn't realize how much I'd enjoy being their dad, but it's truly an incredible feeling."

I lean in close and wrap my arms gently around the back of his neck, pulling him closer for a quick kiss. "Even after this morning?" I tease.

He smiles, a mischievous glint in his eyes, and leans in to plant a soft kiss on the tip of my nose. "Even after this morning," he echoes.

"Can you two quit kissing? We're *ready*," Eric moans.

I chuckle. Eli clasps my hand in his and guides me toward the door, where my family is waiting to say good night. We exchange hugs, and soon, Eli, the kids, Thor, and I step outside. It's so nice that we chose to walk tonight. Eli wraps an arm around me as we head down the rocky path leading home.

On nights like this, beneath a sky full of stars, watching the kids ahead of us, I feel incredibly blessed for having been given another chance at my own happily ever after.

Chapter
Thirty-Four

Walking up the path to the house after a long day at work, the toe of my shoe snags on the porch step, sending me flying forward under the weight of my duffel bag and the heavy sack of dog food I picked up on the way home. The wooden planks meet my chin with a punishing thud. Pain shoots through me, and I roll onto my back, staring blankly at the sky above.

Today has been one of those days I wish I could escape from.

This morning, my phone rang while I was at the station, not out on a call, so I picked it up. On the line was Mr. Darcy's office with an update about our upcoming court date. According to the report they received, the visits with Bryant are going well. They mentioned that if things continue in this manner, there might be a possibility for the judge to grant my ex shared custody. My heart was still weighed down from the conversation when the bell rang, signaling an emergency call.

The call that broke the thread I was clinging to.
A heavily pregnant woman had been in a fatal head-on collision. No matter how hard I try, I can't shake the mem-

ory of the scene. The rescue team managed to free her passenger and the two children in the back, but she was trapped. Being the rescue paramedic on scene, I crawled into the mangled car to treat her, as the Jaws of Life tried to free her from the wreckage. No matter what I did, though, it wasn't enough. Moments before she drew her last breath, she brought a six-pound precious baby girl into the world, leaving behind a single kiss on her daughter's head.

Returning to the station after that call, I was a shadow of myself, drawn only to a long, punishing workout and a scalding-hot shower. Now, as I lie here on the porch steps, my body protests. All I want is the quiet of my bed, where my tears can fall without being questioned.

Today, that newborn baby girl lost her mother, and in about a month, I stand the chance of losing my children.

Life just isn't fair.

"Oh my God, Janie, are you okay?" Mom's voice breaks through the haze I'm in, sounding urgent and worried. She bursts through the door, rushing to where I lie. "Eli! Get out here!" she calls back into the house.

I wipe the tears from my cheeks with the back of my hand and start to push myself up as Eli runs out, leaping over my scattered belongings with practiced ease. "I'm okay." I press against his chest for support and manage to stand up, though I stumble slightly before finding my balance. The thought of being held in his arms right now is too much to bear; a single touch could unravel the progress I've made in piecing myself back together.

"Here, Janie," Mom interrupts. "Let Eli help you into the house. You might've hurt yourself."

"I'm fine, Mom," I retort. My voice comes out much sharper than I intended. "I'm the paramedic here; I'd know if I was injured." Guilt gnaws at me internally, but I can't seem to stop myself from snapping.

"Mom?" Sage's voice is filled with concern, causing me to look her way.

"I'm okay, angel. I just fell up the porch steps, that's all. Nothing a long soak in the tub can't fix."

Though her face is filled with worry, she doesn't argue. Instead, she nods. "While you do that, I'll make dinner tonight."

Mom bends down to gather my bag from where it fell onto the stoop, and I slowly climb the stairs. Eli stands close to make sure I don't fall again.

"Kids, get your coats on," Mom says. "You can join Grandpa and me for dinner. We'll bring some takeout back for your parents when we're done."

Eli shakes his head slightly. "You don't need to do that, Marie," he replies. "I'll just get Janelle in the tub and then come down to help with dinner."

Mom starts to argue, but I ignore them as I inch my way toward the stairs, each step feeling heavier than the last. I need to get upstairs to my room before I lose my cool on someone else without meaning to. I don't know what's going on with me. I've handled these kinds of accidents before, but the one today has clung hard to me. At work, before I left, I was told to take the rest of the week off to get my head straight. I've already called Katie, who set up an appointment for me first thing tomorrow morning.

I'm halfway up the staircase, my hand gripping the banister, when I hear the thud of the front door closing, then footsteps approaching from behind.

"The kids went out with your parents," Eli says. "Why don't you let me help you?"

"Because I don't need your help. I'm fine. I've managed this long," I add. The grip I have on the banister tightens. "I can get myself into the tub."

There's a quiet pause before I'm being lifted into Eli's arms and carried toward our room. "You can be mad at me all you want when you're lying in a hot bath. I don't know what's going on, but I wish you'd talk to me instead of snapping."

When he makes it to the bathroom, he sets me on the counter and kicks the door closed behind him. He then walks to the tub and turns on the water, sprinkling in a generous handful of Epsom salt. Returning to me, he crouches down to remove my socks and shoes, his touch remaining gentle.

I want to speak to him so badly, to explain the chaos playing in my mind, but the words just won't come. Tears fall rapidly down my face, my head at war with itself.

Quietly, Eli rises and opens the medicine cabinet behind me, retrieving a couple of Tylenol tablets. While it's open, I reach my shaky hand out and grab my anxiety medicine. It's been so long since I've needed to take these, I quit carrying them everywhere I go.

After I swallow the pills, Eli helps me settle into the warmth of the tub. He leans in and plants a soft, reassuring kiss on my lips. "Take all the time you need. I'll be in the bedroom when you're ready. I think my beautiful wife could use a massage tonight."

"I don't know what you see in me. There's nothing beautiful about how I look. Is it my stretch marks? The extra weight? Or maybe it's because I can't even sneeze without crossing my legs? I don't understand how a man like you could ever fall for a train wreck like me."

Eli sinks down onto the edge of the tub. He gently lifts my chin, brushes back the strands of hair that cling to my face, then leans in and leaves another soft kiss on my forehead. "I don't know what happened to you today or why you're pushing me away, but I'm not going anywhere. You're the one I want. Do you really think your stretch marks bother me? They're a testament to a life lived with love—proof that you have given so much of yourself that you would create another life. I adore your curves—hell, I love every part of you. You're never afraid to enjoy life, to savor every moment, every bite. I could never be with someone who hides their spark from the world." His thumb wipes away the tears still falling on my cheeks. "There isn't a single thing about you that I don't love. Now . . . I can see you need some space. I'm going to grab a pillow and blanket and take them to the guest room so you can have it. Remember, you promised me no more running away, and I intend to hold you to that." Before leaving, he leans down to press one last kiss on my lips. "I will love you until my final breath, Janelle. You know where to find me when you need me."

The instant I hear the click of the bathroom door shutting, I raise my hands to my face and let out a scream filled with all the pain left in me. I have the best man anyone could ever ask for, yet I'm the one pushing him away. I can't help but feel I don't deserve the love that Eli so freely gives.

It is now well past ten o'clock at night, and despite feeling much better, I still haven't left my room. My cheeks heat with embarrassment as I remember my earlier outbursts, making me reluctant to even crack open the door. About two hours ago, Eli's soothing voice drifted through the door as he read a bedtime story to Eric, followed by saying good night to the older two.

Eli has truly become an incredible husband and father.

I hear the soft click of the door to the hall bathroom closing, followed by footsteps halting just outside my door, sending a fresh wave of tears down my cheeks. How did I become such a terrible wife? It's hard to fathom that so soon after getting married, Eli feels too intimidated to come into our own room.

I need to make things between him and me right.

With a sigh, I crawl out of bed, my muscles groaning in protest, and shuffle towards the door. With a determined breath, I leave the room to find my husband.

Carefully, I tiptoe down the dimly lit hallway, mindful of every creaky floorboard, not wanting to disturb the kids. The guest room door is slightly ajar, so I push it open gently. The soft glow of a bedside lamp casts a warm light on Eli, who sits at the edge of the bed, absentmindedly twisting his wedding ring around his finger. As I step inside, his eyes meet mine.

"Can I come in?"

Eli pats the bed beside him, making space for me, but instead, I choose to kneel before him. I take his hands and hold them close. "I can't begin to tell you how sorry I am for my behavior earlier. Do you think you can ever forgive me?"

A soft smile tugs at his lips as he helps me to my feet. He wraps his strong arms around my waist, pulling me close until his head rests against my chest. The embrace feels like a soothing patch, mending the fractured pieces of my heart. "You've already been forgiven," he murmurs. "Would you like to share what got you so upset?"

"I would. But I think we need to get comfortable for this."

Eli releases his hold on me and shifts to the head of the bed, fluffing the pillows before patting the space beside him. I crawl over and nestle against him, resting my head on his shoulder. The warmth of his body is comforting as I begin to unravel everything, starting with the phone call from the lawyer's office, then sharing the details of the accident that claimed the life of that mother, each word feeling like a weight lifting from my chest. By the time I finish, my cheeks are wet with tears, and I find myself sobbing once again.

Eli holds me in a firm embrace.

Minutes later, once my tears have finally stopped, Eli turns to face me, his eyes filled with understanding and concern. "I can't even begin to imagine what you went through," he says softly. "I'm so sorry. I shouldn't have walked away earlier. You needed me."

"You did the right thing," I reply. I reach over to take his hand in mine. "I took my pain out on you." I pause. "When I was with my ex, he made me his punching bag in every way. No matter how many different outlets he had, I was always the one he used. Tonight, I realized that I did that very thing to you. I may not have hit you, but my words still cut deep." I look into his eyes, searching for understanding. "I want us to make a vow to one another right now."

"Okay." He nods. "What do you have in mind?"

"I vow to you that if I ever have a night where I cannot control my emotions like tonight, I won't bring that mess home to you and the kids. Instead, I'll find somewhere else to stay until I can rein in my emotions." When his eyebrows knit together in confusion, I elaborate. "After everything that happened with Bryant, my therapist prescribed me anxiety medication. It's been almost a year since I last needed to take one. The other pill I took tonight was from that prescription. I'll put the bottle in my bag and plan to keep it with me when I go to work. If I start to feel overwhelmed again, I'll take another pill and find a quiet spot to park until I feel steady enough to drive back home."

"Even though I hate not being there for you in the moment, I understand not bringing it home." He takes my hand in his, linking our fingers. "I promise you that I won't let the stress from work seep into our home life either. When I feel tension following me, I'll send you a quick text saying that I'm heading to the gym to blow off steam and that I'll be home late. I won't walk through our front door until I've let go of that frustration and cleared my mind."

After being with Bryant for so long, a man who would have never made this vow to me, hearing Eli so easily agree warms my heart. "I love you, and I really am sorry about earlier."

Eli wraps his arms around me, pulling me close enough that I can feel the warmth radiating from his chest. He gently presses his lips against my neck, sending a shiver down my spine. "I love you too," he murmurs softly. "You really don't have to keep apologizing, Peach." He plants another tender kiss just below my ear, before pulling back enough to look down at me. "Now . . . can I make out with my wife? I've missed you desperately." His gaze is filled with longing as he tilts his head, inching closer to my lips.

"Please do."

His kiss is soft and tender, a warmth spreading through me that makes my heart race. Thank God for Eli. His kindness and affection are like a soothing balm to my soul. I still don't understand what he sees in me, but when his eyes meet mine, the look he gives me makes me want to believe it when he calls me beautiful.

Chapter Thirty-Five

I step into the pantry, scanning the shelves for a bag of sugar to refill the canister. Eli and I have been busy baking brownies as a surprise for the kids when they get back from Bryant's later today. It's been four days since my breakdown, and although sending the kids off to their father's shortly after didn't ease the strain, I feel more at peace now.

The pantry door closes with a soft click, plunging the small space into darkness. I pivot, only to bump into the solid wall of Eli's chest.

"What do you think you're doing, sir?" Even with me trying to be firm, there's still a hint of laughter in my voice.

Instead of answering, he wraps an arm around my waist, pulling me closer. His nose nuzzles into my hair as he trails a series of kisses along my neck. By the time his lips reach my ear, my knees threaten to buckle. If not for his steady grip, I'd be a heap on the floor.

He chuckles softly. "Have you never thought about those pantry make-out scenes in the movies?"

Oh, I have. The idea of sneaking away from the kids to steal kisses like teenagers carries its own allure.

"I'll take that as a yes," he murmurs.

"Who hasn't?" Reaching around him, I flick the light on, then gaze up into his eyes as he leans in, his hand resting on the shelf behind me, and I nearly consider switching the light back off. Instead, I grab his shirt collar and pull him down until our lips meet in an electrifying kiss. As he takes control and deepens it, I lose my footing. My foot lands awkwardly in an open case of soda. I chuckle, the sound echoing in the small room sending Thor into a barking frenzy in the kitchen.

Eli rests his forehead against mine, letting out a low grumble. After I stop laughing, he leans in and kisses the tip of my nose, then pulls back. "We better get back out there. The brownies are in the oven. I'll let Thor out, then I have something for you."

"What's the occasion?" I ask.

"Does there have to be an occasion for me to do something nice for my wife?" he replies.

"I guess not," I concede.

"I'll meet you in the living room in two minutes." He leans in for one last toe-curling kiss before retreating from the pantry, leaving me with a fluttering heart and a smile.

I swear, I love that man. He may have heard the stories about my past, but he has no clue just how profoundly he has transformed our lives. Before he came along, I could never have envisioned a life filled with such warmth and stability.

The beep of the oven timer jolts me back to the present, reminding me to get moving. I grab the oven mitts and head toward the oven. As I open the door, a cloud of sweetness washes over me. I set the tray of brownies on the cooling rack, then make my way to the living room.

By the time I make it to the couch, Eli's on his way down the stairs with a wrapped gift in his hand. He walks over and sinks into the cushions beside me. Placing the gift on the coffee table, he reaches for my hand.

"I've been thinking about this for a long time now," he begins. "When I said you deserve the world, I truly meant it, and I've been trying to figure out just how I could give it to you. Turns out, that's not exactly possible." His eyes twinkle with a hint of mischief as he lifts my hand to his lips and plants a tender kiss, prompting a chuckle to escape my lips.

What is he up to? I wonder.

"The closest I could come to it is this," he continues. Eli takes his hand from mine and hands me the gift.

With anticipation tingling in my fingertips, I peel back the wrapping paper to reveal a framed certificate. *This star has been named Janelle Cameron Boyd.* Below the precise coordinates and a registration number is an inscription. My eyes fall onto the personal message.

If I could give you the entire world, I would. But since that's not possible, I hope this little piece of the universe is enough. This star sparkles brightly, even with all the city lights. So whenever you look up and see it twinkling, I want you to know just how much you mean to me. Janelle, my love for you is as endless as the sky.

The love I have for Eli is so overwhelming that it sometimes makes me question if it's normal to feel this way. The whole time I was with my ex, I never felt this kind of intensity. Was what we had really love? I'm not sure, but despite everything he put me through, I wouldn't change having ever been with him. We have three amazing kids because of it. But what I share with Eli? It's on another level entirely.

I place the gift aside and gaze at my incredible husband, tears streaming down my face without bothering to wipe them away. "You're seriously the best man a woman could ever ask for," I say. "I hope you know that. The way you've walked into my mess and loved me and the kids regardless is something special." I lean in and press my lips gently against his, hoping the warmth and tenderness of the kiss convey all the emotions and sentiments that my words fail to express.

Eli hooks his hands firmly under my arms and leans back, drawing me along with him, our lips locked in a passionate kiss. Time seems to slip away as I lie wrapped in his embrace, the warmth of our kiss intensifying with every passing second, until the urge to pull back becomes necessary. His lips, soft and insistent, never leave my skin. They travel a gentle path from my lips to the curve of my neck, sending shivers down my spine. In one fluid motion, he flips us over so that he's now hovering above me, his presence both commanding and tender as his lips find mine once more, igniting a renewed spark between us.

Before the heat between us can amp up any further, my phone rings.

Eli pulls back, his eyes meeting mine briefly before he lays his head gently on my shoulder. His warm breath tickles my neck. "You better get that."

I lean forward just enough to grab my phone from the coffee table while keeping a hold on Eli. The screen lights up with Sage's name, and I sit up straight, nudging Eli back. I answer and bring the phone to my ear. "Hey, angel. Are you ready for us to come and get you?"

"Mom? I'm scared," she cries. Her voice trembles through the phone, making my heart sink. "Can you come and get us? Please?"

I glance over at Eli, who's already reaching for our shoes. I put the phone on speaker as I take my sneakers from Eli and slip them on. "Of course." I try to infuse my voice with a calm I don't feel. "Eli and I will pack up now. Are you guys okay? What's going on?"

Theres a muted scream in the background followed by a rustling on the phone. "Peter, no!" Sage yells. "Get back here."

"Sage," Eli cuts in, "Honey, what's going on? Where did your brother go?"

"Pete!" Eric yells out as a door slams.

"Please hurry," she pleads. "Dad's hurting Milly. I tried to stop Peter, but he won't listen. He pushed me and Eric into the bathroom. Mom, he ran after Dad, and there's a lot of yelling. I need to stop him." There's more rustling, then I hear Sage tell Eric to stay there and lock the door.

Eli snatches the car keys from the hook near the door, his jaw clenched with determination, and follows me to the car. As we climb in, I take his phone from his pocket, my fingers trembling as I type in Hugh's number and dial. My kids know him. If he can get there as the police do, they'll have someone with them until we get there.

"Sage, I need you to stay there with your brother and call 911. Let us be the ones to stop him," I say. "Eli and I are on the way now. Don't come out, no matter what, unless it's one of us. Okay?"

"Momma," Eric's trembling voice cuts in, "I'm scared. Sage left me too. What if Dad hurts them?"

I glance at Eli, his expression tense. He reverses out of the driveway and accelerates down the road, kicking up rocks and leaving a trail of dust behind us.

Oh my God. My stomach sinks and I feel bile threatening to rise. If Sage were there, I could have her call the police, but Eric . . . I don't know if he would be able to with how scared he sounds.

"This is Hugh." Hugh's voice crackles through the speaker.

"Stay on the phone with me, bud, but keep it quiet. Don't let anyone know where you are, okay? I'm going to let Hugh know to call it in."

I mute my call with Eric, take a deep breath, and try to keep my thoughts together as I relay everything I know to Hugh, detailing the situation and rattling off the address where they can find the kids and Milly. My hands shake slightly, but I focus on the task at hand. "Eric was left alone in the locked bathroom. Eli and I are on the interstate. Can you call this one in for me?"

If I hadn't already called Hugh, I would have called OKCPD myself.

"Got it," he replies, the sound of scribbling just audible over the phone. "I'll radio it in now and head that way. Drive carefully. I don't want to get a call to come save you too."

"Thanks." I put Eli's phone down and then unmute mine. "Hey, bud, we're almost there, and Hugh and the police are on their way too. Be a big boy and stay hidden for me."

"Okay, Momma. Please hurry though. There's a lot of noise and it's scaring me."

Eli's going at such a high speed already, but when he hears that, he presses on the gas a little harder, so much so that I have to grip the panic bar to keep myself steady when he passes a slower driver. As he maneuvers through traffic, I pull Dad's name up on my phone and shoot him a text.

Me: *Sage just called. Bryant hit Milly, and Pete and Sage ran out to confront him. On the way now.*

Almost immediately, the familiar three dots appear, indicating he's seen the message and is typing a response.

Dad: *Mom and I will get ready in case you need us to head that way. Call me as soon as you know something.*

That's when my brothers come to mind, and I send another message.

Me: *Call the boys and let them know please.*
Dad: *Will do.*

Moments later, Eli exits the intestate and enters Bryant's neighborhood.

"You doing okay, bud?"

"Yeah. I'm just scared."

"I know, baby. I'm sorry. But Eli and I are pulling in now. Stay in your hiding spot until I come and find you. Be brave just a little longer."

"Okay."

Before the car comes to a full stop, I unbuckle my seat belt, fling the door open, and run toward the house. What I find the moment I enter the door—thank God it was unlocked—nearly takes me to my knees. Lying on the floor, barely able to move, is Milly, reminding me of myself all those years ago. But the scream I hear as Sage falls over the back of a chair has me moving. Bryant is approaching Peter, and from the blood on my son's lip, I see he's already had more than his fair share of violence.

"Get your filthy hands off my kids!" I nearly scream. In seconds, I'm across the room and throwing every bit of my body weight against my ex, tumbling to the floor right along with him.

Before he has the chance to move, I'm on my feet again and ushering the kids down the hall toward their brother. "Don't open the door for anyone but me or Eli. I'll be back for you in a minute."

"But, Mom—" Sage argues.

"Angel, you and your brothers were so brave. But I'm here now. Let me take care of you. I'll be right back. I promise."

Reluctantly, they go into the bathroom with Eric and lock the door after it's pulled shut.

I walk back into the living area and see Bryant in Eli's face as Eli stands over Milly.

"Get away from her!" Bryant shouts. "This one is mine. Go have fun with my leftovers."

I can't recall a time I've ever seen Eli mad enough to hit. Until now. He pulls back and knocks Braynt's screws loose. My ex falls to the ground with a loud thud.

I don't condone violence in any way whatsoever, but Bryant had that one coming.

"Don't you ever talk about my wife like that again. And if I ever hear about you touching her or my kids again, I'll hunt you down myself."

"Whoa," I hear a voice say from the doorway. "Eli's pretty alright."

I turn just in time to see all three of my brothers walk in. They head over to join Eli, each giving me a nod along the way. I'm sure it's their way of keeping my husband from beating my ex senseless.

I walk to Milly and kneel in front of her, taking her hand in mine. I check her pulse, and though it's a bit erratic, it's her labored breathing that worries me. "Help is on the way," I say.

She coughs and winces. "If I had known he was capable of such anger, I'd never have invited the kids to stay in my home. I'm truly sorry," she sobs.

"None of this is your fault. Don't go down that road like I did. You'll heal and get a lot of therapy, but I promise, there are happy times to come, if you let them." I look up at Eli and smile softly, then look over my shoulder when I hear a commotion.

As Heather, Val, and Hugh walk through the open door, I meet Hugh's eyes and nod in thanks before standing and heading down the hall. Now that help is here, I'm free to wrap my kids in my arms and never let go.

I knock and let the kids know it's me. When they open the door, I'm wrapped in three sets of arms so tight I might not be able to draw my next breath. Tears fall as I pull back and see the marks on my kids' faces.

"We'll let Heather have a look at you two before we head home." I can't trust myself not to overreact right now.

As we turn, Eli is standing there, a step away. The kids run over and give him a hug of their own. As they're in his arms, my brothers walk my way and wrap me in theirs.

We have a lot of healing ahead of us again, but with my family and Eli by our side, I have no doubt that we'll get there.

Chapter Thirty-Six

Four Months Later

I stand in the bathroom, my gaze landing on the timer. Throwing my hands in the air, I start pacing, attempting to distract myself from the ticking of the seconds, as my footsteps quietly echo on the floor. It's hard to believe how much life has changed in just four months.

After Bryant was arrested again for attacking Milly and hitting the kids, Mr. Darcy quickly filed to strip him of his parental rights. Eli didn't waste a moment either—he filed the adoption papers the instant the ink dried on the court documents.

Since then, our family has been busy choosing paint swatches for the house renovation we have planned once we return from our trip to Charleston next week. This is our chance to make this house ours, turning it into a space that reflects us as a family, not Bryant.

The timer goes off, and instantly, my nerves ramp up. Today marks three weeks of being late. Eli and I hadn't planned on having another child—in fact, he mentioned he was perfectly content with our three. Yet, I can't shake this intuition that our family might be growing soon.

At last week's ladies' lunch, there were plenty of tears over babies, some happy and some sad. Leah broke down and shared the news of her miscarriage just after Kim announced that she and Pat are expecting. Leah tried so hard to be happy for them, but she just couldn't handle it and went home in tears.

Though I understand this is a part of life, it's still a part that I would never wish on anyone. My heart goes out to Leah and Cam right now. I hope she can eventually find happiness for Kim and Kayla, who is due to have her baby boy any day now. It won't be easy, I know that, but if she leans on us for support, she'll get through this in time.

There's a knock at the door before it opens slightly. "Are you okay?" Eli asks. "You've been in here for a while. I have something for you before we head out to the site." Today is my baby brother's wedding day, and I'm supposed to walk down the aisle with Eli.

"Yeah, I'm fine. Where are the kids?"

"They're downstairs with Mom and Grandma."

His mom and grandma both flew in last week and have been staying with us ever since. Having them here has been a blast, filling our home with laughter and the smell of so many different dishes from Eli's home.

My husband comes up behind me as I stand at the counter and wraps his arms around my waist, pulling me into his warmth. He leans in, his breath tickling my skin, and places a gentle kiss on my neck, sending a shiver down my spine. "As much as I would love to stay here, holding you like this," he murmurs, his voice a soft whisper in my ear, "we really should get downstairs."

I turn in his arms, lean closer, and kiss him softly on the lips. "There's something important we need to talk about first." I take a deep breath, gathering the courage to share the news. "Eli," I start, "I'm late."

A look of confusion crosses his features. "No, we're not. The wedding isn't for a few more hours."

I can't help but laugh. "I'm not talking about being late for the wedding. I mean, my period is late."

His eyebrows furrow for a moment, and then realization dawns on him, his eyes widening. "*Oh*," he responds.

"Exactly."

"Okay, we're okay," he says. Eli lets go of me and shakes out his hands as if to release nervous energy. His eyes search mine, a mixture of excitement and apprehension. "Do you know . . . if you know . . . Are we?"

"Are we pregnant?" I echo.

I watch his expression closely as he nods, his anticipation palpable.

"I don't know yet. I took a test, and I was just about to find out when you walked in. Would you like to look with me?"

"Can I?"

I smile warmly at him. "Of course you can." I reach out and take his hand, feeling its warmth as I tug lightly to lead him over to the counter. "Would you like to do the honors?"

He hesitates, his voice tinged with uncertainty. "Are you sure?"

I nod, my smile widening. "Yeah. This is your chance to be a dad from the start. I think it would be nice for you to have this experience." A wave of emotion washes over me as I realize how close I came to depriving him of this moment. I point to the pregnancy test resting on the counter and explain what he'll need to do. "You'll want to touch that side and flip it over. It should say 'pregnant' or 'not pregnant.' It's pretty simple, really." I turn to meet his eyes, searching for any hint of hesitation.

Eli's fingers wrap around the test, a slight tremble in his hand as he lifts it from the counter. He glances at me, his eyes wide and filled with a mixture of hope and fear. Taking a deep breath, he flips the test over in his hand. The instant he sees the result, he drops it. Without a word, he sweeps me into a big bear hug, laughter mingling with tears as he spins us around the bathroom. I pat his shoulder gently, feeling a wave of dizziness. Sensing my discomfort, he halts and carefully sets me back on the floor, a broad smile lighting up his face.

"I don't imagine that I could ever love you more than I do right now," he says. "We're having a baby." He kneels down, pressing his lips tenderly against my stomach. Looking up, his eyes shine with happiness before he plants another kiss. "Hang in there, little one. Your daddy loves you so very much already. I just know your siblings will too. I'm going to give you the best life possible." Suddenly, his eyes widen with a mix of excitement and realization. "Mom and Grandma are here," he says. "We should go tell them." He stands swiftly, intertwining his fingers with mine, and tugs gently, eager to share the news.

I pause, my hand resting on his. "Don't you think we should see the doctor first and confirm that everything is okay?"

"I guess if you really want to, we can, but I'm so unbelievably happy right now that I feel like I could shout it from the rooftop."

"How about I make you a deal? We can tell your mom and grandma, but *only* if they promise to keep it under wraps for the time being. I don't want to steal the spotlight from Tom and Maddie's wedding."

He pulls me closer, his lips meeting mine in a kiss so electrifying that it sends a tingle down to my toes. When the need for air becomes too much, he pulls back, taking my hand gently in his. "Deal." Without another word, he guides me downstairs.

When we get to the family room, I spot the patio door standing open. As I move to close it, Eli takes my hand, halting me. "Just so you know, this was all planned long before anything you said upstairs."

"What was planned?" I ask.

He grins and leads me out. There, standing in a semi-circle, are Mom, Dad, the kids, Anna, and Ms. Emmy, all beaming back at me. Eli guides me to the corner of the patio I hadn't noticed yet. The floor is covered in roses and dozens of tea light candles. But what takes my breath away are the life-sized, illuminated letters behind them spelling out, *Marry me.*

Eli and I pause in front of the display. He clasps my hand in his, looking deeply into my eyes. "From the moment I first saw you, I knew you were the one for me," he begins. "I believed that if I was patient and showed you I was worth the chance, you'd come around. I'm so glad I waited. You, Janelle, have transformed my life in so many ways. You've given me a wonderful family and a love like no other." With that, Eli kneels, revealing an eternity band. "Janelle Boyd, will you do me the honors of marrying me? Again."

I nod eagerly, feeling a rush of warmth spread through me. "Of course I will," I reply. I reach out and pull him up, our lips meeting in a tender kiss. "I can't believe you did all of this. It's beautiful."

"I had some help," he murmurs. "I'm sorry I ruined it the first time."

"You didn't ruin anything," I assure him, squeezing his hand gently. "But thank you for giving me this memory to look back on."

Just then, Mom and Dad approach us with wide smiles, their arms outstretched for a hug.

"Congratulations, you two," Dad says, his voice filled with pride. "We're going to take the kids, if you don't mind, and go help set up for the wedding."

"That would be great, thank you. We'll be over within the hour."

Moments after they leave, Eli clasps my hand and guides me back into the house. He calls out to his mom and grandma, asking them to join us in the family room. As we reach the center of the room, Eli halts, turning us both to face the women whose expressions are filled with curiosity.

"Mom, Grandma, we have some news," Eli announces.

His mom raises an eyebrow, a playful smile tugging at her lips. "More than you guys getting married again?"

Eli nods, a grin spreading across his face. "When I went upstairs to grab Janelle, she told me that I'm going to be a dad again."

The room is filled with gasps, and tears glisten in their eyes.

Eli continues. "You cannot tell anyone just yet. We don't want to overshadow Tom and Maddie getting married. Plus, we really would like to go see the doctor first."

Anna nods, her eyes locked on Eli. "You've got my word, son."

Ms. Emmy chuckles softly. "For the first time, you've got me thinking that I might finish out my retirement in a new state."

I glance at Eli, a smile spreading across my face. If I wasn't a believer before, I am now. Mom always said that your true partner will meet you in your mess and help carry the weight of it. I used to think she was just trying to make me feel better. But Eli, standing beside me through every storm, has shared the burdens of my past and woven them into the beautiful tapestry of the life we have now. I can't begin to imagine a world without his hand in mine.

Standing here with my husband wrapped around me from behind, I gaze out over the slope of the hill. The horizon is painted in hues of orange and pink as the sun dips below the skyline, casting a warm glow over another hot July evening. The wedding was as beautiful as we had hoped, with twinkling lights strung up and flowers everywhere. The kids are still twirling around the dance floor with their grandparents.

"How are you feeling?" Eli asks.

"I'm good," I reply. I tilt my head slightly to press my lips to his in a quick, affectionate kiss. "Just lost in thought is all."

"Hey now, none of that," Tom teases. He approaches us with his new bride nestled in his arms. He stands beside us, looking out over the hill with a grin. "It's my wedding. If anyone's going to be making out, it'll be me."

"See, that's where you're wrong," Cam interjects. He walks over, joining us with Leah on his arm. They settle just on the other side of Tom.

"I have to side with Cam on this one," Pat adds. He steps up beside Eli and me, nudging my shoulder playfully, as Kim joins him on his other side, linking her arm in his.

I laugh. "I swear, no matter how old you guys get, you'll never change."

Memories flood back of a rare Fourth of July moment before any of us has partners, many years ago. Much like tonight, we had a similar exchange after a friend of ours had gotten married.

"In some ways, we've changed a lot," Pat begins. "Each one of us has faced our own challenges and come out the other side to be where we are today."

"You know," Tom interjects, "I was thinking about Mom's plan to keep us all close and on the farm. She really was smart in doing that, but—"

"Oh Lord, help us. Tom's thinking again," Pat teases.

Tom rolls his eyes, his expression turning serious. "Would you stop it? I'm being serious here."

Pat nods, his amusement replaced by genuine interest.

"I think she was on to something by making sure we stayed together. But what are we supposed to do when we're outnumbered by kids? I can see it already with the older ones. It's a little intimidating. A whole new generation of Cameron kids. We gave Mom a run for her money growing up. I can only imagine what's in store for us."

Pat leans forward, looking down the line at the others. "The way I see it, between the eight of us, we've already done just about everything there is to do. These kids don't stand a chance at getting one over on us."

Eli throws his head back in laughter, the sound rich and infectious. His eyes sparkling with amusement, and I can't help but stare at him. He really is a thing of beauty, with his tousled hair catching the light of the setting sun, reminding me of the first time I met him. Pat might be oblivious about what lies ahead, but with my family close and my husband by my side, I'm certain we can tackle whatever challenges come our way.

H K Brown's *Running Scared* is book four in the
Baycliff Valley Series.

This concludes the series.
Or does it?

A Get-Together at Cameron Farms—a Baycliff Valley
Series novella, told through Kim's POV—coming soon.

Ready for a standalone?

Our Journey—coming in 2026.

Follow the author for up-to-date information.

Facebook: @authorhkbrown
Instagram: @authorhkbrown
TikTok: @hkbrown_author
Website: authorhkbrown.com

Subscribers get sneak peeks into cover reveals and other
exciting information earlier than the general public.
Follow along at:

https://hkbrown.eo.page/mailing-list